AF256929

Wild Savannah

Spiderwize
Remus House
Coltsfoot Drive
Woodston
Peterborough
PE2 9BF

www.spiderwize.com

Wild Savannah

The adventures of two safari guides…

Acknowledgements

My thanks go firstly to Laura Conneely and her team at Spiderwize for their help and advice, and to my friend Samantha Dunmore for her proof-reading expertise. Thanks also to my partner Rosie for her encouragement and support.

It would be remiss of me not to mention here, and record my appreciation of the clients, real and imagined who have unwittingly supplied a portion of the material for this narrative.

I acknowledge with gratitude the kind permission of Mr. Chris Brown of Take That Ltd. to reproduce the image of a solar eclipse.

However, and most important of all, my thanks go to Steve Maidment, Andy Dott and Heiko Genzmer of Africa, without whose brave decisions to give me a chance, this book would not have been possible.

Contents

Dedication

This book is dedicated to my friends Christopher and Karen Henderson of Lusaka, Zambia; two of the most courageous people I have ever met.

Introduction

Sam and Gabriel had been the best of friends for as long as either of them could remember. Although born in different regions of Botswana, a beautiful country in southern Africa, they went to school and grew up together from the age of five.

Sam was actually born in Francistown, a large urban city in the east of Botswana. Both of his parents were schoolteachers. However, just before Sam was due to start his first school, he and his parents moved to Maun, (which means "The Place of Short Reeds" in the local language of Setswana) on the edge of the Okavango Delta and near to the great game parks of Botswana.

Gabriel however, had been born in a small village just outside Maun, within the Moremi Game Reserve, where his father was employed by the Wildlife Authority of Botswana as a senior Game Warden. Whilst Sam had been playing in the streets of Francistown, Gabriel's playground had been the bush, with all its beauty and danger. After they first met, it was here, in the bush that they forged their friendship, which only became deeper as they grew older.

They were similar in many respects, both tall, strong, good looking, and they were roughly the same age. Sam however, was slightly older, but even so, they had been in the same class as each other at primary and secondary school. They were both intelligent young men and took their studies seriously, but neither of them had entertained the idea of attending a university. Indeed Sam proved to be something of a rebel, defying his parents' wishes for him to follow them into teaching, rather than constantly disappearing on adventures with his best friend. Gabriel was probably more academic than Sam, but Sam was better at sport, although both played for their school at rugby and cricket. However, the thread that bound them together more than anything else was their deep and abiding love for the wildlife and culture of Africa, and Botswana in particular.

As young boys, they could most often be found in the bush, sitting in a hide they had constructed themselves, waiting silently and excitedly for any animal that happened to wander past. They took large reference books with them and whenever either of them spotted an animal or a bird they hadn't seen before, they quickly skipped to the relevant page in the book and devoured all the information on that particular species. They studied the trees and bushes of the region, reading as much as they could and learning the Latin names of everything as well as the common names. Very soon, there wasn't a bird, animal or tree that either Gabriel or Sam wasn't familiar with and couldn't identify from a mere glance.

Gabriel had been exposed to the more sinister side of Africa when he was still a small child. His mother died from the bite of a venomous snake. She had been walking along a track with Gabriel when they were suddenly confronted by a huge, dark grey snake called a Black Mamba, widely regarded as the most dangerous in Africa. It had felt threatened when Gabriel and his mother approached and had reared up to a height of over a metre, hissing its warning and opening its mouth wide to show the frightening black colour inside.

Gabriel had been walking just in front of his mother when the mamba reared up. She immediately stepped in front to protect him, but the snake interpreted her actions as an attack and with lightning speed, the mamba struck, several times. Gabriel watched in horror as the vicious, venomous fangs sank deep into his mother's leg, injecting a poison into her bloodstream that would affect her muscles and nervous system. There were no hospitals where they lived and certainly no medicine, called anti-venom with which to treat the poison. Although she knew that without medical help she would soon die, she struggled to reach home with Gabriel. By the time she got to her house, the venom had taken its deadly effect and she died a few hours later.

Gabriel was always aware that his mother, although getting weaker by the minute, had taken him to safety before thinking of herself. From that time onwards, he had a healthy respect, as well as a fascination for all reptiles and snakes, especially the Black Mamba.

After she died, Gabriel's father would take him on long, instructive walks into the bush, deepening his knowledge and love of the fauna and flora of the region. He seemed to sense rather than know that his son would finish school and immediately start work where he could, eventually following in his own footsteps along the well trodden tracks of animal welfare and conservation.

With this in mind, Gabriel's father took him on safaris whenever he could, to capture game animals and move them to a different part of the park. Sometimes, sadly, it was also necessary to cull, or shoot a number of animals where the bush could no longer support them and they couldn't be captured and moved. When his father had to do this, he took his son along and made sure Gabriel understood precisely why it was being done. He made him swear an oath that he would never destroy an animal unnecessarily for sport purposes. Gabriel gave his oath gladly, knowing he would never break it.

He taught him to use a rifle safely and where he had to shoot an animal to cause the least amount of suffering. Gabriel's African friends employed by his father, taught him how to recognise certain animal tracks, which direction they were headed in and what they were eating by examining their droppings.

There were many other aspects of the African bush that Gabriel learned in his early years; he was being educated by experts in a subject he loved dearly.

Apart from handling a firearm, whatever Gabriel was taught, he passed on to Sam, who unfortunately didn't have the opportunities that his best friend had. This did not however affect his passion for Africa. From the age of around twelve or thirteen, both Sam and Gabriel took every opportunity to wander in the bush, camping out for several days at a time. They would track animals, especially predators where they could and document their adventures in logbooks and diaries.

After leaving school at age sixteen, both boys worked in various safari camps and lodges for a few years, taking clients from every part of the world on day-long game drives, deep into the bush. They would meet each other occasionally, chatting excitedly about their most recent adventures and the days they spent in the bush when they were younger.

They were both now just nineteen years old.

One day, Gabriel heard that a safari company based in Maun was searching for suitable people to act as safari guides, taking clients camping in the bush for anything up to three weeks at a time. Anybody taken on by the company would need to have extensive knowledge of birds, animals and trees, be able to cook on a bush-fire, be able to drive a large truck safely over very rough ground and be ultimately responsible for the safety and well being of clients unused to the ways of Africa.

He immediately contacted Sam and suggested they both apply for a position with that company, called "Drifting Ways Safaris" and Sam agreed. The two owners of the company were both ex-safari guides themselves and they listened intently to Sam and Gabriel's obvious passion for and knowledge of the fauna and flora of the region.

Regarding them as mature young men, and knowing that both Sam and Gabriel would give their clients the best and most memorable experience of Africa they could, Drifting Ways immediately employed them both as Safari Guides.

These are some of their stories.

Adventures

THE PRIDE OF LIONS

Daylight had barely broken through the darkness of the African night when the lions began to hunt. Predators, such as the big cats, instinctively use the greyness of the early morning as an aid to concealment. But the prey animals, such as antelope are wary, they know that this is a dangerous time for them.

On Chief's Island in Botswana's Okavango Delta, the huge male lion with the thick, black-tinged mane, the Alpha Male of the pride, lay on the slightly raised ground of an old termite mound and watched disinterestedly as the five females in the group began to stalk a lone waterbuck antelope.

Very near to him on the mound, the two small lion cubs he was father to played and romped together. Later in their lives, they would learn from their mothers how to hunt successfully, but for now, they knew nothing other than how to play-fight. Near to them lay a second male lion. Fully grown but smaller and younger than the other, he knew his place in this pride would always be behind the Alpha. If he ever wanted to lead a pride, he would either have to fight and defeat this Alpha, or leave and form his own.

The five females walked around in a wide circle to be able to approach the unsuspecting waterbuck from behind and downwind. Unless the wind changed direction, the scent of the approaching lions would never reach the antelope. It carried on grazing on the sweet, dewy grass as the lions spread out in a semi-circle around the antelope. Once the chase began, the waterbuck would be forced to run unknowingly left or right, straight towards some of the lions waiting in ambush.

The Alpha Male looked on as the lion directly behind the waterbuck crept stealthily through the bamboo coloured elephant-grass, her tan hide camouflaging her form perfectly. Her ears were laid back against her massive head, which was almost in a straight line with her back as she concentrated entirely on getting as close as she could to her quarry before exploding into action. There was a long second or two when she stopped and remained absolutely still, now only a matter of ten to fifteen metres away from the waterbuck. Her eyes never left her prey.

Suddenly, and for no apparent reason, the waterbuck sensed her presence and began to bolt away from its attacker. A fraction of a second later, the lions were crashing through the undergrowth in desperate pursuit of their meal. Ordinarily, the lions would gain valuable ground on their prey by starting the chase first, but this time, they had been outsmarted by their prey.

The lions' plan to ambush the waterbuck would have succeeded spectacularly had the antelope not shown a remarkable turn of speed. The African lion can accelerate from a standing start to full speed quicker than any other animal, but this waterbuck managed to get away fast enough for it to cover a hundred metres or so straight ahead. The lions waiting in ambush closed in on it from both sides and were almost within touching range of its grey, hairy body; another few metres and they would be able to bring it down. Then, quite unexpectedly, there was a huge splash as the antelope plunged into one of the many water-filled channels criss-crossing the Okavango Delta, and safety. The predators would not follow it there.

Panting from the ferocious exertion of the chase, the five female lions paced up and down on the bank alongside the channel, staring at their prey. A strong swimmer, very used to deep water, the waterbuck was able to swim easily across the channel to the other side, where it climbed out and, after throwing a casual glance back at the now distant threat of the lions, carried on grazing the rich Delta grass.

Later that same morning, the female lions caught a small warthog, which was devoured almost as quickly as it had been caught. Although taking no part in the hunt, the males always feed first, and in this case, left precious little for the females and the cubs to eat.

They would hunt again in the same area the following morning.

Sam was on a short four day safari with five clients, Marcus, Dieter, Bonnie, Cathy and Steve, exploring one small part of the beautiful Okavango Delta region of Botswana; the same area occupied by the pride of lions. It was near the end of the month of February and the rains had been falling steadily since the previous November. The group had stayed overnight at Crocodile Camp, a sprawling hotel-type venue with restaurant and bar facilities, chalets, swimming pool and an area for safari tents, in a small town on the outskirts of the Delta called Maun, leaving shortly after breakfast to head for the Delta.

On the way to the village of Ditchipi, where they would leave the Land Rover, Bonnie asked Sam, 'Will we get rained on today?' It was still only the middle of the morning but Sam could see wispy clouds already forming. He spoke more from experience than certainty.

'Probably,' he replied with a sigh. 'Here in Africa,' he went on, 'the "rainy season" starts around late October with a few small showers in the afternoon. Gradually, the rain builds in intensity, until between November and March, it can become torrential and persistent. We often have clients who say they've never seen rain like it before, and it's probably right that they haven't. Sometimes, it rains so hard and long here, the gravel roads are washed away, small streams become raging rivers and the local houses made with mud and wood are simply destroyed.' Bonnie looked up at the still blue sky.

'We're ok for a few hours yet though,' said Sam, 'it won't start raining till this afternoon, and quite late at that!'

Sam turned his concentration back to guiding the Land Rover along the narrow, sandy track through the bush that led to Ditchipi.He drove through a small clump of trees and then, quite suddenly, they stopped in a large, sandy, open area at the water's edge.

Sam jumped out of the Land Rover and went immediately to a tall, strong-looking man. 'Dumela, Mr. Landy,' he called out in greeting in Setswana. He was fluent in several local dialects as well as English and Africaans.

'Dumela, Mr. Sam,' replied Landy, grinning and holding out his hand for Sam to shake. They had met several times before and liked each other enormously.

Sam turned to his clients on the Land Rover and said, 'Everyone, this is Landy from the local village. He and some of his fellow villagers will be taking us into the Delta.' The clients climbed down from the vehicle and greeted Landy one by one.

As they unloaded the equipment and luggage, Dieter pointed to some wooden canoes lying at the water's edge and asked, 'Sam, are those what we'll be travelling in?'

'That's right, they're called "mokorros". Every man and woman in this part of southern Africa can use one of those. The villagers cut down a hard-wood tree known locally as a mokwa tree and then hollow out the trunk. They straighten the sides and flatten off the bottom to make it more stable and then carve the front and rear.'

'Doesn't look too stable to me,' remarked Bonnie, eyeing the craft nervously.

'Trust me,' said Sam, 'these guys are experts, they've been doing it all their lives; they won't tip over unless you start messing about, and if you do, well, good luck with that!! And,' he carried on, 'they are probably the most environmentally friendly craft you'll come across, no engine, no fuel, no fumes, no "footprint" and they'll last a generation. Ok, let's get the gear off and stowed ready to go.'

Landy and Sam then spent the best part of the next hour negotiating! They had to agree on the number of mokorros Sam would need and consequently, the number of people Sam would need to employ for the trip. The more mokorros Landy could persuade Sam to use, the more money they could earn. It was a little game they played each time they met before travelling into the Delta, and both enjoyed the hard, but fair bargaining.

Landy had begun, 'You have five clients and you. That's six persons with equipment and luggage, I think you need ten mokorros, one for each person and four for equipment!'

Sam knew that Landy was exaggerating the number and he would play the game by going in the opposite direction. 'No, no,' he said, 'I only need four, two for people and two for the equipment and luggage.'

He knew that three people could easily travel in a mokorro, but the arguments about how many people *should* actually fit into one, or just how much equipment and luggage could fit, raged back and forth for some time, until at last, they both agreed on six mokorros and six polers. They both knew from the start that would be the number, but they enjoyed the challenge of negotiation too much to agree straight away!

'Good,' said Sam, 'now that's sorted out, let's get going, the day is wasting and the first camp is far!'

With that, they set off for their adventure into the Okavango Delta.

As leader of the safari, Sam would ordinarily have a mokorro to himself, along with equipment, but on this occasion, he'd paired himself up with Dieter.

Not long after setting off, Dieter said 'Sam, every other delta I've heard of is at the mouth of a great river, such as The Nile in Egypt. How come there's a delta this far inland?'

'Good question,' replied Sam, realising Dieter thought deeply about things. 'Millions of years ago, a Rift Valley formed across the course of the Okavango River. There must have been a massive shift in the earth's crust and a section of land just dropped. Over time, the vertical sides of the valley were eroded by the river and wind-blown sand until eventually, a large basin began to form. It carried on forming by having river silt deposited in ever wider areas, and that silt layer got higher and higher until it reached the level of the land at the top of the valley sides. Geologists reckon that the original floor of the Rift Valley is some 300 metres below where we are right now. That "basin" is now the Okavango Delta. The river still flows as it always has done and the silt has created thousands of channels for the water to flow along, most of which evaporates. The water that does get down as far as Maun drains into the Thamalakane River which then flows into other rivers in the region.'

He went on to explain, 'The water that flows into the Delta comes from rain-swollen rivers in the north of Botswana, Angola and Namibia. Bearing in mind the actual Delta was formed by silt being deposited, the land is really flat and level, so the water takes many weeks and months to flow southwards towards where we are at the moment. Over a distance of around 250 kilometres, the drop from the top end of the Delta to the other is only about 62 metres. The water level is quite low at this time of year, but even so, there is still plenty in most of the little channels that make up the Delta. Landy and his pals know every little twist and turn of this region, they know where the water is, but the area won't actually flood till around May or June, probably three months after the rainy season finishes.'

Cathy and Steve were in another mokorro and overheard what Sam was saying. 'Is this the best time of year to be here then, when there's less water?' asked Cathy.

'In Africa, February is summer, so it's an ideal time to explore the region, providing you don't mind getting wet on occasions! When there's less water, the animals tend to be concentrated in those areas where the water remains. We should be able to spot hundreds of species of animals and birds in and around these waterholes and channels, unlike in non-Delta areas where it gets so dry, the animals have to walk long distances to find water and grazing.' replied Sam. 'By the way,' he went on, 'this water is clean enough to drink. The current is so slow, all the sediment and such, drops to the floor, leaving the water clean and pure. You must take it from the middle of a nice wide stream though, and then only when you have to. There are too many nasties deposited by animals lurking in the small channels to risk taking a drink from there.'

'Thanks,' said Steve, 'but I don't think we'll bother with that!!'

They travelled on for the rest of the day, meandering through the many channels and waterways, accompanied by the almost unique sounds of the Okavango Delta, the soft swish of the pole in the water, the occasional and unmistakeable "honking" from a group of hippo, or maybe the eerie cry of the magnificent Fish Eagle perched high in a tree. It rained a little in the afternoon, but not so much that the group's spirit was dampened. Landy eventually headed the group up a small channel and they made camp for the night in a grove of trees on an island. It was the end to an almost perfect day!

The next morning was much the same as the first, hot and peaceful. Around lunchtime that day, all the mokorros pulled into the side of the channel.

'Ok, everyone off,' said Sam and then he and the polers began to unload the equipment needed for lunch. The clients were mystified however, when Sam carried the aluminium dining table into the middle of the stream and set it down onto the sandy bottom. The polers brought out the food for lunch and set the chairs around the table.

'Let's call it lunch,' announced Sam with a huge grin, inviting the clients to sit in mid-stream. 'Oh, cool!' announced Marcus, splashing his way noisily to the table. Everyone ate a super lunch under a hot sun with the clear, warm water of the Okavango Delta lapping around their ankles.

'Can anyone think of a better way to enjoy lunch?' asked Sam, leaning back in his chair and lazily tipping his favourite safari hat down over his eyes.

Later that afternoon, they had reached the main camp from where, the next day, Sam would take the clients on a guided game-walk on the neighbouring Chief's Island; the same day and in the same location that the lions would once again hunt in the early morning. The rain that Sam had predicted the day before, arrived after the tents had been erected, accompanied by a thunder and lightning storm that seemed to shake the air. The clients watched and listened under a large tarpaulin Sam and Landy had slung over the camp. 30 minutes later, the rain stopped.

After dinner, Sam gathered the clients together around the campfire and told them what to expect the following day. 'We'll be up and out of our tents around 5am,' Sam announced.

'Why so early?' asked Marcus.

'Because', replied Sam, 'early morning is the best time to see animals. The sun hasn't become too hot and so the animals don't need to find shade until later in the day. Even 5 o'clock may be a little late.'

Sam explained that they would walk in single file in order to do as little damage to the environment as possible.

'Landy will lead the walk as he knows the island like the back of his hand. If animals are around, he will find them. I'll be walking right at the back of the group to make sure we all keep together.'

'What can we expect to see?' asked Bonnie.

'It's possible that we could encounter any number of animals as we walk,' Sam explained, 'some of them could be dangerous, but we won't under any circumstances take unnecessary risks. Most species of predator and large animals such as buffalo and elephant are present on the island. Whether we'll see them is another matter, *but*' and Sam emphasised the word, 'if we find ourselves in an awkward situation with any animal, it is imperative that if Landy or I say to do something, or not to do something, you obey without question. It could just save our lives.'

Sam allowed the point to sink in and watched the expression on some of the clients' faces. They were clearly excited about the following day's walk, but at the same time, maybe a bit apprehensive.

'Will you be carrying a gun?' asked Steve.

'No, I won't,' replied Sam, 'for two reasons. One, although I can shoot, I'm not licensed to carry a firearm and two, between Landy and I, although it can never be guaranteed because this is a wild area, we have enough knowledge and experience of animal behaviour to avoid dangerous situations wherever we can. If however, we do get into a sticky problem, both of us know what to do and that's when you must obey us without question. It could be that in the future, walks won't be allowed, or only guided walks with armed Rangers, but for now, it's just us.'

Sam went on to tell the clients about what to wear, or more importantly perhaps, what not to wear.

'Bright colours, such as yellows or reds or oranges must be avoided,' he explained, 'they tend to spook animals, and besides, we might need to blend in with our surroundings and look like a bush! And lastly,' said Sam, 'no loud talking or laughing whilst we're walking. We have to remember we are in the animals' environment and we should respect that. If you want to talk at all, you must whisper!'

After a delicious dinner of lamb chops barbecued over an open fire, rice and salad, the clients went contentedly to their sleeping-bags. Each of them was looking forward to the game-walk they would experience the following day.

4-45am! Sam was already up and making sure the clients were all awake. There were various comments from inside their tents, ranging from a cheery 'Good morning' to a rather blunt instruction to whomever it was shaking the tent to, shall we say, go and do something else!! They had a small breakfast of cereal and milk and then went to the water's edge to board the two mokorros to cross the channel onto Chief's Island. Sam looked around at his clients and was pleased to see that each one had heeded his warnings about not wearing brightly coloured clothing; everyone was dressed in clothes one could only describe as dull!

Once everyone was aboard a mokorro, Sam said 'Good, the clothing is perfect. Now,' he went on, 'does everyone have at least three litres of water with them, a hat and some sunscreen?' Everyone muttered a tired and sleepy 'Yes,' and then they set off.

As soon as they landed on Chief's Island, they began their walk around the area. Just as they had been told, Landy took the lead and Sam walked at the end of the single file. Every so often, either Sam or Landy would stop to point out a bird in a tree or a distant antelope such as a red lechwe or a brindled gnu, otherwise known as a wildebeest. At regular intervals, they quietly explained to the clients the differences between various animals, especially antelope, which to the untrained eye, could look remarkably similar.

At one stage, Landy led them very near to a small grove of trees. He held up his hand to signal a halt and gestured everyone to gather around.

'Listen,' he said. Everyone heard a faint rustling sound coming from the trees. 'I think there's an elephant in there, feeding,' he said quietly.

'We'll walk round the outside of the trees and see if we can spot whatever it is. No talking anyone!'

Walking as softly and carefully as they could, Landy led the group in a wide circle. Sure enough a few minutes later, through a gap in the bush, everyone could see a huge bull elephant with tusks around a metre and a half long, ripping leaves from the topmost branches of a tree. Although they hadn't realised it, Landy had led them down-wind of the elephant and they had approached so quietly, it didn't know they were there.

Sam stood in the middle of the group and whispered, 'This is a male elephant, a bull. He's obviously left the herd to spend his last years alone, that's what they do.'

'Could he be attacked by poachers if he spends his time out of the herd?' asked Cathy.

'Oh yes', replied Sam, quietly, 'any elephant with tusks that big is under threat from poachers whether they're in the herd or not.'

'Who could possibly want to kill such a magnificent animal?' said Dieter.

Before answering, Sam led the group to a spot away from the elephant but from where they could still watch it.

'Well, poaching aside, sometimes, sadly it's necessary.' he said, 'Elephants eat around two hundred kilograms of food, leaves, twigs, shoots, berries, grass etc, per day and can destroy an awful lot of bush to achieve this. They'll drink maybe 90 to 100 litres of water per day and in times of drought, will dominate a waterhole so completely, other animals are not able to drink; the elephants will chase them away. No matter who was here first, man or animal, the fact is, we and all the other animals have to live together in this land. If elephant numbers are allowed to get out of control, they would destroy the bush for everyone and everything else. We have to control them by having a very occasional cull to reduce their numbers.'

'Is hunting allowed in this area?' asked Marcus.

'No, not here, but there are hunting concessions in other countries such as Zambia. People like Landy and myself don't support shooting animals purely for sport in any way, but the fact that we have professional hunters, men and women, in charge of the hunts, at least means that it's done in a controlled way. And the money generated by hunting licences goes a long way to conserving the area. Until such time that hunting for sport is outlawed, that is the best we can hope for.'

Sam allowed this to sink in, then carried on, 'Look how he uses the tip of his trunk to wrap around the leaves and tear them off the branch. It's called a "prehensile" trunk, and he uses his tusks to strip bark away from the trees.' They carried on watching the elephant for some time, taking as many pictures as they could before Landy indicated they should move on.

After some hours, Sam looked at his watch and quietly sent word along the line to Landy that they should return to the mokorros and to the camp for a late breakfast. Sam was sure that everyone would be in agreement. They had been walking for around five hours but had seen relatively little game, apart from birds, several species of antelope and of course the elephant, but even more disappointingly, no predators. Oh well, thought Sam, that's how it goes sometimes!

He didn't appear to alter his course at all, but Sam knew that Landy knew exactly where he was and that the mokorros would not be too far away.

A short time earlier, Sam had noticed one or two large birds flying high above the ground not far away from where they were. He recognised the distinctive style of flying instantly, gliding in large circles and identified them as vultures. He gathered the clients together and pointed to the birds, which were off to the left of where they were.

'Those birds over there are vultures, probably whitebacked as they are the most common' he explained, 'they're circling around, waiting to drop onto a carcass that's been left by predators, possibly cheetahs or lions, earlier this morning. It's most likely a kill from hours ago, and more than likely after we passed this area, but there will still be dozens of birds around the carcass, picking it clean of flesh. Those up there', he said, pointing skywards, 'may be just too late for breakfast!' Everyone laughed at Sam's little joke. 'Landy, take us up to the top of that little rise over there and we'll see if we can spot the kill.'

Landy immediately led the group off in the direction that Sam indicated and a few minutes later, they were standing on top of a large mound that rose above the otherwise totally flat ground of the Delta for only a couple of metres. Landy's keen eyes soon spotted what they were looking for, on the open plain, about a kilometre away from where they were.

'Over there,' he said, pointing. A lot of dust was being thrown up by the birds and animals squabbling to get the best bits and Sam had spotted it at the same instant.

'Yes, that's it,' he said, looking through his small field-glasses, 'I can see that it was a wildebeest that was taken and now there are vultures and hyenas feeding from the carcass and, wait, yes, I can see a couple of jackals hanging around as well. The main predators, probably lions, will have eaten already and gone.' He handed the field-glasses to each client for them to witness the scene of death supporting life, played out every single day on the African savannah.

Looking into the distance, Sam pointed out the channel, about two kilometres away, curving around a bend where the mokorros would be waiting. They set off once more and although both had seen that their path would take them through some tall elephant-grass and near to a clump of trees about one hundred metres from the water's edge, neither Sam nor Landy paid it any attention, the whole island was made up of such grass and trees. Even though they were tired and had seen very little game, the two guides and all the clients were in good spirits as they walked along.

That was about to change, rather abruptly!

By this time, it was about 11o'clock in the morning and the sun was beating down mercilessly on Sam and the others. He looked ahead under the wide brim of his sweat-soaked safari hat and watched Landy idly swishing his walking stick at stalks of chest-high, yellow coloured grass they had walked into. He's bored now, just as well we're heading back to camp, thought Sam, smiling. He then started thinking about the breakfast he was going to cook for the clients on the fire when they returned to camp. The only sounds he could hear were the footsteps of the people walking ahead of him and the gentle rustling of the wind in the long grass they had walked into. 'What a lovely, peaceful day,' Sam murmured to no-one in particular.

Then, suddenly, without warning, his thoughts evaporated in an explosion of noise and chaos ahead of the party. He was taken completely by surprise but became instantly alert, his experience telling him that, although he couldn't see anything, there was real danger.

He stopped in his tracks and looked around him. It seemed as though the long grass had come alive. He could see the tops of the stalks bending and swaying crazily in all directions and he could hear the sound of animals crashing through the undergrowth away from where they were standing.

'What's happening, what's happening?' he heard one of the clients saying, more than a little panicked by the sudden noise. After only a few seconds, Sam knew exactly what was happening. He didn't need to hear the snarling or to see the animals to know that his party had inadvertently walked into a pride of lions, chilling out in the shade of the trees and hidden by the long elephant-grass.

Without actually thinking it, Sam knew that these lions would be responsible for killing the animal that the vultures were circling earlier. Landy had stopped only a matter of a few metres from where the lions had been, and he also knew immediately what was happening, but the clients between him and Sam understandably, did not. They were confused and scared at the sudden and frighteningly loud mixture of noise and action, knowing instinctively that there was a threat to their safety! They were looking all around, but seeing nothing, which only added to their fears.

Sam acted instantly and began to hustle the clients together into a tight group.

'Close up, close up,' he urged them, grabbing some of their garments and physically pulling them in. He knew that the lions would be watching them from a distance and he knew also that by grouping everyone into this cluster, the lions would view them as one big animal.

'Keep quiet everyone,' Sam whispered urgently, but calmly 'don't break away from here, stand perfectly still. We've disturbed a group of lions. They've run away from us but we must stay alert. Don't worry, stay together and do exactly as Landy or I say.'

Although Sam was giving urgent orders, the clients trusted him and knew that if they followed his instructions, all would be well.

He knew that his main task now was to keep the clients safe and not to let them panic. He spoke in quiet, measured tones to try and reassure them.

'Keep perfectly still, we'll be just fine. They don't recognise humans as prey and they're the ones that killed the animal we saw on the plain. So, they won't need to hunt again. If we keep together like this, they'll see us as an animal bigger than they are, but if we threaten them in any way, we may have a problem.'

All the time he was talking to them, both Sam and Landy were frantically looking around to see if they could spot where the lions had bolted to. At last, Landy saw them, their heads just visible above the top of the grass, milling around nervously on an ancient termite mound where the stack had collapsed, only about fifty metres off to the left of where they were.

'There they are, over there, look,' and pointed them out to the clients.

This was still not far enough away to be safe. Sam and Landy kept everyone standing still for a few moments longer, Sam's eyes never straying from where the lions had gathered and then, still whispering, he said to the others, 'Start to back away from where we are. Keep watching the lions, stay together in our group and do everything slowly, very slowly. They mustn't think we are a threat to them, and if we convince them we're bigger and stronger than they are, they'll leave us alone!'

They had taken only a few steps backwards, when Sam heard the noise he had been dreading, the plaintive cry of a distressed lion cub. The danger level had just been increased, dramatically! In her haste to get away, the mother lion had abandoned her cub in the grass, and now she would want it back!!

He had an idea where it was by focussing on the sound. He knew it was close, disorientated and puzzled by the sudden abandonment by its mother. The lioness however, knew exactly where her cub was and how close to it Sam and the others were. The cries of the cub were becoming louder and more urgent as the infant called for its mother. Everyone could hear it scrabbling through the long grass, frantically searching.

'Landy, how many did you count over there?' whispered Sam.

'I counted five females and two males, and one of them is definitely the Alpha.' replied Landy.

'Yeah, I counted the same.' Sam looked up at them now and thankfully saw that all were still on the mound, but as he watched them, one of the females dropped to the ground and began to return to the long grass. This was obviously the mother lion coming back for her cub!

The clients in front of Sam had seen the female leave the old mound and became even more nervous, shuffling around and understandably trying to get further away.

'Oh God, one of them is coming back, look!' said Cathy, trying to keep her voice under control, 'she's going to attack us.'

'No she won't, stay calm, she just wants her cub,' replied Sam, trying to reassure the frightened group, although he knew perfectly well that this lioness could easily attack if she thought her cub was in danger; that would be natural for her.

'Keep moving back, keep moving back, slowly, don't panic, everything will be ok, we just need to move away,' urged Sam, whispering as loudly as he dared. 'Landy, can you see anything, do you know where the cub is?'

Landy would have the best idea on where it would be as he had been in front. 'I think about 10 metres over there', he said, pointing in the direction of the lions. If Landy was right, this was a stroke of luck for the party, as the mother would not have to cross in front of them to find it.

Still whispering encouragement to the group, Sam now started to walk backwards with them, a little faster, as he thought the distance from the cub was becoming safer. After a few more agonising minutes, which seemed to the clients like hours, they had emerged from the long grass, back out onto the open plain.

Sam kept the party creeping slowly backwards, away from the danger. They were no longer watching the lions, concentrating instead on the rustle of the grass in front of them, mingled with the pathetic cries of the lion cub.

Suddenly, the cries stopped and Sam knew then that she had found it and had picked it up in her mouth to carry it to safety. 'She's found it!' he said with relief, knowing that the lioness would take her cub back to the others for safety.

Although he knew the young lion was now safely back with its mother, Sam still strained his hearing for the cries of any other cubs abandoned in the grass. He glanced up at the group of lions on the mound. They were still watching Sam and his group just as intently as before, but there was something wrong!

'I can only see three females,' whispered Sam. Another of them had slipped away whilst they weren't watching, probably just a second or two after the first lioness, and Sam had no idea where she was or why she had left the pride. Then, as if to explain the reason, he heard the desperate cry of a second cub.

'Another female is coming to collect her cub,' he whispered urgently to the clients, 'stay tight in our group.' He listened again for the cries of the cub. 'It's over there,' he said, pointing to the right of where they were, 'and the mother is coming from the other way. She's going to cross right in front of us, but hopefully, she'll stay in the grass and leave us alone.'

He scanned the long grass in front of him, hoping to catch a glimpse of where she was, and hoping beyond hope she would simply pick up her cub and retreat to the old mound.

Then he saw her! Sam's breath caught in his throat as he watched her walk slowly out of the grass, about forty metres in front of them. She was huge, measuring well over a metre at her shoulder. Her tan coloured skin was flawless and seemed to shimmer as she walked, her limbs bulging with muscle. Sam had never seen one so large or powerful. She placed each foot in front of the other, very carefully, as if she was testing the firmness of the ground, and she never took her eyes off Sam and the others. To all intents and purposes, she was stalking Sam's group.

She didn't have the cub in her mouth and Sam knew that first, she would deal with what she thought was a threat to her and her infant. Just by looking at the way she was moving and staring at the group, Sam knew she was different from the other female lion, menacingly dangerous.

'She's far more aggressive than the other one,' he said, hoarsely. He feared the worst but hoped that they would still appear to be bigger and stronger than her, and not a threat. 'Get behind me, get behind me,' Sam said as he tugged roughly at the clients' clothing to get them behind him. Landy had moved to the rear of the group in order to keep them together in a tight formation.

After taking just a few steps out of the grass, the lioness stopped but continued to stare at the group, her pale yellow eyes narrowing slightly making them appear cruel and sly.

'Stand perfectly still, nobody move!' whispered Sam urgently, 'she's weighing us up, asking herself if we're a threat. She may charge us, but without the others, it will only be a warning. She *will* pull up before she gets to us.'

As long as they all stayed in their tight little group, he and Landy both knew from their experience that this would be a mock charge. She would be telling them that they should go away and leave her and the cub alone. She didn't understand that was precisely what Sam and the others were trying to do anyway.

But even though he was convinced she would pull up, Sam knew that this wasn't an exact science; that she could very easily be bold enough to carry through her attack. The most frightening aspect for Sam was that he simply couldn't know for sure, he just had to hope that he and Landy had it right, and he had to convince the increasingly agitated group behind him of that.

The clients were understandably nervous and shuffling about. Sam had just told them that they might be charged by one of the top predators in the world.

He heard various comments such as, 'She's going to kill us,' 'Oh my God, she's going to attack.'

'No she's not, shut up,' snapped Sam.

He and Landy were doing their best to keep them together and to stand still, but the group was becoming more and more nervous, more and more difficult to control. Sam knew that he had to make the lion think that he and the group were a large enough animal for her to leave them alone, but she could still charge at them if she thought her cub was in danger and to show she wasn't afraid of them.

Sam watched her movements intently. His nerves were at breaking point as he looked for any indication she was going to attack. He prayed she wouldn't, but they were in an incredibly dangerous situation and the signs were getting worse.

Then, seemingly without reason, the aggression appeared to leave her. She lifted her head more upright and, although she still never took her eyes off the group in front of her, the cruel stare seemed to disappear. Sam visibly relaxed a little, convinced that she had decided they were no threat to her and her cub.

'She's backing down,' he whispered, 'she's backing down, thank God.' Sam felt the tension in the group ease as the female continued to stand in front of them and watch Sam and the others but not so threateningly.

For the first time in many minutes, Sam realised that it was deathly quiet. No birds were singing, there was no sound of distant animals such as the gentle lowing of buffalo, the wind had died down to nothing. It was as if the day was holding its breath.

And then Sam knew why! From his left, he watched in horror as the Alpha Male crept out of the elephant-grass and stopped on the edge of the clearing. He and the rest of the group had been so preoccupied with the female in front of them, no-one had spotted this male leaving the termite mound.

At any other time, Sam would think he was magnificent, fully grown, beautifully proportioned and standing about a metre and a half tall at his shoulder with a mane so thick and dark, it made his head seem even larger than it actually was. Now, however, he thought only of surviving the day.

This was now a far worse situation for Sam and the others than with the female. She was only acting in the interests of her cub, but this lion's responsibility was to protect the entire pride, that was why he was the Alpha Male.

'Hold still, hold still,' he implored the group, 'he obviously sees us as a threat, but we must stay together.'

The big male stood there for a few seconds, head raised high, sniffing the air.

'Look at the tail,' Sam whispered, to no-one in particular. 'Look at his tail!'

The lion was waving the jet black tip in the air, from side to side and in slow, deliberate circles, almost as if he was trying to distract the group. Sam was determined not to fall into that trap.

The Alpha continued to stare at the group for what seemed like an eternity, and then Sam saw the unmistakeable signs he was going to charge at them!

Slowly, the male lion sank down into a low crouch. He pushed his head forward and lowered it so that it hung below his shoulders, his ears flattened against his mane. The cruel, yellow eyes took on a fierce new intensity as the Alpha focussed totally on Sam and the others, his breathing resulting in a series of low snarls and grunts. As the lion shifted his position slightly, Sam knew he was making sure he had a good purchase on the ground before launching himself forwards. The attack was only seconds away!

The black tipped tail was still waving from side to side. There was no possibility now that he would leave them alone, he'd obviously decided to show them he was superior. Then, the black tipped tail bobbed up and down two or three times....

Sam's throat was dry and his voice hoarse from the urgent whispering to the clients to stand still and keep together. He could hear and feel his heart pounding in his chest, harder and faster than he had ever known. He was afraid but he knew he needed these precious few seconds left to keep control of the group. The clients behind him were panicking, some of them were openly crying, some were trying to break away. Sam had to keep them together, they must stay as a group. If any of them broke away now and tried to run, he or she would definitely be attacked and killed by either the lioness or the Alpha Male.

He grabbed hold of the clothing of the clients on either side of him and held on tightly as they shuffled nervously around.

Suddenly, it was happening! 'Here he comes, here he comes!' shouted Sam. His eyes never leaving Sam at the front of the group, the Alpha Male exploded into action, a full-blooded charge towards them. He ate up the distance between him and the group at an alarming rate, running at full speed towards them, his massive paws the size of dinner plates thumping into the hard, dry ground. Sam could feel the earth beneath his feet shuddering as each paw slammed down.

Closer and closer he came, his yellow eyes seemed to blaze with hatred and his tail was thrashing around wildly as he thundered towards the terrified group. Two of the clients began to scream and Landy had to struggle to keep hold of them, preventing them from running away. Sam was almost shouting, 'Stand still, don't move, don't move! He'll stop, he'll stop!'

Others were now desperately trying to break away and it was taking all Sam and Landy's strength to keep them together. Everyone in the group was now screaming as loudly as they could. Sam and Landy were doing the same but they were trying to make as much noise as possible to deter the lion from a full attack.

On and on, the Alpha thundered towards them. Sam would remember later how everything at this stage seemed to be happening in slow motion. He could pick out the muscle groups in the lion's superbly conditioned legs as they rippled with effort, and the dark mane around the head seemed to flatten itself out with the wind rushing through it.

Then, when he was only a matter of around three or four metres in front of Sam, the Alpha pulled up sharply, his paws skidding him to a stop in a cloud of dust and sand which completely enveloped Sam and the group.

With his head held high, the Alpha gave a mighty roar at the group just in front of him from his huge, gaping mouth. Through the cloud of dust, everyone could see his long, vicious-looking front teeth, his canines, teeth that could tear massive lumps of flesh from bones in an instant.

Finally, satisfied he had demonstrated just how superior he was, he stared at the terrified group for a few long, long seconds, then turned away and trotted back towards the grass.

All this time, the female had stood motionless in front of the group, leaving the charge to her far more frightening leader. When he turned back towards the long grass, she did the same. Sam heard, rather than saw her find the cub. In complete contrast to the terrifying charge towards Sam and the group, he knew she would pick it up gently in her mouth and make her way back to the safety of where the others waited.

Some of the clients were whimpering, some were crying and some were shaking uncontrollably. Sam couldn't blame them. Only when the lion had been up-close to them could they appreciate just how enormous and awesomely powerful he really was.

The charge of the Alpha lion had been a terrifying experience for everyone there, including the two guides. It had been a very close call with one of the largest and most fearsome predators of Africa, and it was thanks to the skills and courage of both Sam and Landy, that they had all survived it.

Sam kept the clients walking backwards slowly for another 50 or 60 metres, until he deemed it safe enough to turn around and walk forwards.

'Landy, get us back to the mokorros quickly, please.' he ordered.

Landy took them in a wide circle around where the mock charge had taken place, but within minutes, the group arrived at the edge of the channel they had crossed and Sam could see the mokorros waiting for them about a hundred metres upstream. There was a small pathway along the bankside.

'Sam, you and the others wait here,' said Landy, 'I'll go and fetch the two mokorros. We don't know that all the lions are still on the termite mound and this path goes very close to where they were. If anything happens, I can jump into the water, they're not likely to follow me there.'

'Good idea,' said Sam.

A few minutes later, Landy and one of the other polers arrived with the mokorros. Still keeping a watchful eye in the direction of the lions, Sam made sure everyone was safely in the canoes before getting in himself and pushing the craft away from the bank, and danger. As soon as he was in the channel, he let out a long, slow breath. He glanced over to Landy, who smiled approvingly at him.

When they got back to camp, Sam immediately set about cooking a monster breakfast for everyone. He listened to the clients talking animatedly about their adventure, which would probably be just about the scariest thing that would ever happen to any of them.

He knew they would remember the day they were charged by a huge, fully-grown and angry lion, and survived to tell the tale, for a very long time to come.

THE MIGHTY ZAMBEZI

'The "Mighty Zambezi",' said Gabriel, 'is possibly the only river in the world where you have to wait for the water level to drop after the rains before you can go rafting.' He was explaining this to the clients on his safari through the game-parks of Botswana. 'You would not believe the volume of water that goes downstream at the height of or just after the big rains, it's far too dangerous for water sports. This time of year though, it's perfect'

It was the month of November. They were near the end of their trip and had made their last bush-camp at Serondela, alongside the Chobe River, which, at this point forms part of the border between Botswana and Namibia, 50 metres to the north. They would cross the river a little to the east of where they were camped, but their final destination however, was not Namibia; instead, they were headed for the bustling town of Livingstone, (named after the famous explorer David Livingstone) in Zambia.

They had enjoyed a delicious dinner of barbecued lamb chops, pasta and salad, and everyone was now grouped around the campfire, listening to Gabriel's briefing about the following day's activities.

'After breakfast tomorrow, we'll break camp and drive out of the park and into a town called Kasane. We'll pick up some water and supplies then drive onto the border crossing into Zambia at Kazangula. After we've set up camp at Livingstone, I'll organise the rafting for the following day for those of us who want to go.'

He knew already that at least three of his clients would go rafting with him, they weren't going to miss out on one of the most thrilling experiences they would encounter in their lives.

'Just a quick word about the Zambezi and the Victoria Falls themselves,' he continued, 'The river rises from a tiny spring in the far north-west of Zambia. I've been there and I can tell you, it's tiny. From Zambia, it flows to the west getting bigger all the time, and after meandering around Angola, it eventually reaches the geological fault that forms the Falls between Zimbabwe and Zambia, and at that point, from a spurt of water coming out of the ground, the Zambezi stretches for well over one and a half kilometres across the width of the waterfall. There are five sections, Devil's Cataract, Main Falls, Horseshoe Falls, Rainbow Falls and the Eastern Cataract.

'We're here before the high water period and so this is the best time of year to see the falls, and to go rafting. To give you some idea of the size of Victoria Falls at the end of the rainy season, around 550 million litres of water flows over the falls every minute, more if the rains have been really heavy.' He explained this very slowly, emphasising the words, "every minute," to allow the enormity of the volume of water to sink in.

'To put it into modern terms, that's like filling the fuel tanks of about 10 million family cars every minute, and some bright spark,' he continued, 'has even worked out that if that 550 million litres of water, was poured into empty coke cans, which were then placed end to end, they would stretch for around 200,000 kilometres, very nearly halfway to the moon, or around 4 times around Earth at the equator!

'So much water,' he continued, 'flows into the Zambezi from other rivers along its length, that the rapids down here become much too big and dangerous to raft during the high water, and you can't see too much of the actual falls themselves because of the spray. That's why the locals call the falls, Mosi-oa-Tunya, The Smoke that Thunders'.

The clients couldn't wait to view this magnificent, natural spectacle.

Most of that last day had been taken up with driving along sand roads to reach Serondela, their camp for that night. Gabriel was driving his favourite safari vehicle and trailer, a powerful old Mercedes Benz Unimog lorry, adapted to carry most of what they needed and affectionately known as "BJ", the two letters of its registration number. Whatever didn't fit onto BJ, was packed away in the trailer.

The tracks Gabriel had to negotiate were narrow and the banks at the side were simply where the sand had piled up. The tracks were so narrow in fact, that Gabriel could easily take his hands off the steering wheel and let the steep sides keep BJ going straight.

On one occasion, the sand was so soft and powdery that, as hard as Gabriel tried, poor old BJ simply ground to a halt. Even though Gabriel had done what he should have, let the tyre pressures down to allow them to have more grip in the sand, there was just too much even for BJ to power her way through.

'Ok,' Gabriel had said, 'everyone off, we have to push!'

From previous off-road driving experience, he knew this could be potentially dangerous for the clients. In their enthusiasm to help, clients could position themselves wrongly to push the truck. Gabriel jumped down from the driver's seat and approached the group of six.

'Nobody pushes from here!' he stated emphatically and pointed to the rear of the Mercedes, between it and the trailer.

'If someone is here and BJ suddenly lurches forward on firmer ground, that person could be thrown to the ground and run over by the trailer wheels. You only push from behind the trailer, is that clearly understood?'

He didn't really expect an answer and the clients were in no doubt that this instruction was not to be disobeyed.

Even though the vehicle was that much lighter without the clients and with all six of them helping to push at the back of the trailer, old BJ just about managed to pull herself forward a few metres and onto some firmer sand. That happened two or three times on their way to the campsite and on one occasion, Gabriel had to cut branches and place them under the wheels to enable BJ to get enough grip.

The day had been long, hot and tiring, especially for Gabriel. 'What a day!' he said to himself, as he crawled gratefully into his sleeping bag that night. He was sound asleep in less than a minute.

The next day dawned bright and clear, it would be another hot one! He and the clients soon had the camp broken up and on their way to Kasane. When they arrived at the border crossing, a short way outside of the town, the clients were dismayed to see dozens of huge, fully laden articulated lorries, all lined up waiting to cross the river by the ferry.

Gabriel however, surprised them all when he simply drove off the road onto a dirt track and slipped past all the trucks, right to the front of the queue.

'It's quite simple.' he said, 'This ferry crossing is the best way to get to Zambia. The only alternatives are to drive about 150 kilometres west of here, enter Namibia and cross the Caprivi Strip to Sesheke in Zambia and then the same distance back, or drive into Zimbabwe and then into Zambia. Neither is an option and each of them is a bureaucratic nightmare. This river crossing is a sort of pinch-point, where the Chobe and Zambezi rivers join together and where the borders of Namibia, Botswana, Zimbabwe and Zambia all meet in the middle.

'The reason there are so many lorries here is simply because they've come from all over southern Africa and this is still the most convenient way to get to other places such as the Copperbelt area of Zambia or even Mozambique.

'We need to cross the river to the Zambian border control at Kazangula on the other side. The ferry can only take one lorry at a time and I counted 43 waiting to cross. Sometimes, there are two ferries operating, but mostly it's just one that shuttles back and forth across the river, providing it hasn't broken down. It'll do about two, maybe three trips an hour, so it can take days to get a place on the ferry! The rest of the space is allocated to local vehicles and tourists.

'Not many people would bother with this area if they had to wait in line behind all these lorries, or drive into and out of countries they had no intention of visiting. We wait here with the locals but the ferrymen usually try to get us on first; tourism means foreign currency income for Botswana and Zambia, and that's a big deal for them.'

Almost immediately, Gabriel was ushered onto the ferry. A massive lorry and trailer was loaded after him and lastly, all the foot passengers, and then they were off. Around two hours later, Gabriel and the clients had completed the crossing, gone through the chaos of Zambian Customs and Immigration and were on their way to Livingstone.

They made camp that night at a site specially reserved for campers at one of the riverside hotels. The best thing about the campsite, the clients said later, was that it had proper toilets and showers; there would be no more standing under a bush-shower or making their way to the toilet tent, which simply surrounded a deep hole in the ground!! These same clients also said however, that they would miss standing naked in the open-air under a shower, using water warmed over a log fire and surrounded by beautiful African bush! The toilet tent however, would not be missed!!

Gabriel spent the afternoon making arrangements for the clients' activities the following day, including of course, the white-water rafting!

Only four of the six clients actually wanted to experience the Zambezi rapids, so after a hurried breakfast, Gabriel and the others made their way to the rafting briefing area. The two remaining clients would explore the historic town of Livingstone and barter for the goods on offer in the markets.

'Don't forget or be afraid to haggle a lot,' said Gabriel as he and the others were leaving camp, 'it's expected. Good luck and enjoy your day.'

As there were only five of them, the rafting company, appropriately named "Zambezi Rafting" asked Gabriel to take a lone traveller with them, a guy called Hans from The Netherlands, just to make up the numbers to a full crew.

The all important safety briefing and paddling instructions took about half an hour and at the end, they were told to expect a) "to get wet," b) "to fall out of the raft," c) "to be scared," but most of all, d) "to have a lot of fun!!"

Finally, the briefing was over and they all then trooped down a narrow little path to the water's edge. As they made their way down to the river, Gabriel couldn't help but marvel at the gorge they were descending. He tried to imagine the same scene millions of years ago. He wouldn't have been descending into a gorge, he thought to himself, as it probably wouldn't have existed.

At some time in the history of the region, a major geological event had formed a deep vertical crack, a "fault", across the path of the river, which interrupted its flow. The force of thousands of tonnes of water, sand and rocks constantly battering the sides of the fault, caused a scouring effect and eventually, the river found the weakest points and began the process of escaping the fault which had formed the Falls themselves.

Gradually, over the following eons, the never-ending flow continually forced itself through cracks in the rocks, gradually wearing them away to form the zig-zag pattern of gorges he was now admiring. It continued to do so at that very moment Gabriel was thinking about it, and it would continue to do so for as long as the river flowed.

When they finally reached the water's edge, only one raft-guide was left waiting, a tall African woman. As she approached the group to welcome them, she held out her hand for Gabriel to shake, and said, 'Good morning everyone, my name is Mukazi and I'm going to be your guide on the river today.'

Gabriel knew that it was culturally unusual to have an African woman acting as a guide on the Zambezi. However, the strength of her handshake won him over instantly and Mukazi's smile did the same job on the rest of them.

Everyone was captivated by her beauty, especially Gabriel. She stood almost as tall as him, but her long, slim legs made her look even taller. The green colour of her eyes was accentuated by her flawless, honey-coloured skin. She had what Gabriel would later describe to his friends as a "slash of a smile, which seemed to stretch from ear to ear, perfectly sculptured lips and nose and beautiful, white teeth." He made a very definite mental note of Mukazi!!

Pointing to various parts of the raft lying at the edge of the river, she continued, 'This is the raft we're using. It has eight separate inflated compartments, around the sides, the three thwarts in the middle and the floor, so we're definitely not going to sink. We'll probably end up upside down at times, but we won't sink! I'll sort out where you'll all sit in just a moment but first I want to check your helmets and buoyancy aids are done up correctly.'

Although never having rafted with him before, she knew that Gabriel had done several trips previously. After completing her equipment check, she pointed to where she wanted him to go, 'Gabriel, you sit at the front left position please, you know what to do.'

'Sure,' he replied. Gabriel immediately bounced over the thwarts and sat down on the side tube. This important position is known as the "stroke seat" and everyone else would take their paddling timing from him.

The others were seated according to size and weight, making three on each side. 'Remember your briefing everyone,' said Mukazi, 'paddle together and watch Gabriel for your timing. I want to emphasise just one point from the briefing; absolutely no-one is to deliberately drop over the side of the raft into the river, either to go for a swim or just to cool off. There are currents and eddies in this river that are lethal, people have died simply by having a dip in the wrong place. Is that understood?' Everyone nodded.

'Okay, make sure you all ram your toes securely under a tube when we set off; it may just make the difference between you staying in the raft or falling out.'

She then checked that everyone had their paddles, and shouted, 'Are we ready?' and when everyone shouted back, 'Yeah,' she said, 'Ok, let's go and play with some of the most dangerous rapids in the world, on one of the mightiest rivers in the world, in one of the most beautiful places in the world. And remember,' shouted Mukazi, 'it's meant to be fun!!'

Then they were off. From this point on, there would be no turning back.

The moment after they pushed away from the riverside, the swift-running current had them in its grip. The raft immediately picked up speed as they raced along through the steep sided gorge. Only a few minutes later, Mukazi, sitting in her position on the back tube of the raft and slightly to the right, shouted to the others, 'We're coming to the first rapid 200 metres ahead. It's not a long drop over the edge, but it will wake you up if you've fallen asleep!' She smiled at those who nervously looked around at her.

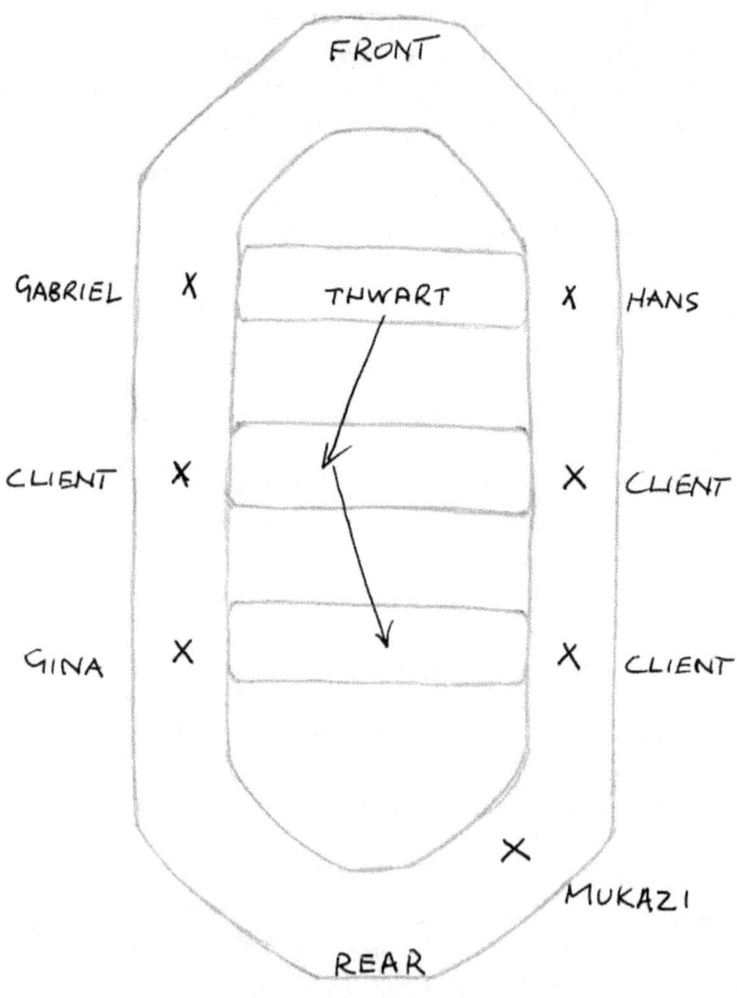

Mukazi's seating plan

At first, there was very little to disturb the peace on the river apart from the lazy swishing sound of the paddles in the water, but gradually, as they got nearer, the air was filled with a thunderous noise; the rapid!

'When I shout to hold on, make sure you grab the safety rope running around the outside of the raft,' said Mukazi, pointing.

The river divided slightly at this point and the water was being channelled either side of a large, rocky island which only appears when the water level has dropped. Whichever way the water was flowing, it simply disappeared over a ledge of rock.

Mukazi had to choose which side of the river she was going to follow. She knew from experience that, at that time of year, the right side was the correct way to go. As the water level had dropped over the previous months, dangerous rocks were exposed to the left side. Any slight miscalculation in direction could spell disaster over there.

As they approached the rapid, the current was being squeezed into an ever tightening channel and flowed faster and faster. As a result, the raft began to pick up even more speed. The crew had seen the water going over the edge and understandably had stopped paddling, not wishing to hasten their arrival at what was obviously going to be extremely scary.

Gabriel however, knew what was coming and he kept paddling to help keep the raft on a straight course towards the rapid. Mukazi concentrated hard on trying to keep the raft in the centre of the current, making small alterations with her paddle. She was shouting orders at the crew, 'Keep paddling, keep paddling, watch Gabriel!'

Suddenly, everyone could see that the river would shoot them over the ledge and drop them some 3 or 4 metres down, where the river simply turned into a frenzy of white spray.

Following the current, the front of the raft began to tip forwards, down towards the chaos at the bottom of the rapid. Mukazi shouted, 'Hold on, hold on, here we go!' Everyone on board, including Mukazi, made a grab for the safety rope running all the way around the raft.

As they slid over the edge and hurtled downwards, someone shouted, '*Sh* …..', but the voice was lost in the thunderous noise of tonnes and tonnes of green water crashing over the ledge and into the river below. The raft hit the river's surface below the ledge and immediately capsized, spilling the rafters and Mukazi into the fast-flowing current, arms and legs flailing helplessly. Gabriel surfaced a few seconds later and was relieved to see Mukazi had already climbed back onto the raft and was in the process of turning it the right way up. The yellow helmets of the other rafters bobbed up to the surface one at a time and everyone began making their way back to the raft, their bulky buoyancy aids dictating that the only stroke they could attempt was the "doggy-paddle".

'Help me get everyone in,' Mukazi shouted as she grabbed Gabriel's arm and pulled him back onboard. By the time every bedraggled client was back in, coughing and spluttering Zambezi river water, the raft had drifted about two hundred metres away from the rapid and into calmer water.

A few seconds later, everyone was back in their places, each shouting their excitement at having survived the first rapid, if a little wet and more than a little scared! An unofficial competition began amongst the clients to see who had had the worst experience underwater. Surely there would be nothing worse than that, each secretly thought. How wrong they were, for some at least!!

The crew were much too excited to notice how far they had drifted downstream. Mukazi decided it was time to re-focus them.

'Ok, everyone,' she said, 'we're coming up to number two in a few minutes. It's every bit as bad as the first and maybe worse. This will test your paddling skills. We have to get it right or we start crashing into the rock faces. If we do that, we start to spin and we might have to go down the last part backwards. Not a good idea.'

To form this rapid, the Zambezi had found weak spots in the rocks and a gently curving, backwards 'S' bend had been shaped. At this point, the gorge narrowed significantly and the current, as in the previous rapid, was squeezed into a tighter space. The water was slammed against the solid rock wall with tremendous force, throwing the course of the river to the right. 40 metres or so further on, after once again crashing against a solid rock face, the river was turned back to the left. At every point, the wall of rock at both sides of the gorge was waiting to catch the adventurers unawares and bounce them off course.

'If we avoid the walls and stay in the current, we'll shoot down a slope and back out into the main flow of the river. I'll have very little time to make any adjustments to our course through the gorge. Make no mistake people, 'she shouted, 'this is a dangerous section, make sure you keep paddling and do everything I tell you, when I tell you. I don't get a second chance with this rapid, we have to get it right first time.'

It didn't happen that way!

The current raced them along into the narrowing gorge. A gigantic boulder on the riverbed about 25 metres in front of the first rock wall was going to be an additional hazard for Mukazi. The water was being channelled either side and once again, she would have to choose which route to take to pass the boulder, there would be no opportunity to change her mind.

100 metres to go!

'When I shout for it, you guys on the left side keep paddling forwards and you guys on the right paddle backwards *hard,* to try and turn us around the corner. Paddle backwards for all you're worth and paddle together. We have to slow down the right-hand side and turn the raft to avoid the wall.'

50 metres to go!

'After we've turned, I'll call for everyone to paddle forwards. Give it everything you've got, we have to avoid the walls.' shouted Mukazi, as she steered to the left side of the huge boulder, giving herself the best possible chance of turning the corner. Suddenly, the raft shot forward, accelerated by the current.

10 metres!

'Here we go!!' she shouted, struggling to make herself heard above the roar of the river.

They had slipped past the big rock with only centimetres to spare, but now everyone could see they were hurtling straight towards the sheer side of the gorge directly in front of them.

'Left side keep paddling forward, right side back, paddle backwards together, now, **hard!** shouted Mukazi.

As one, everyone on the right-hand side of the raft leaned back and pushed their paddles through the fast-flowing current from back to front. They dug in deep, trying to get as much purchase in the water as they could.

Mukazi had her feet firmly secured into the foot-straps on the deck and she was leaning as far out over the back of the raft as she could, sweeping her paddle from left to right, desperately trying to push the rear over to the left, so that they would "skid" around the corner and stay in the centre of the current.

Eventually, she and her crew had managed to turn the raft to the right. 'Everyone, paddle forwards, now!' she shouted above the din of the river, 'keep paddling together!'

However, in spite of all their efforts to paddle away from the wall on the left side, they had gained too much speed. The river was just too powerful and they were slammed side-on into the unforgiving rock face.

One of the clients, Gina, an Italian lady sitting on the left side, just in front of Mukazi, suddenly realised why they wore safety helmets. The unexpected shock of the collision had caught her off-balance. Her head struck the solid rock as she was pitched over the left side, into the swift-flowing river between the raft and the rock face.

As she slipped over into the water, Mukazi lunged forward and managed to catch hold of the back of her life-jacket before she disappeared under the raft. She held onto Gina tightly as the current grabbed them again. The force of being catapulted off the rock started the raft spinning wildly.

Now they were heading for the second turn, where the river flowed round to the left. There was nothing Mukazi could do, she had to hold on to Gina's life-jacket or she would be swept away and possibly drowned or dashed against rocks. But holding onto Gina meant she had no control of the raft.

Suddenly, a vicious undercurrent dragged Gina further down into the water. Mukazi held on grimly, but she could feel Gina slipping out of her grasp.

'Help me here, help me,' she called out. Hans responded instantly and his big hands found a part of Gina's life-jacket and between them, he and Mukazi managed to pull her head clear of the water. But that was all they could do, there was no time to pull Gina back on board properly, she would have to ride out the rapid in the water. The raft however, had almost stopped spinning by now, but they were heading for the second turn to the left, fast!

'Hold on to Gina,' Mukazi shouted at Hans and returned to her place at the rear of the raft. In the confusion, one or two of the clients were still paddling, making their situation even worse.

'Stop paddling, stop paddling!' Mukazi shouted to the other clients. She knew there was now no chance she could line the raft up properly to descend the slope forwards into the rapid, the current was too strong and swift.

Her only choice was to allow the river to slam them into the rock face ahead, but she had to protect Gina. The powerful current and the paddling of some of the clients had twisted the raft slightly so that the left side would strike the wall. Gina would be squeezed between the raft and the rock face, possibly with disastrous consequences. Mukazi had a split second to alter the situation.

'Left side, backwards now, together, paddle backwards, *hard,*' she shouted.

Immediately Gabriel and the other client, (there were now only two paddling on the left side) responded and dug their paddles deep into the water behind them. They were only a matter of metres away from the rock face, but mercifully, the raft began to turn and they slammed into the wall with the right-hand side of the raft, protecting Gina.

'Everyone, grab hold of the safety rope,' Mukazi shouted as they rammed into the rock face. Hans hung on grimly to Gina as the force of the collision threatened to rip her from his grasp.

Again, the raft bounced off the rock wall spinning them round.

Then, suddenly, they found themselves around the corner and back in the grip of the current, which was speeding them down the slope, backwards towards the thundering water at the bottom of the rapid. Hans' arms ached with the strain of holding onto Gina's life-jacket.

There was absolutely nothing Mukazi could do to turn the raft to the front.

'We're going down, hold on, hold on!' she shouted as the raft hurtled down the slope. The clients looked behind them nervously as they all grabbed the safety rope.

Suddenly, the raft stopped dead as they hit the water at the bottom of the rapid, known as a "stopper". (Over the eons, water racing down the slope and crashing into the bottom of the rapid had gouged out a depression, or hole. The water flows in and around the depression in a circular motion and is then forced back on itself, against the current, creating a "standing-wave.")

Not expecting the sudden halt, the clients at the front, including Gabriel were all tipped backwards, some falling into the people sitting at the back. Everything was chaos, arms, legs and paddles pointed in every direction. The impact finally forced Gina out of Hans' grip and she was swept into the rapid.

The action of the raft being tossed around in the standing-wave prevented the clients from getting back to their seats for the first few seconds. The force of the water racing down the slope was pushing the raft backwards into the wave and that same wave was pushing the raft forwards towards the slope. As a result, it wasn't going anywhere.

Mukazi's main focus now however, was to recover Gina as quickly as possible.

'Look for Gina, look for her life-jacket underwater,' she shouted, desperately. 'She's caught in the wave and we must get her out!' There was just an edge of panic in Mukazi's voice.

'There!' cried one of the others, pointing to a flash of yellow just under the surface. Mukazi lunged for the side of the raft and reached over and down as far as she could to try and grab the material of the jacket, but her feet were trapped by the bodies that had tumbled into where she was sitting and she couldn't reach far enough. She missed and the flash of yellow, although tantalisingly close, disappeared and Gina was gone again.

For the next few seconds, chaos reigned as people scrambled to return to their seats and the raft slowly flattened from its near vertical position to a more horizontal one. The raft, still trapped by the wave, was bobbing around in the rapid like a little cork. For those few seconds, it seemed as though the river would never let them go. Water poured into the front of the raft from the rapid and water from the wave crashed over Mukazi from behind.

Suddenly, a hand shot out of the foaming white-water, straight up into the air. Hans was nearest and he saw it first. 'There,' he shouted.

'Grab her, grab her,' called Mukazi, urgently. Hans had already reached over and managed to get a firm grip of Gina's wrist and pull her head clear. Fortunately, he was a strong man and he held on until she was hauled back onboard a few minutes later.

Although by this time the raft was completely full of water, Mukazi eventually managed to get it out of the grip of the wave and into calmer water, where the special holes in the raft were able to do their job and bail the water out and back to the river.

Hans and Gabriel took an arm each and yanked Gina out from the Zambezi. She lay in a crumpled heap in the bottom of the raft, coughing up water and completely exhausted. Finally, she stopped spluttering, and plucky lady that she was, she started to laugh and whoop. Everyone was really excited about taking the rapid backwards, and getting bounced around in the wave, something none of them had ever imagined would happen.

'Well, I'm grateful to whoever it was who pulled me out, but I reckon I had the best ride of all,' Gina said, laughing.

Mukazi said, 'I think you probably did Gina, but good job everyone, that was great fun, don't you think!' She was especially grateful to Hans, and nodded her thanks to him.

Gabriel and the rest of the crew carried on shooting rapids, getting drenched, falling overboard and generally having a lot of fun, for the next two or three hours. There were several other rafts on the river at the same time as Mukazi's, including some from other rafting organisations.

'I suppose all you guides know each other,' asked Amy, an American lady.

'Yeah, mostly,' replied Mukazi, 'but we also get private rafts, ones owned by individuals on the river and we don't really know who they are. The golden rule is though, no matter who it is, we all look out for each other.'

The raft carried on drifting lazily down the Zambezi while the crew chatted amongst themselves.

Eventually, Mukazi brought them back to reality. 'This next rapid,' she said, 'is easy as long as you all paddle together, in time with Gabriel. It's a straight course through the middle, but if we go off-course, we could well get beached on one of the large rocks to either side.'

By this time, all the clients were used to Mukazi's voice, describing the rapid accurately and encouraging them in their efforts to paddle together.

'Why is it so important for us to paddle together?' asked Marc.

'It's like this,' replied Mukazi, 'I only steer this raft, it's you people in front of me that get us to where we have to be. If all six of you dip your paddle in the water at different times, in effect, only that one paddle is creating any forward motion. If you all dip your paddles in at the same time, there's six times more energy to push us forward, or backwards as the case may be.'

'Oh I see, makes sense really doesn't it,' commented Marc.

They paddled along for about 5 minutes before Mukazi began to line them up for the run through the rapid. Ahead of her, she could see another raft with 8 clients on board, all wearing different coloured life-jackets.

'Just paddle backwards for a while,' said Mukazi, 'we'll let that raft up ahead go through and get beyond the rocks before we go.'

She knew this was a private raft, and just from watching the guide's actions, she wasn't at all sure he knew exactly what he was doing. Even from a distance of 200 metres or so, Mukazi could see that the guide wasn't steering the raft in a straight line. When they entered the rapid, they were much too far to one side and the raft was immediately thrown off course.

Mukazi knew that disaster was about to strike and she shouted for action from her crew.

'Let's go, let's go, all together,' and instantly, the raft accelerated forward and into the rapid.

Up ahead, the other crew was in trouble. As well as steering her own raft, Mukazi was watching the one ahead of them.

'He's going to crash into the rocks, ...whoa! There he goes,' she shouted as the guide from the other raft was suddenly thrown into the water as they hit one of the boulders. The now guide-less raft bounced off the first boulder and shot across the stream into another smaller rock, the top of which was just sticking out of the water. They hit the second rock at such speed that the raft simply rode up over the top and became stranded, unable to go forward or backwards. The force of the current ensured that they remained there, marooned.

Mukazi watched all this happening and knew instantly what she had to do. She just hoped she had enough time.

'Gabriel, come to the back, Hans take Gabriel's place,' she ordered. Both knew that Mukazi was deadly serious.

'I'm going to steer straight for that raft up ahead,' she said, 'and when we get there, I'm going to jump from here into the back.' She turned to Gabriel, 'I know you can handle this, I want you to steer the raft through this rapid and then downstream, ferry across the current and eddy-out on one side or the other. If you can pick up the guide from the river, great, but if not, just wait for me at the side. You have to steer a straight line to avoid the other rocks. Got it?'

'Ok,' replied Gabriel. He wasn't about to question Mukazi's faith in him, even though he wasn't too sure about it himself. Thankfully, he thought to himself, I am at least familiar with the rafting terms "ferrying" and "eddying-out".

Immediately after Hans had taken Gabriel's position, they approached the stranded raft. Gabriel knew that they weren't going to stop and that Mukazi would jump from one to the other.

'Get me as close as you can Gabriel. Watch out,' shouted Mukazi to the other crew, 'I'm jumping in.'

With expert timing, she launched herself from the back of her raft across the small gap and landed in a heap in the middle of the stranded crew. There was a loud clunk as the paddle she was carrying struck one of the others on the helmet, but Mukazi was much too pre-occupied to notice.

His job partially done, Gabriel steered the raft through the rest of the rapid without incident. Once they were through, he began to look ahead for a suitable place he could swing the raft around to wait for Mukazi. As it happened, he could see a raft already eddied-out behind a boulder close to the right edge of the river a little further ahead and knew that this would be the best place for him to wait.

'This is going to be fun' he muttered to himself, not at all sure he was going to manage it. 'We're going to stop up ahead, where that other raft is,' he called to the others. 'When I shout for it, the right side has to paddle backwards and the left side has to paddle forwards. I'll steer us round and then when I call for it, everyone has to paddle forwards, hard, to get us across the current and into the eddy.' There was no time to explain the intricacies of the manoeuvre.

Moments later, Gabriel's voice rang out, 'Now, right side back, left side forward, paddle now together.' Completely opposite to Mukazi's confident and composed manner, there was more than a little uncertainty in Gabriel's tone as he shouted his commands, but thankfully, everyone paddled as one and the raft began to turn. He took a wide sweep out to the left of the raft with his own paddle to help them turn around into the teeth of the current and closer to the side of the river.

Just at the correct moment, he shouted, 'Everyone forwards, *now*, paddle hard, get us in.' Miraculously, the raft had turned round completely to face the oncoming current, but Gabriel had his paddle in the water at such an angle that the front of the raft was pointing in slightly towards the bank. With the powerful paddling of the crew, they entered the eddy, just behind the other raft. As soon as they were in, everyone noticed that, curiously, the raft began to drift forwards, effectively against the flow of the river.

'Phew, made it,' said Gabriel, more to himself than anyone else. But the others heard him and gave him a rousing round of applause.

A few minutes later, Mukazi entered the same eddy with the crew she had rescued. Their guide had been picked up by the raft that was already there when Gabriel arrived. He jumped back aboard his own raft after shouting his thanks to Mukazi, and so, everyone was back where they should be.

'How do these eddies work then, why do we seem to go against the current?' asked Gina.

'It's a question of water flow and obstacles,' replied Mukazi, as she prepared to push back out into the river. 'Imagine a big boulder sticking out of the middle of the riverbed. Water will generally follow a straight course until it comes to an obstacle. It can't go through the boulder so it passes either side and continues on its course. This creates an empty space in the current directly behind the boulder, and like a vacuum, something has to fill it. Water that has passed by is sort of sucked back to the rear of the boulder, effectively creating a current in the opposite direction, understand?' she enquired of everyone. Without waiting for an answer, she carried on, 'Where we just stopped, the flow of water has to go past the big rock sticking out into the current, but then something has to fill in that space behind the rock, so the water is drawn into that space and begins to flow in the opposite direction to the main current. Eddies are really cool places, they mean we can stop safely without having to fight the current all the time.'

'Fascinating,' remarked Amy.

'How do we think Gabriel did getting into the eddy?'

'Brilliant,' replied Amy, and everyone agreed.

The rest of the morning was taken up with shooting more rapids, some exciting and some not so exciting. By lunchtime however, no-one on the raft had managed to stay on board through every rapid. At some stage, each of them had tasted the cold Zambezi water.

Eventually, Mukazi steered the raft to the side of the river and tied it securely to a rock.

'Ok, lunchtime,' she said, 'food and cold drinks, let's go.'

Gabriel and the rest of his fellow rafters followed her a short distance from the water's edge to a cleared area, where company staff had prepared a lunch of sandwiches, fruit, cakes and, best of all, some ice-cold drinks. Although taking a ducking in the river allowed people to cool off a little, the African sun soon got to work again and nothing became so welcome as a can of drink so cold, it was painful to swallow.

After a relaxing lunch and exchanging stories with others of how they had run the rapids, every story becoming more and more life-threatening with each telling, Mukazi gathered all her crew together and then set off once more down the "Mighty Zambezi".
'Mukazi, all the other raft-guides at lunch were young men, mostly African. I didn't see any other women guides, are you the only one?' asked Amy.
'No,' replied Mukazi, 'there is one white girl from South Africa who guides here but only occasionally with private trips. I'm the only female here in Livingstone regularly employed as a raft-guide, and what is even more unusual, as you can see, I'm an African woman.'
'Why is that so unusual?'
'It's as much cultural as anything else, it just isn't seen as something that African women do. We would generally look after the family or work in the fields tending crops, but as my country, Zambia progresses and modernises, those old beliefs are dying out and we women are becoming more and more active, socially and culturally.'
'How did you get into it?' asked Leon, a quiet and unassuming South African.
'Originally, I'm from a suburb in Lusaka, the capital, called Leopards Hill. My father is a Zambian but my mother moved from Ethiopia to Lusaka, where she met and married my father. When I finished school I didn't really know what I wanted to do, so I came to live with my auntie here in Livingstone. I've always wanted to work on the river, so I contacted several companies and Zambezi Rafting was the only one which seemed to be interested in me. They eventually agreed to give me a trial and as a result of that, they took me on and trained me. Some of the male guides were a bit peeved I was working with them, one or two did their best to make me quit but I got through and to be fair, they now treat me as an equal. I never intended to do this forever though and when I finish here at the end of this season, I'll go on to

university. By the way,' she went on, 'in Nyanja, my native language, my name Mukazi means "friend".'

'Well, good for you, *friend*' said Marc, 'hope you do well, you clearly know what you're doing on the river.'

'Thanks.'

At one stage, they glided past a huge, vertical wall of rock with a strange shape drawn onto the side facing the river. It appeared to have the body of a snake and the head of a serpent.

'Mukazi, what's that?' asked Gina, pointing to the drawing.

'That,' she replied solemnly, 'is Nyaminyami, the "God" of the Zambezi River. The local Tonga people believe that Nyaminyami protects all who travel on the river or who live by her side. Traditionally, animal sacrifices were made to make sure that Nyaminyami kept people safe and provided food from the river. They don't make sacrifices anymore, but if you don't keep paddling, I could make an exception with some of you lot!!'

As they drifted lazily down a calm stretch of water, Mukazi told them about the next rapid, perhaps the worst they would encounter on the river.

'The power of this river is awesome and the best advice I can give here,' she said, 'is to hold on tight and not to fall out in this one. First of all, the current will speed us up as we shoot through a gap in the rocks. After that, we go down a gentle slope for around 15 metres or so, going faster and faster all the time. At the bottom, we can't avoid bouncing off some rocks; this is where you must hold on. I can steer us through some of it, but as I avoid one, I'll be crashing into another straight away.'

'If you fall out, the current will suck you under and release you three times, before the river finally lets you go. Each time you surface, you will have maybe a second or two to breathe some air before you get sucked down again. When the current has you under, it will toss you

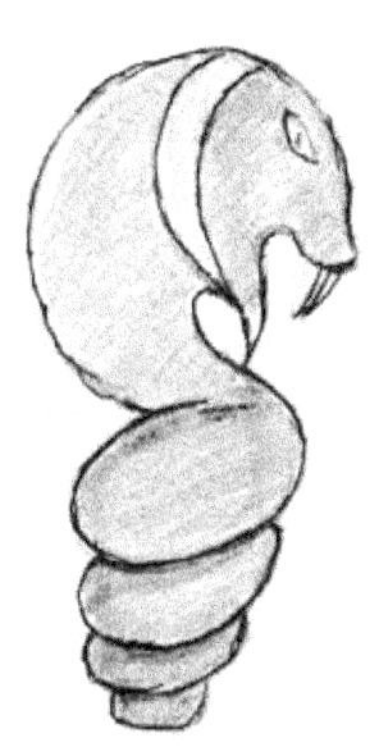

Nyaminyami

around and turn you over and over and over. Don't fight it, you'll exhaust yourself. Just let the river do what she wants, she will let you go in the end. Your buoyancy aids will do their job and float you to the surface but it's scary down there, don't fall out!'
Everyone exchanged nervous glances as they paddled towards their possible doom!
Mukazi steered through the gap expertly and then careered down the slope. 'Here come the rocks, hold on tight,' she shouted.
She managed to avoid the first rocks and it seemed as though they would make it through without hitting any. Indeed, Hans thought exactly that and, disastrously, had not only let go of the safety rope but had stood up in the raft.
'Yeah, we made it,' he was shouting, turning round to the others.
'Sit down and hold on to the rope,' shouted Mukazi, more than a little annoyed.
Her warning however, came too late. The raft clipped the edge of a large boulder at the left side of the river. The force of the collision halted the raft for the briefest of split-seconds and compacted the inflatable tube just a little. It was enough however, to act like a giant spring, flinging the raft back away from the boulder.
The sudden stop-start motion caught Hans completely unawares. The force of hitting the rock and then being bounced away, catapulted him across the raft, over the side and into the water. In a desperate attempt to stop himself falling overboard, he had grabbed onto Gabriel's buoyancy aid, but Hans' momentum was too much and he pulled the unfortunate Gabriel over with him. There was nothing Mukazi could do; she had to hope that the river god, Nyaminyami would look after them!
Gabriel was taken completely by surprise as he was dragged over, but as he hit the water, he managed to take a lungful of air. For a brief second, his head was above the water, then he felt the current sweep his legs away and drag him under, just as Mukazi had said it would happen.
Under the surface, Gabriel forced himself to open his eyes and try to peer through the green murk of the river water. It seemed as though

his body was being assaulted from all sides as the current twisted him round and turned him over and over, seemingly endlessly.

He caught fleeting glimpses of light through the darker green and knew that this was the surface. It was the only way he could orientate himself in this strange environment. Gabriel was a strong young man, fit and healthy, but the brutality of the underwater currents was beginning to sap even his strength.

He had no idea how long he'd been held captive by the river, but suddenly, he felt the hot sun on his face and knew he had surfaced. He instinctively opened his mouth to breathe, but in his haste, instead of all air, he took some water in as well. Then he was dragged under again and thrashed around helplessly by the strong current.

Gabriel could feel the burning pain in his lungs and because he had taken some water into his wind-pipe, the urge to cough became overpowering. As the swirling currents twisted him this way and that, he not only had to try and keep the surface light in sight, he had to fight and defeat the urge to cough up the trapped water. He felt himself getting weaker by the second.

Just as he thought he was going to have to cough underwater, he popped out onto the surface once more and immediately spluttered and spat out the water, but in doing so, he couldn't take another breath before he was sucked down for the third time.

Each time he had been underwater, it seemed longer than the last, and this time, he thought he was never going to re-surface. The current was twisting him round and round, turning him over and over without mercy. He was helpless, he couldn't resist, it was as though he was a little toy being worried by a big dog.

The advice of Mukazi to relax underwater and not to try and fight the current was completely forgotten as Gabriel fought to make sure he could see the surface light through the deep green of the water.

His increasingly desperate efforts however, were draining his strength, weakening him more and more, but Gabriel's mind was spinning round even more than his body. He was in such confusion, remembering what Mukazi had said, would be impossible at this time.

Sometimes he caught flashes of the light above him and then the river snatched it away again, twisting him round and round, each time more cruelly than the last. He knew he desperately needed to breathe, his lungs were aching with pain. His arms and legs now felt like lead weights and he could feel the fight going out of him, his limbs moving slower and slower.

He knew the "Mighty Zambezi" was winning the battle. If he didn't manage to get to the surface within seconds, he knew he would drown in the current that held him captive.

After what seemed like an eternity, he stopped struggling, not through some sudden memory of what Mukazi had said, but simply because he had no strength left. Everything now appeared to be happening in slow motion, even his confused mind had cleared a little. He'd all but given up trying to keep the light green of the surface in sight. Instead, he watched the endless streams of bubbles created by the maelstrom, floating to the surface.

By now his arms and legs were moving only in time with the unpredictable current. He thought the fight had gone out of him, he didn't realise that the river was actually giving him up.

Is this it, he wondered as he drifted along, am I going to drown? It was the only thought he had at that time.

And then, mercifully, he felt the glorious heat of the sun once more, the river had surrendered him. As he floated on the surface, helpless, his mind still full of thoughts of drowning, he heard someone shouting, 'Grab hold of the rope! *HEY!* Grab the rope!'

It took two or three seconds for Gabriel to realise that the voice was directed at him. He had become so disorientated and confused by his underwater beating, nothing was making sense. He was lying in the water, floating on his back and gazing with unseeing eyes at the clear blue, cloudless sky.

Eventually though, the shouted orders got through to him and he saw the safety kayak alongside him.

'*Hey*, grab the rope!' the voice was repeating. He reached out weakly for the length of rope trailing from the back of the kayak, which then towed him down to where Mukazi had stopped the raft in an eddy to wait for him and Hans. Gabriel was pulled into the raft, where he collapsed in an exhausted heap, on top of Hans who'd been pulled in seconds earlier.

'Told you not to fall in,' said Mukazi, smiling. 'Now you know why we call that rapid "Stairway to Heaven"!'

After trying, and failing to adequately describe to the others on the raft what being underwater and thrashed around by the merciless current was like, Gabriel and Hans were ready to start paddling the raft again and they continued on down the Zambezi.

At one stage, Mukazi stopped the raft at the river's edge just before a thunderous rapid where the river gathered speed down a long slope and then dropped over a rocky ledge into the river below, creating a huge cloud of spray. The sound of the river crashing into the water at the bottom of the drop-off was deafening.

'You are not allowed to remain in the raft for this rapid, it is simply too dangerous,' she told the clients. 'I have to take the raft down alone, and meet you at the end.'

Gabriel had seen this rapid before and he knew the dangers. Even in the hands of experts such as Mukazi, guiding the raft safely through this rapid was extremely difficult, one small mistake could spell disaster for the guide and the raft. The volume of water was awesome and the current, swift and unforgiving.

Out of the raft, Gabriel and the others made their way along the rocky path at the side of the river. From here, they watched Mukazi and the other guides take their crafts down this most dangerous of rapids.

Once empty of clients, the rafts pushed back out into the flow of the river, one by one. The first 25 metres or so was a not-so-gentle slope, where the current accelerated them to an incredible speed. Rocks lying just under the surface were sending the current in all sorts of different directions.

'Look how she has to fight to keep the raft going in a straight line,' remarked Gabriel, 'that's how vicious the currents are there.'

A few seconds after setting off, Mukazi's raft was on the edge of a terrifying drop into a storm of spray and thunderous roaring.

'She probably can't even see the bottom,' ventured Gina, as they watched the raft slip gracefully over the edge and drop through the air, seemingly in slow-motion.

Mukazi was holding her paddle aloft with one hand and holding on tight to the safety rope with the other, eventually disappearing in the curtain of spray.

There was a loud thump as her raft crashed down onto the river surface. Everyone, including clients from other rafts, stood transfixed. Nothing happened for several long seconds and everyone held their breath, desperate to see that she had made it safely.

'There she is,' shouted Gabriel, pointing to where Mukazi was casually paddling the raft out of the spray and over to the small ledge at the side of the river where he and the others were waiting.

Remarkably, none of the guides were thrown from their rafts and none had flipped over at the bottom of the rapid; Gabriel thought this was a testament to their skills. For Mukazi however, it all seemed to be completely routine as she came alongside the ledge and beckoned all her clients to get back aboard and start paddling down the river to the next rapid.

'Ah, for us it's not so difficult,' she remarked casually, 'remember, we do it every day. Scary the first time, but after that, it's real fun!!'

By now it was mid-afternoon and everyone was getting just a bit tired. Mukazi warned them all about the next rapid they would encounter, named "Washing Machine".

'Fall out of the raft in this rapid, and you'll find out why we call it that,' she remarked, mischievously. It was more of a warning than an invitation, but Amy did just that! When the river seemed to get tired of her and the exhausted Amy was eventually pulled back into the raft, she described her experience.

'Now I know how you guys must have felt through that long rapid, what did you call it, Stairway to Heaven? It was just a battle down there because the current battered me so violently, turning and twisting me round and round and round. It felt like I was being kept within a spiral of churning current underwater, no matter what I did, I just couldn't seem to break free. It was almost as if the Zambezi was getting revenge for something, maybe it was because she didn't manage to drown either of you two!! I simply had no idea where I was when I popped out onto the surface. How long was I down there, it felt like a couple of minutes?'

'About 15 to 20 seconds,' replied Mukazi.

'Is that all!?' shouted Amy, 'My lungs were agony, I honestly thought I was going to die. 15 to 20 seconds!!' she repeated, shaking her head in disbelief.

It may not sound a long time, but Gabriel knew just how brutal the current could be and how it would seem like an eternity underwater.

From his previous rafting experience, Gabriel knew that they were nearing the end of the trip. They plunged through some further rapids where the water cascaded over the entire raft as they crashed through, and once, they collided with a rock in the middle of the river.

Gabriel suspected that Mukazi ran into the rock deliberately, to give just one more bit of excitement. She could easily have avoided it but Gabriel saw that she steered straight for it and the raft came to rest directly on top of the rock. The clients in the raft clung on to the side safety ropes and looked round, rather bewildered at Mukazi. They had become thoroughly used to careering through rapids and spray, negotiating obstacles and surviving the churning waters of the "Mighty Zambezi". They were not used to being stranded high and dry on a rock!

Mukazi had a huge smile on her face, indicating to Gabriel that she was very satisfied as to how she had run into the rock.

'OK, everyone,' she said, 'I'm going to show you how I got that other raft off the rock. Carefully and slowly, make your way to the back with me.' As the clients clambered over the thwarts that were the seats in the centre of the raft and piled up in the back, they could see that the front was lifting off the rock. Eventually, with the weight concentrated in the rear, there was nothing to pin the front of the raft to the top of the rock. The river current simply twisted them off and back into the stream, albeit, going backwards.

'See, nothing to it,' said Mukazi cheerily, steering the raft round to face forwards. All the clients were laughing as they scrambled to get back to their seats to carry on paddling.

A few minutes later, the river bent slightly to the left and they passed a vertical stretch of rock face, about 10 metres high from the river to the top of the cliff, worn smooth by the scouring action of the current.

The river had slowed to a lazy meander and as they paddled the raft past, Mukazi said, 'On your right is a good example of why people in rafts should *always* do what the professional guide says, or in this case, what the guide says not to do. Looks pretty flat and even, yes?' she asked, pointing to the flat surface of the rock face, 'the current here looks slow, yes? Well, it isn't. Last year, a raft came down this far. All the clients had been briefed as you were, "no jumping off the raft". Two of them however, a man and his female partner thought they knew best and jumped over the side to go for a swim. The under-current at this point in the river is vicious and what they didn't know is that just under the surface at that point over there,' she said, pointing to a spot on the rock face where the current was colliding into the wall, 'is an underwater ledge that goes back into the rocks about a metre and a half. It's a softer rock than the rest of it and the ledge has been scoured out by the action of the river. Within seconds of being in the water, both of them were swept against the rock face and then sucked down and into the crack underwater. The force of the current kept them there and they didn't come out. Neither of them was ever seen again, even when the river level dropped enough to reveal the ledge, no bodies were ever recovered; no clothing, no buoyancy aids, no shoes, but someone did find a battered helmet later on, further downstream. We reckon that after drowning, their bodies were eventually torn apart by the constant grinding effect of the current and what was left was eventually swept downstream and taken by crocs or tiger-fish.'

There was an eerie silence and nobody spoke, as they glided gently past the rock face.

Eventually, they reached the point in the river where the rafts are taken out. This was obviously the finishing point for everyone as there were several other rafts at the same place, all being worked on at the same time. Gangs of porters were busy packing up equipment, deflating rafts, folding them up, stuffing as much equipment as they could into large bags.

As soon as they had picked up as much as they could carry, each porter set off up the incredibly steep, zig-zagging paths on the slopes of the gorge. Gabriel and the rest of his colleagues were very tired from the trip but they still had to slog their way up to the top.

At one stage, as he wearily trudged his way up one path, Gabriel remarked, 'That's the second time those two porters have passed me. I'm carrying nothing and they're carrying a whole raft on their heads!'

'They're much fitter than you are, Nkosi and they get paid by the load so they don't hang around nattering like you do, get a move on,' joked Mukazi behind him. All Gabriel could think of however, was the ice-cold beer he knew was waiting for him at the top. It kept him going!

Finally, when all the equipment had been loaded onto the waiting lorries, the clients from all the rafts scrambled on board. There would be a party that night when film of all their trips, including the successes and the disasters such as rafts being stranded on rocks, flipping over in rapids, the sometimes comical attempts by clients to get back into a raft would be shown to an appreciative but increasingly raucous audience. There would be no secrets, it would all be there, followed by dancing into the night.

 For the entire journey back to Livingstone, there was excited chatter and much laughter. Everyone on board the lorry had a tale to tell, scary, thrilling, funny and sometimes, moving tales.

However, they all had one thing in common, they told of the day that these adventurers rose to the challenge of the "Mighty Zambezi", and survived.

Maybe Nyaminyami was watching over them that day!

THE ZEBRA FOAL

The trees on the far horizon seemed to dance and shimmer as the searing African heat bounced off the savannah. Animals that had grazed and browsed during the cool early morning now lay dozing in any shade they could find.

It was the middle of March and despite the heat, the rainy season was in full swing. From early morning until around mid-afternoon on most days, the sun burned its way into the African landscape. But above the land, the massive thunder-head clouds told a different story. Darkening all through the day, becoming more and more dense with water-vapour, they would finally shed their watery burdens around late afternoon.

In the space of minutes, savannah that had become dry and parched from the day-time heat, suddenly found itself almost drowning in the deluge. Trees bowed under the enormous weight of rainwater that clung to their leaves and branches, plants and bushes were pounded almost flat against the earth. Any slight hollow in the landscape was immediately filled to overflowing, joining others to form gigantic puddles. Waterholes were replenished, streams flowed stronger than ever and the animals rejoiced in the abundant water supply.

This is the annual cycle of life-giving rain that Africa depends on. And during this cycle, new life is born.

The female zebra barely noticed the huge raindrops that pounded down on her as she lay on her side, breathing heavily from the exertion of trying to push her foal from her womb. She had carried it inside her for over a year and now it was time for it to exist on its own. It was the time of year that zebras usually gave birth and this would be the mother's second foal. She knew she had to keep trying and that the birth was very near.

Suddenly, with one last enormous push, the 30kg bundle of legs, head and striped body slipped from its warm hiding place, out onto the rain-soaked earth. The mare, although exhausted from the effort of giving birth to her offspring, immediately began the process of cleaning the infant zebra, licking away the mucus of birth and stimulating it into life.

It was only a matter of minutes before the foal, a thin but beautifully marked male jerked his way up from lying on the ground to standing, albeit a little wobbly at first, on his four spindly legs. He fell back to the ground straight away, but on the second attempt, the foal began to take his first tentative steps towards the mare and his first drink of her nourishing milk.

A few minutes later the mare and her foal were walking along with the rest of the herd. Now all the young zebra had to do for the next year or so as he grew to adulthood, was survive the predators and pitfalls of life on the open African savannah. It would not be easy, danger surrounded him wherever he and his mother went.

Eight months later and 7,500 kilometres away, Helena stared out of the first floor window of the large, elegant terraced house where she and her parents lived, in Winchester, England. It was a dull, depressing day, no sun and a cold wind that seemed to penetrate all layers of clothing. In less than five weeks' time, she would celebrate her 16th birthday and Helena was wondering about what her mother Catherine had said to her the previous day.

'Don't make any plans for a week before your birthday, we're doing something special.'

Helena was intrigued and tried desperately to get some better information out of her father, Lance, who had simply said, rather unhelpfully in Helena's opinion, 'Wait and see.' And today was the day that she would find out.

Later that evening, over dinner, Helena's mother handed her an envelope. Inside was the printed itinerary for a camping safari that she and her mother would undertake to Botswana, Africa. The trip was a way of saying, 'Well done, we're proud of you' to Helena for her support of a close friend of hers suffering from leukaemia. Helena had been passionate about helping her friend through her very personal crisis, raising money to help with research and stimulating awareness of the tragedy the illness creates.

Helena had also been passionate about environmental issues for as long as she could remember and now this safari, would be her chance to experience the unique ecology of Africa, and see up close some of the wildlife that she had only previously studied in pictures.

Helena couldn't remember being so excited about a holiday before, and she would be there for her birthday, 22nd December.

Four weeks later, four of the longest weeks that Helena had ever experienced, she and her mother Catherine joined the safari that Sam was leading in Moremi Game Park in Botswana. There were six clients in total, all from different parts of the world. Nicola and Frank had travelled from America, Werner from Switzerland, Johannes from South Africa and of course, Helena and Catherine from England. One other person made up the team, Aupo, Sam's assistant, who had lived and worked all his life in and around the bush. When running a safari together, he and Sam made a formidable team!

They had spent most of one particular day travelling to an area known as Serondela, setting up camp not far from the water's edge of the Chobe River. Throughout the journey, the sun beat down mercilessly as they drove along the dusty tracks and the breeze, far from cooling everyone down, made the air feel hotter than ever. Catherine thought at one stage it felt rather like having a hair-dryer blowing directly into her face.

'Make sure you drink some water every few minutes,' Sam had told them, 'this heat and breeze will de-hydrate you in no time at all, you must drink.'

Later that afternoon, after everyone had rested, Sam gathered the clients together on the Land Rover. 'OK,' he said, 'now that everyone has had chance to cool off and rest, we're going into the bush to try and find some game. It's been really hot today and the animals would have found shade somewhere, but now they'll be out grazing, so we should see quite a lot.' That, after all was why all the clients were there, to view as many animals of Africa as they could, and it was Sam's job to know the best times to look for animals and try and make their experience as memorable as possible.

Helena had already taken dozens of photographs of animals of all descriptions and she probably had as many photos of birds.

'I can't believe the variety and colours of some of these birds,' she remarked to her mother.

'Which is your favourite?' asked Catherine.

Without hesitation, Helena replied, 'The Carmine Bee-eater, it has to be the most gorgeously coloured bird I have ever seen. Mind you,' she carried on, 'the Paradise Fly-Catcher comes a very close second. Which is yours?'

'Oh, I think that would have to be the Glossy Starling.' replied Catherine, 'I just love the way its plumage seems to shimmer and change colour in the sunlight.'

Helena turned her attention to Sam. 'Are we going anywhere in particular?' she asked.

'I thought we'd go to a waterhole I know about,' said Sam. 'It's large enough to have some crocodiles living there permanently. We've had a fair number of thunderstorms recently and I reckon the waterhole will be full, with lots of animals using it.'

Sam went on to explain how animals had to search for water in the hot season and would make the most of finding a full waterhole. 'There's also a small stream that runs into it from the Chobe River. Crocodiles and birds, such as the Giant Kingfisher and Fish Eagle feed on the fish the stream brings.' He looked up at the sky and noticed the darkening clouds. 'We might be in for some rain in a little while, better take your waterproofs.'

Sam drove the Land Rover slowly along the meandering track, avoiding where he could, the football-sized boulders, potholes and tree-roots lying in wait to puncture tyres and wreck suspension on just such a vehicle. He stopped regularly to point out animals and birds his keen eyes had picked out and to explain their various characteristics.

At one point, he sniffed the breeze that was blowing into his face through the open windscreen.

'Smell that?' he asked, stopping the vehicle and turning round to the clients.

'Yeah, I thought it was different, what is it?' asked Nicola.

'It's not the usual African smell, it's much more sort of, musty and really strong,' remarked Nicola's husband, Frank.

'Any ideas?' said Sam, looking around at the blank faces facing him. 'Elephants,' he exclaimed, 'and lots of 'em I'll bet. It's so typical of a large herd, it's a mixture of their raw animal smell and dung, can't mistake it! They'll be around here somewhere.'

Sure enough, a few minutes later when they arrived at the circular shaped waterhole, which measured about 50 metres across, Sam and the clients were treated to the sight of a large herd of elephants, males, females and calves, drinking, washing away the dust and playing in the water. Sam stopped the Land Rover a safe distance away from the elephants and settled down to watch them.

'Which of them is the leader?' asked Catherine.

'That large female over there,' said Sam, 'she's the head of the herd, the Matriarch as she is known'.

'How do you know that's a female, they all look the same to me?' asked Catherine.

'Unfortunately, you can't distinguish between cows and bull elephants by genitalia because they carry it all internally. But, if you look at their heads, you'll see a bony angle at the top on some of them. Those are the females, or cows. The ones without the bony lump, with a much smoother and more rounded forehead, are the males, or bulls. That's generally how we tell them apart. Can you all see that?' explained Sam, looking around at the clients. 'The other elephants will be part of the Matriarch's extended family, other females with calves, juveniles and adult males. See how the mothers fuss around their calves, making sure they don't wander off or drown themselves'

As he watched some of the elephants using their trunks to spray cooling water and mud over their bodies, he noticed that parts of the edge of the waterhole had been trampled into fairly large mud-holes by the massive feet of the adults. One or two of these mud-holes were at the base of a one metre drop from a raised bank of earth to the water's edge, and they were being made worse by the elephants' antics.

Eventually, after about half an hour or so, the herd had obviously had enough and began to withdraw from the water, plodding their way through the sticky mud they had created at the side of the waterhole.

As the elephants departed, Sam noticed a herd of zebra and wildebeest approaching the waterhole to drink. Pointing them out to the clients, he explained, 'They've probably been hanging around for ages. Elephants in the numbers we've just seen, won't generally tolerate other animals at the water when they're there, including lions. I've seen fully grown lions being physically chased away by bull elephants. Now that the elephants are going though, the other animals figure it's their turn to drink. We should see some other antelope soon and maybe, if we're lucky, a predator or two.'

'Do they always stick together, zebra and wildebeest?' asked Werner.

'They do often, yes, they're both very sociable animals, they have the same grazing habits, they like the same grass and some experts think they stick together for safety. These are Burchell's Zebra, notice the slightly darker stripes in between the black ones. They're called shadow stripes'

The zebra and wildebeest spread themselves around the water's edge for a few minutes. There were so many of them, some couldn't find a space to start drinking. There was a lot of squabbling, kicking and shoving each other out of the way, and all the time, the mud-holes were getting wetter and muddier.

In amongst the bad tempered adults, Sam noticed a young foal, no older than a year trying to suckle from its mother, who in turn, was at the top of the bank-side, trying to get to the water. Those lucky ones that had found some space were drinking as much as they could, but keeping a close eye out for the ever-hungry crocodile.

Suddenly, Sam heard the unmistakeable, urgent braying of a young foal in trouble. Having heard the sound before and witnessed the speed at which a crocodile strikes, he immediately put the two together and began to look for the stricken foal, which he thought would be thrashing around in the water trying to escape the powerful jaws. Older zebra were still milling around the edge of the waterhole but Sam couldn't see where it was happening. The clients had heard it too.

'Can anyone see what's happening?' Sam asked, reaching for his field-glasses. Others scanned the scene, but all replied they couldn't see where the foal was.

Sam was focussed on a small group of zebra, which appeared to him to be panicking. Suddenly, they parted and through the gap, Sam could see that a large part of the bank-side where he had seen the foal trying to suckle, had collapsed, plunging it and the young zebra down about a metre and a half into the largest of the mud-holes created by the trampling adult elephants.

He knew from experience that the wet, clinging mud would hold the foal tightly and the more it struggled, Sam knew its plight would worsen to the point where the poor animal would simply give up through exhaustion, and drown.

He and the clients watched as the foal struggled desperately to get out of the mud, its braying becoming more and more urgent, its body twisting this way and that, straining every muscle to get itself out, not realising of course, that with every movement, the mud was tightening its grip.

Everyone on the Land Rover was becoming distressed at the sight of the struggling foal, Helena was close to tears. Unfortunately, Sam had to tell them that this is the sort of thing that occurs in nature, uttering a well-used phrase in his part of the world, 'This is Africa, this is what happens here. It's not pleasant I know, but it is part of the survival cycle on the savannah. The foal is doomed, it's going to die and then other animals will feed off its carcass. Death and life, life and death, that's how it works here.'

Sam knew that what he was saying was the truth, but even so, the tragic scene unfolding in front of his eyes was causing even him to examine his own integrity. Should I intervene? was the question spinning around in his head. He knew he shouldn't, all his training and experience was telling him that nature must take its course. If he did intervene, he knew he would be interfering with how things have happened on the African savannah, probably since time began. If he didn't, could he live with the memory of the helpless foal slowly drowning in thick, slimy mud, and him not doing anything to prevent it?

'Believe me,' he said to the clients sitting behind him on the Land Rover, 'I wish this wasn't happening or even, if it has to die, let it be taken by a crocodile, at least its death then would be quicker than this way!'

'Can't we do something to help, anything at all?' pleaded Nicola.

'Surely, we have to try and get it out, we can't just let it drown.' added Frank.

'No,' said Johannes firmly, 'I'm from South Africa, I understand what is happening here and I know why Sam is refusing to help. He's right, we have to let this play out, it's nature.'

Sam appreciated the arguments both for and against their taking action to save the foal and he knew that he shouldn't.

'No,' he insisted, 'we're not going to interfere, we're not going to help the foal but then, neither are we going to watch it die.' With that, he started the Land Rover and began to drive away, the screams and braying of the struggling foal had become too much to bear. The clients behind Sam were silent.

They had driven about a hundred metres away from the waterhole, when Sam drove over the crest of a small hill. A slight movement to his right, on the horizon attracted his attention, and effectively changed his mind for him.

His keen eyesight had made out the hulking shape of a spotted hyena, the most efficient scavenger on the savannah. The huge shoulders and sloping back made it unmistakeable. He knew that more would be close by, and sure enough, one by one they appeared, being attracted to the scene by the frantic screams of the foal, knowing it would be in trouble.

The doomed zebra foal would most likely drown in the awful mud, but even if by some miracle it did manage to get itself out, it would be so weak from exhaustion, it wouldn't be able to get away and the hyenas would immediately attack and kill it. There was nothing unusual about this, the foal was quite simply a meal for the hungry hyenas.

Sam knew that all he had to do really, was simply to keep driving away, ignoring what was about to happen. But the memories of the struggling and screaming foal would remain, along with the clients pleading with him to help. Could he live with that?

He slammed on the brakes, causing some of the passengers to pitch forward out of their seats. Sam didn't even realise he'd done it, his mind was reeling from his dilemma. On the one hand, his basic humanity was telling him he desperately wanted to help but on the other hand, his experience and knowledge told him he shouldn't.

He agonised for what seemed like an eternity. Then, he came to a decision. 'Ok, sorry Johannes, I've changed my mind, we have to at least try to get it out of the mud, give it a fighting chance to survive. We'll make sure it can at least run before we leave, but then that'll be it, nature must take its course after that.'

The clients realised he wasn't asking their opinion! As he turned the vehicle around, there was much whooping and clapping from the clients, even Aupo, the man who had lived and worked in the bush all his life, was relieved they would try and help. The hungry hyenas would have to find something else for dinner!

The first thing Sam did was to drive the Land Rover up close to the mud-hole, scattering the rest of the zebra herd, which no doubt included the foal's mother. 'You two,' he shouted, pointing to Nicola and Frank, 'get up on the roof and watch the water for any signs of crocodiles. They'll be in the water by now and probably eyeing up the scene, be alert.' He spun round and pointed towards the hyenas, 'Werner, Johannes, watch them, shout to me or Aupo if they start to get too close,' and finally, to Catherine and Helena he said, 'You two stay on the vehicle and look out for lions. If they pitch up, we'll have to abandon the foal, it'll be too dangerous with them around, they'll probably be hunting at this time of day.'

Running towards the mud-hole, he shouted, 'Aupo, get the thick rope out from under the seat and bring it to me please.' There was urgency now in Sam's voice and his orders would be obeyed without question!

Sam himself grabbed a shorter length of rope, for no reason other than he figured he might need it. He sprinted from the Land Rover and stopped at the edge of the mud-hole at the same time as Aupo arrived with the thick rope. Taking it from him, Sam quickly tied a slip-knot to form a loop, a sort of lasso, then standing away from the edge of the bank-side, he tried several times to throw the rope over the foal's head, about five metres away. But it was struggling so much in the mud that every time Sam threw the rope, he missed. His attempts to lasso the foal became more and more desperate as he could see it sinking lower and lower into the deep mud.

Eventually, Sam realised he had no option. 'Aupo, this isn't working, I'll have to get into the mud-hole and get the rope over its head. Make sure you stand on the bank with that other rope ready to pull me out if necessary.'

'Tie it round your waist now, it might save precious seconds,' said Aupo.

As soon as he slipped into the hole, Sam could feel the awful mud clinging to him. He knew enough not to move around too much, but even so, he had to manoeuvre himself close to the foal and it became a real effort simply to try and move one leg in front of the other, such was the grip the mud had on his legs.

As Sam was preparing to slip the noose over the head of the foal, he heard an urgent shout from Frank sitting on the roof of the Land Rover. He was pointing to the water, 'Sam, Sam, look out, a crocodile has just surfaced!!'

Sam's head immediately swivelled round to the water's edge. From a distance, it looked just like a bit of wood floating on the surface, but Sam studied it intently for a few seconds and then made out the two eyes, characteristically situated at the top of the head. He watched it moving very slowly towards the back of the mud-hole.

'It can feel the foal's distress through the water,' said Sam, to no-one in particular.

He knew that apart from the one he could see, there would be others. Just like the hyenas, they would be waiting their chance to strike. As if to confirm his thoughts, Sam saw another crocodile surface, further out towards the middle of the waterhole. It watched what was happening but wasn't making its way to the mud-hole, not yet!! Sam knew it would eventually.

The battle to save the foal now took on another degree of urgency. He knew that if the crocodiles got hold of the foal, their power would be too much to resist and they would drag the animal into the water and it would be lost. 'Not if I can help it,' he muttered to himself.

Although he had been initially reluctant to intervene, Sam's fight to save the foal was now becoming almost personal.

Nobody noticed the thick, black clouds that now filled the sky. Suddenly, there was an almighty crash of thunder, so loud and sudden, Sam instinctively ducked his head, and a streak of lightning flashed across the sky.

'That's all I need now,' said Sam, looking up as the first few spots of rain began to fall. This was going to be a big storm, short maybe, but violent, and out in the open, everyone was in danger from a lightning strike. Although trying to save the foal, Sam still had to think about the safety of his clients. 'Everyone,' he shouted to get their attention, 'everyone, back inside the Land Rover, now!! You and I have to stay, Aupo.'

Looking beyond the waterhole, Sam could see the curtain of rain that was heading their way. Trees and bushes that were plain to see in normal daylight, quickly faded from view as the rain cloud engulfed them. Not even the flashes of lightning penetrated the murky cloud. The thunder grew ever louder and seemed to roll along from one end of the sky to the other as the storm approached.

They barely noticed the sudden drop in temperature that always accompanies a rain-storm of this size. Within a few seconds, the rain began to hammer down on Sam and Aupo, making it even more of a struggle to save the foal. The dry earth at the top of the bank-side suddenly became a slippery mass of mud, huge puddles formed everywhere. But crucially for Sam, the heavy rain was making the mud-hole, already dangerous, even more treacherous, and the plight of the stricken foal ever more hopeless.

There was a disgusting sucking noise as Sam managed to drag one of his legs clear of the mud in his attempt to get near to the foal. Risking injury from its flailing head, he managed to slip the rope noose around the neck of the foal. Taking a firm grip on the other end, he tried desperately hard to pull it towards him, but his muddied hands couldn't grip on the wet, slippery rope and he could feel himself sinking deeper into the mud. He pulled his feet out one by one and moved back a little to try and get a bit more purchase for his legs. He tried again to pull the foal clear, without success. He threw the end of the rope to Aupo and shouted, 'Pull with me when I call. Now, *heave!*' But it was no good, the foal was stuck fast and its struggling wasn't helping it to get free.

As both Sam and Aupo pulled on the rope, Aupo pointed beyond the foal and shouted, 'Sam, look!'

The nearest crocodile had now come completely out of the water and was approaching the back of the foal. Laboriously, it slithered its way towards the foal, its long, slender body and outstretched legs preventing it from sinking into the mud.

The foal knew the reptile was there and its instincts were screaming at it to get away from this fearsome creature with its terrible jaws and rows of yellow, bacteria-stained teeth. But now the struggles of the foal had sapped its strength to the point where it simply lay on its side, its head resting on the muddy surface. Sam knew it was close to death from exhaustion and shock, and he desperately didn't want to lose the foal to the crocodile.

'No, no!' he cried, 'you're not going to die on me! Come and help me,' he shouted to the other clients sitting on the truck. The rain was still coming down in torrents but thankfully, the thunder and lightning had stopped, the clients would only get a little wet.

Frank and Johannes were the first to get there. As they arrived on the side of the mud-hole, they each grabbed a part of the rope. Aupo took charge of them on the bank-side and called out, 'Heave, pull, pull, PULL!' All three of them started to tug desperately and Sam could see the foal inching out of the mud, but so, so slowly, much too slowly!

Just as it began to emerge, Sam looked behind the foal to see the second crocodile making its way out of the waterhole and onto the mud. Then he watched, transfixed, as the first crocodile, a big fat one, about three metres in length, raised itself from the surface in preparation to strike at the foal. With its mouth wide open and head twisted sideways, it lunged towards the foal. There was a soft crunching sound as the crocodile's powerful jaws snapped closed on part of its leg.

The foal shrieked in pain and the sudden shock seemed to shake it back to life. It struggled wildly and the crocodile lost its grip.

'This isn't going to work, it's too slow, we're going to lose it to the crocs,' Sam shouted to the others. 'I want to try something else.' He knew it was risky but he'd made up his mind.

'Aupo, bring the Land Rover nearer the edge and tie the rope to the front crash-bar!' His voice had become more of a shout, such was his urgency. The second crocodile was now completely in the mud-hole and Sam knew that one of them would try to grab the foal again within seconds.

'Quick, get some stones, rocks, bits of wood, anything,' he shouted to Helena and Catherine standing at the side of the mud-hole, 'chuck them at the crocs. We have to keep them away for a little longer.'

They grabbed anything they could off the ground and began pelting the crocodiles. Sam picked up big handfuls of mud and threw them at the crocs, aiming specifically for the eyes.

'Get away, get away,' Helena shouted at the ancient looking reptiles.

'It's working, keep throwing,' shouted Sam, and for those precious few seconds, it did work. But then Sam could see they were approaching the back of the foal once more, completely ignoring his, Catherine's and Helena's missiles.

Sam knew that pulling it out of the mud using the Land Rover risked the life of the foal, but it would be his last chance before the crocodiles managed to grab it and drag it away into the water.

Suddenly, the nearest of them lunged forward again and its massive jaws clamped around the foal's tail. Immediately, the crocodile tried to twist its body around to tear it off, but with only a partial grip on the tail, it didn't work. Instead, the crocodile began to tug the foal towards the water's edge. If it got there, the foal was as good as dead.

Everything was happening so quickly, Sam and the others barely had time to breathe, but until Aupo had attached the rope and started to pull it out, there was almost nothing anybody could do except watch in horror as the crocodile began to win the battle for the foal.

Sam looked at the dying animal, its eyes wide open with terror, its lips drawn back against its teeth and listened to the desperate, ear-piercing screams as it was being dragged away to its death.

'It's tied on,' shouted Aupo at last. Sam knew that Aupo would have used a good knot to tie the rope to the crash-bar. He'd taught him how to do several knots, not just well, but also quickly for an emergency situation, just like the one they were in right at that moment.

'Ok,' shouted Sam, 'jump into the Land Rover and start to reverse gently. We'll see if we can pull the foal away from the croc.'

There was a tense moment as the rope tightened and the immensely powerful jaws of the crocodile versus the equally powerful Land Rover, created a tug-of-war.

Sam's fear was that the foal would suffer unbearably during this battle and may yet not survive. Its cries of pain were becoming almost unbearable as it felt itself being literally torn apart by two forces, one that wanted to eat it and one that was trying desperately hard to allow it to live.

Tears filled Helena's eyes and her cheeks flushed red with the effort of flinging missiles at the crocodiles. But now, she watched in horror as the crocodile had grabbed the foal's tail and had begun to drag it into the water. She watched the battle between the crocodile and the Land Rover and tried to block out the cries of anguish and fear from the foal.

Suddenly, Helena knew what she had to do!

Without a word to her mother or to Sam, she immediately bolted back to the Land Rover and opened the driver's door. She knew that Sam kept his machete in a sheath lodged just inside the door. Ordinarily, Sam would use this to maybe cut firewood for the evening fire or to cut away branches and other bushes that blocked the track for the vehicle. This time, Helena would use the machete for a very different purpose.

She withdrew the long knife from its leather sheath and ran straight back to the mud-hole.

The battle for the foal was still raging, the crocodile holding on grimly to the tail at one end and the rope attached to the Land Rover, pulling the foal's head and neck in the opposite direction.

Sam saw her approaching and immediately called out, 'Helena, what're you doing!' He thought he had it figured out when he saw she was holding the machete. Attacking the crocodile in its own environment would be madness.

'Stop,' he shouted to her, 'it's too dangerous. Helena, stop!!'

Without a thought for the danger she was about to place herself in and ignoring Sam's warning, Helena ran straight towards the zebra foal. Catherine tried in vain to stop her but she managed to evade her mother's outstretched arms and jumped straight into the mud-hole, at around the rear of the foal where the crocodile was tugging it into the water. She immediately sank up to her knees in the soft mud, and for a fleeting moment, regretted her rash action. Then she steeled herself.

Taking a deep breath, Helena raised the machete high above her head and slashed down at the tail of the foal, slicing it off near to its rump. A tiny spurt of blood splashed onto Helena's face, but she didn't notice it, she was too pre-occupied with her actions. As the tail parted, she fell back against the side of the bank, unable to move her legs in the mud. Being suddenly released from the tug-of-war, with the foal's tail still lodged in between its teeth, the crocodile turned away and headed for the water.

The second crocodile was even bigger than the first and now it turned its attention to Helena, helpless and completely at the mercy of this prehistoric looking creature.

It began to move threateningly towards where Helena had trapped herself against the side of the mud-hole, unable to get out. The crocodile seemed to sense Helena's helplessness, its movements were slow and deliberate, almost as if it was relishing the final attack, which would surely come.

Watching in horror as it made its way towards her, Helena twisted her body round as best she could and grabbed desperately at clumps of grass on the top of the bank. She screamed in terror as she glanced over to where the crocodile had crawled to within just a couple of metres from where she was trapped.

Adrenaline roared through her body, giving her almost super-human strength. With a massive effort, she managed to pull herself half out of the clinging mud, but she knew she wasn't going to make it, the lower half of her legs remained stuck in mud that seemed reluctant to let her go.

Catherine was screaming incoherently as she tugged at Helena's clothing, trying to pull her free.

Suddenly, Catherine was shoved roughly aside and Helena felt strong hands wrapping themselves around her arms.

Seeing what was about to happen, Johannes and Frank had dashed around to where Helena was struggling to free herself. Lying half on the ground and half in the mud, she was kicking her legs wildly, trying to push herself out and at the same time, was tugging desperately at the clumps of grass she had gripped.

The crocodile was only a metre away now and had opened its terrible jaws, preparing to strike and clamp them around Helena's legs when the two men made a desperate grab for her arms and with a Herculean effort, pulled her clear of the mud, just as the reptile made its lunge.

Johannes, Frank and her mother dragged Helena unceremoniously at least five metres away from the edge and then all four collapsed on the ground, the wonderful, firm and safe ground, panting from the exertion.

It had all happened in a matter of seconds. From the moment she ran around her mother, no-one, not Sam, not Aupo, and especially not Catherine had had any time to appreciate just what Helena had in mind, until she had done it. They could all however, see just how dangerous, whatever she was planning, her efforts would be.

The instant the tail was cut, the battle for the foal was won. The Land Rover was able to start to drag it clear of the mud. Defeated, the hungry crocodiles retreated into the murky water from where they had come, the foal's bushy black tail disappearing beneath the surface.

During the tug-of-war between the vehicle and the crocodile, Sam and all the clients had seen how the foal had all but given up. The screaming had stopped, its struggling had stopped and it was uttering no sound, but its eyes were still wide open in terror, as if waiting for that bone-crunching clamp of the crocodile's jaws.

Now, as it started to come clear of the mud, its head was no longer thrashing from side to side, its eyes had closed and its body had gone limp. Sam figured that at best, the foal was clinging on to the very edge of life.

'Hold on, little one,' he called out, 'just hold on for a while longer.'

Aupo carefully eased the Land Rover away from the side of the hole, dragging the foal out of the mud and its potential grave. It made no sound as it was dragged a few metres across the stony ground. Its legs seemed to be lifeless, and the plucky animal appeared to everyone to be dead from its ordeal.

When he judged it was safe, Sam released the rope from around its neck and he, Johannes and Frank heaved the foal, which was actually about the size of a small donkey, unceremoniously up onto the bonnet of the Land Rover, its head lolling down to one side.

'We'll take it about 50 metres away,' said Sam, breathless from the effort, 'let's stay well clear of the crocs.'

As he ran alongside the vehicle holding the foal in place, Sam saw the concern on some of the clients' faces.

'I know this is not the best way,' he said, 'I don't like it, but we have no choice, it's too heavy to carry and if we drag it, rocks and stones could well break bones, this is the only way to do it quickly and efficiently. We have to get the foal away from the mud and the crocs as quickly as possible. The rest of you keep your eyes open for lions.'

It was a gamble for the life of the foal he had taken on in the beginning and he was determined to see it through to the end.

'What about the hyenas?' Catherine asked, glancing round to see them pacing impatiently around in the distance.

'They're ok,' said Sam, 'we've got the Land Rover between them and the foal. We'll keep them scared away, but just to be sure, you keep an eye on them.'

Finally, they reached a spot well away from the mud-hole and the lurking crocodiles. Sam and the others took the foal off the front of the vehicle and gently laid it down on the sandy ground. Being dragged out of the hole had completely covered its body, face and head with the thick mud. Sam immediately started to clear it away from its mouth and nose by pouring water over its face and scraping it away with his hands.

'Someone pass me a blanket,' he demanded. The foal lay on its side, not moving and Sam was unsure whether it was breathing. With the blanket and water, he rubbed away most of the mud covering its body. As he cleaned the foal's rump, he was relieved to see that there was no bleeding from the severed tail. It was mostly gristle and cartilage with no main arteries or veins to worry about. With most of the mud gone, Sam continued to rub the foal's body vigorously with the blanket, hoping to stimulate it into life.

'Aupo, take hold of the head please and just pull it forwards a little.'

'What will that do?' asked Helena

'It may do nothing at all, but basic first-aid means ensuring a proper airway to be able to breathe. I'm just trying to make sure it has one.'

Sam watched the foal carefully and finally saw a tiny sign of life, a slight up-and-down movement in its chest. As he watched, the movement became more rhythmical, the foal was breathing but only just. Sam and the clients retreated to the truck, if the foal did recover, they didn't want to scare it any more by standing close to it.

'Keep a close eye out for the hyenas behind us' he told the rest of the clients, 'shout if they look as though they might approach!'

All anyone could do now was watch and wait to see if the foal recovered. Being stuck in the mud and attacked by the crocodiles, not to mention having a rope round its neck and being carried and dragged for fifty metres or so, had been terribly traumatic for the animal.

'We saved it from drowning or being taken by crocodiles, but we could still lose it to exhaustion or shock. We just have to hope and pray,' remarked Sam.

Seconds went by, and the seconds turned into minutes. Everybody watched and waited, nobody spoke. It was as though everyone's energy was being put into willing the foal to live.

Its condition didn't seem to be improving, when suddenly Helena cried 'Look,' and pointed to the foal's head. Sam saw a tiny flicker of one of its ears, then another and another. The foal opened one eye and gave a huge blast out through its nostrils, spraying a fine, muddy mist into the air.

Sam and the rest of the clients laughed with relief as they watched the foal sit up on its haunches and then finally, finally, get to its feet, albeit a little shakily.

'Come on, Half-tail, you can do it. Come on!' whispered Helena, willing it on. It stood there for a few precious seconds, regaining its strength, looking around at the Land Rover, perhaps trying to work out what had just happened to it.

The braying sound of an adult zebra made Sam look up towards the crest of the hill. A small group were standing there, looking towards the foal. Sam guessed it was the mother calling to its offspring. With a snort and a shake of its head, the ungainly looking foal trotted away to where its mother and the rest of the herd were waiting, as though it had lingered a little too long at the waterhole. Sam wondered to himself if any of the zebra had any idea at all just how close to death the foal had come.

'Oh no,' cried Aupo, 'look!' He was pointing to the side of where the foal was trotting to meet its mother. With everyone's attention fully on the zebra, the hyenas had sneaked around behind the Land Rover and were now running to intercept the foal and attack it before it could reach its mother. Their instincts were telling them this was an easy meal for them. They were only a hundred or so metres away and everyone could see that the foal wasn't going to make it.

'Hold on,' shouted Sam, and the Land Rover's engine roared into life. He immediately stamped on the accelerator and the powerful vehicle raced away towards the hyenas. If he could just get between them and the foal, he might be able to scare them away long enough for the foal to reach its mother. The group of adult zebra would protect it from the scavenging hyenas, now turned hunters.

Fortunately, the hyenas were running as a pack, quite close together and as Sam raced towards them, the massive bulk of the Land Rover with its screaming engine was enough to make them stop in their tracks. They milled around for precious seconds, not sure whether this huge creature, as they saw it, would attack them. It was long enough for the little zebra to finally reach the safety of the waiting herd.

The last Sam, Aupo and the clients saw of the foal was when it disappeared into the crowd of adults, as though curtains had been opened for it to enter, and then shut.

The hyenas, no doubt disappointed at their evening meal being taken away from them, sulked away into the darkening gloom.

When the herd of zebra and the hyenas had gone, everyone on the Land Rover talked excitedly about their adventure. Quite unexpectedly, Johannes put his hand on Sam's shoulder and said quietly, 'I'm glad you changed your mind Sam. I learned something today, things are not always so black and white and we always have a choice. You made the right one. Thank you!'

Sam turned to Helena who was sitting just behind him. She had a look of serene satisfaction on her face, and there was a calmness about her. That was on the outside. On the inside, she was jumping, her heart was pounding and she could barely breathe. She, Helena, a quiet, unassuming 16 year old schoolgirl from urban Winchester, who had never in her life done anything remotely dangerous, had grabbed a machete, jumped into a slimy African mud-hole, sliced off the tail of a trapped zebra foal and escaped the deadly jaws of a huge crocodile by a matter of centimetres. My friends will never believe me, she thought to herself.

'Well,' said Sam, 'I must admit, when I saw you with the machete, I thought you were going to attack the crocodile. That would have been extremely dangerous, the skin of the croc is so thick and scaly, the machete wouldn't have had any impact at all, let alone kill it. Mind you, you ticked them off nicely by taking their dinner away, and you were lucky Johannes and Frank were aware of what was happening. They saved your life by a thread, young lady!' He was trying to sound very angry with her, but he was failing, miserably.

After being dragged from the pit, Helena's mother Catherine had naturally wanted to give her daughter a real telling off for being so stupid, but she realised instead, how incredibly brave she had been. Lying breathless on the ground, covered in mud, she just hugged Helena and whispered 'Thank you' to the two men.

'But you had other ideas. Half-tail,' continued Sam, 'that's a good name, and that was a really gutsy thing that you did. You may not realise it, but today, you saved a small piece of Africa!' Helena gave Sam her most beautiful smile, a smile that can melt glaciers!
'Apart from that bit of tail you gave to the crocodile,' shouted one of the others. Everyone laughed!

Around eighteen months later, Sam was once again on safari in Moremi Game Reserve, Botswana with seven clients sitting in the back of the Land Rover. They had made camp for the night and had driven out into the park to see if they could spot some animals. As they drove over the crest of a small hill, they saw a herd of wildebeest and zebra grazing together a short distance in front. Sam stopped the Land Rover and turned round to the clients, 'I'll try and get as close as I can,' he said, 'but wildebeest and zebra are really nervous. They'll probably run off before we even get close.'
He approached the herd as carefully as he could, or as carefully as one can in a big vehicle like a Land Rover. Looking up in their direction, one of the wildebeest decided Sam was getting a bit too close and snorted a warning to the others. As one, they all galloped off, wildebeest and zebra alike, away from the "danger."
All, that is, apart from one, a magnificent, young zebra stallion.
Whilst the rest of the herd was busy getting away from the humans and the truck, this zebra stood absolutely still and stared at Sam and his Land Rover. At first, Sam simply thought he was just a little more curious than his fellows. He continued to watch, and the stallion continued to stare back.
Suddenly, the zebra swished its tail and Sam's heart immediately began to race and thump in his chest. He saw that the tail was less than half

as long as it should have been, the black, bushy part was completely missing!

'Half-tail!' he whispered quietly to himself.

He was instantly transported back to that evening at the mud-hole and the desperate fight to save the foal. But that was not what was uppermost in his mind. He had no doubt that this was the same foal that had now matured into an almost fully grown adult, but could it be possible that the animal was actually remembering Sam and what had happened?

As the rest of the herd galloped to safety, Sam realised that this zebra knew he had nothing to fear from him or his vehicle.

Instinctively, Sam knew what he wanted to do.

'Stay here', he instructed his clients. Slowly, he opened the door of the Land Rover and stepped down onto the savannah. He stood there for a few seconds, not quite sure how the young zebra would react. Slowly, Sam began to take a few paces forward. As if in reply, Half-tail walked steadily towards him and they both stopped just a metre away from each other.

Sam stood perfectly still and gazed steadily into Half-tail's eyes, who nodded his head several times, as if in greeting.

Sam fought the impulse to reach out and stroke the zebra's neck, he knew that that would be wrong, but this whole scene was somehow "wrong". He should not have been able to stand on the savannah, barely a metre from a completely wild animal and that wild animal should not have been completely relaxed, facing him. Everything about this was "wrong"!

From the moment he stepped down from the Land Rover, Sam knew that something extraordinary was about to happen. Touching the young zebra might very well destroy that, and so he continued to fight the impulse. Instead, he would content himself simply to be experiencing that unique moment in time.

For the best part of a couple of minutes, (Sam would later think it had been merely seconds), the two stood facing each other, Sam talking to Half-tail in a low, measured tone and Half-tail continuing to nod his head.

The clients sitting on the truck, watched open-mouthed as Sam and the supposedly wild and "nervous" zebra stood close to each other, as if they were friends. They knew nothing of the events that had taken place during an evening 18 months ago and the efforts that Sam and others had made to save the life of a very young and frightened zebra. If they had known, they would not have doubted their friendship.

Reluctantly, Sam eventually took a step backwards, and with a final shake of his head, the stallion slowly turned away and then galloped off to catch up with the others.

Sam stood there and watched as the zebra disappeared from view over the horizon. 'Goodbye Half-tail,' he whispered to himself, 'take care.'

That magical, almost surreal moment on the African savannah would remain with Sam for the rest of his life. Whilst always looking out for his friend when on safari, he never saw Half-tail again.

THE ECLIPSE AND THE ELEPHANT

'It's a spectacular event,' said Sam. 'And we only get to see it on rare occasions. There'll be a shadow that moves across Botswana on a track. Stay within that track and we'll witness the whole event. We've worked out exactly where the best place around here is, nice and flat with hardly any trees.'

He was talking to his clients about a total eclipse of the sun by the moon, or in other words, a solar eclipse.

'Because of the positions of the sun, earth and the moon in space, we can see the full eclipse. If we were in say, Zambia, two or three hundred kilometres away to the north, we'd only see part of it. It's all to do with how the sun's rays cast a shadow on the earth's surface'

The company had advertised that they would run a special safari to view the eclipse. Sam and his six clients were spending a couple of days before the event just wandering around the beautiful African bush, trying to spot as many animals and birds as they could.

'I know where I am,' he told his passengers, 'we're in the right part of the park. The eclipse is tomorrow morning and then I'll get to our exact spot using this G.P.S.'

Although he knew that two of his clients had seen an eclipse before, Hamish and Fiona, a married couple from Scotland who travelled the world to watch them, most of the others hadn't. Sam himself was excited about viewing it.

'I've never seen one,' he admitted, 'but then I am only twenty years old!' He grinned at his clients and sipped on his mug of steaming hot coffee.

They had stopped for some lunch under the spreading foliage of an enormous tree. Looking up into the huge branches, Claudette from France asked, 'What type of tree is this Sam?'

'Well,' he replied, 'look at these berries that have fallen to the ground.' He picked up a handful and showed them to the group. 'These green ones have freshly fallen off the tree and the yellow ones are old. Animals pick these up and eat them, they're rich in vitamin C and contain protein in the form of oil. Elephants especially like the berries. They strip the berries off the branches and they use their tusks to strip the tree bark away as it contains medicinal qualities. You've probably heard the stories about how an elephant can get drunk on berries. Well, these are the ones, it's a marula tree.'

'Are those stories really true?' asked Claudette,

'Not exactly," replied Sam, 'the berries can be become alcoholic in a minor way. An elephant would have to eat an enormous amount for it to get anywhere near tipsy even.'

'I'll have some for dinner,' joked Del. He and his wife Hannah were from South Carolina in the United States.

He knew he just loved the little green berries he was ripping from the branches of the tree he was standing under, but the old bull elephant knew nothing of a solar eclipse. He was in his sixties and although he'd experienced a long life, for an elephant, he had never seen the sun blocked out during the day. As far as he was concerned, the sun rose in the morning, which meant he could eat and drink as much as he wanted and then, at the end of the day, the sun seemed to just drift away out of sight, which meant he could catch a few hours sleep in the darkness. That had been the way of his life since he could remember, and he remembered a lot.

He was beginning to feel his years, his temper was short and he just felt generally grumpy. His joints ached as he ambled slowly through the bush and at his age, no more teeth would come along. The ones he had were wearing away rapidly. It was becoming more and more painful to chew the twigs and tough savannah grass that made up his diet. It wouldn't be long now before he would lose the teeth he had and he would no longer be able to chew anything at all. When that time came, he would die, not exactly a painful death, but an uncomfortable one due to hunger. He always thought his great years would mean he could have a more dignified end, but alas, it wouldn't be that way.

So, he continued as he had done for all his long life, wandering the bush, eating and drinking. In his early years, he enjoyed being in the family herd with his brothers and sisters, but now that he had left the others to lead his solitary existence, for that was now all it was, an existence, he could no longer count on the safety and friendship of the herd.

Eating the soft little marula berries was probably one of the last pleasures he had left in his lonely life.

Around the middle of the morning on the day before the eclipse, Sam was driving his Mercedes Benz Unimog safari vehicle along a wide fire-break, a gap in the bush about 20 metres wide to prevent bush-fires from spreading, when he saw a vehicle approaching from the other way. It's the custom in this part of the world that vehicles stop and exchange information about what the people have seen or where the best place is to go to see animals in that part of the bush.

The driver of the other vehicle and Sam both stopped in the middle of the track. Sam used the respectful Setswana language term for a greeting and said, 'Dumela nkosi, hello my friend, where are you headed?'

'Hi,' replied the other man, 'eventually up to Kenya, and you?'

'Well, we've been game viewing for a few days, but we're here specifically for the eclipse. After that, we'll camp and do some more game-driving for a few days and then head back to Maun.'

They chatted on about what they were doing, what they had seen etc. and Sam noticed several baskets woven from long strands of grass on the top of their Land Rover.

'Where did those come from?' he asked.

The other vehicle contained a married couple and the husband replied, 'Well, before we set off for Kenya, we spent a few weeks touring South Africa. We went into the Kruger Game Park and then went down into Swaziland. We bought the baskets in Mbabane market, after a great deal of haggling I have to say. They're great aren't they?'

Several of the baskets were decorated with different coloured grasses. The weavers had dyed the long stems of grass vivid reds, blues, oranges and purples, making them very colourful. Sam's clients thought they were wonderful.

'Are you going to watch the eclipse?' asked Sam.

'Well, yes', replied the other man, 'but we're not sure where the best place is to view it, we don't have the GPS coordinates.'

Sam said, 'Oh, I can help you there,' and passed on the information. 'The path of the eclipse is quite wide, so anywhere within a few hundred metres of those coordinates will do and don't forget, it's scheduled to start at 8-35 tomorrow morning.'

'Ok, thanks for that,' replied the other man, 'enjoy!'

They parted company with a handshake and all the clients wished them a good journey up to Kenya. Sam spent the rest of that day driving around the bush, spotting and describing the various characteristics of the animals they came across.

In the late afternoon, Sam arrived at a flat, sandy area in the centre of a group of trees and said to the clients, 'Here we are, let's get the tents set up and some coffee on the fire.'

The area was a site designated for wild-camping by the Hotel and Tourist Association of Botswana, or HATAB for short.

Sitting at the fireside, sipping a steaming mug of coffee, Sam explained 'In the old days, people drove around the park and just made camp wherever they liked. There wasn't much thought about the environment and they often left rubbish around for the animals to injure themselves on. So, eventually, the authorities stamped down and made these specific camping sites available. There are three or four areas for tents in this one spot alone. No-one can enter the park now without showing that they've booked a campsite somewhere. And if even the slightest piece of litter is left by an organised trip, that company will get banned from entering. Not good if you're running safaris!'

Sam had collected some large leadwood tree branches for firewood and was busy building the fire up ready for the evening's barbecue, when he heard a shout behind him.

'Hello!'

Sam turned and recognised the couple in the Land Rover he had been chatting to earlier in the day. 'We've just been out viewing animals around the large waterhole. We're camped just over there, through those trees. Have a good day tomorrow.'

'Thanks,' said Sam, 'you too.'

Later on, Sam was concentrating on barbecuing the evening meal, when he heard shouting and a loud, crashing noise coming from the direction of the other camp. 'Stay here, all of you,' he instructed his clients and he immediately ran over to see what was happening.

The old bull elephant's gums really hurt him. His teeth were so worn down now, the twigs he picked up with his trunk made tiny little stab marks in his gums and he continually dribbled a little blood from the corners of his mouth. He longed for soft grass that wouldn't cause him so much pain to eat and if he could get that grass without having to move too much, all the better. Large, colourful grass baskets would be just what he wanted.

As he ran into the camp, Sam saw the huge, old bull elephant standing next to the couple's Land Rover. It was using its trunk to tear the baskets away from the roof and stuff them into its mouth. The husband and wife were frantically shouting and making as much noise as they could to try and scare the elephant away from their precious baskets. It was no use, the old bull was determined, and besides, he'd heard it all before. He simply ignored them and carried on eating. Eventually, when all the baskets had been consumed and he couldn't find anything else to eat, he just shuffled away and disappeared into the night.

'We never saw him coming, didn't even know he was there,' said the woman, 'I just heard a noise, turned round and saw him eating our baskets. How can an animal that big, move so silently?'

'It always amazes me as well,' said Sam, 'it's the size of their feet. When they put a foot on the ground, it spreads out so much and the pad under the foot is so soft, it deadens any noise. It can step on dry old twigs but you won't hear anything.'

They could only watch as their baskets disappeared one by one. Once he was finished, the ancient bull seemed to simply melt back into the bush. Sam felt quite saddened that this once magnificent animal was now so old that his spine was showing under the grey, sagging skin on his back, and his head hung low from the weight of his two metre long tusks, stained with the dirt of many years.

It wouldn't be long now before he died, but there again, where death occurs in the bush, there is also life. The bull's carcass would provide food for countless animals, birds and insects for many days and weeks. As he moved away into the darkness, Sam noticed a black, vertical streak on the side of the elephant's head. He knew what it was and, as old as the bull was, he knew that it was potentially dangerous.

After it had disappeared into the bush, the couple examined their vehicle for any damage. There was none, but they had lost all the lovely baskets they had brought from Swaziland, the elephant had left them nothing apart from a few colourful shafts of grass on the ground. 'Well, there's a lesson,' remarked the wife, 'shan't carry stuff like that on the roof anymore!'

Sam returned to his own camp and told the clients what had happened.

'Why was it on its own?' asked Otto from Austria, 'I thought they went round in herds.'

'It's his age,' explained Sam, 'when a bull elephant reaches a very mature age, say around sixty, he'll go off and spend the rest of his life alone. There doesn't appear to be a scientific reason for this behaviour, it just happens that way.'

He carried on cooking the meal, chatting with the clients who were sitting around the fire, answering their questions about what they had seen that day and discussing the solar eclipse they would experience the following morning.

Suddenly, a movement behind the clients caught his eye! It wasn't much, almost like a shadow of something moving in the darkness. There was no sound, other than the clients chattering amongst themselves, but Sam strained his ears for some clue as to what had caused the movement. There was no breeze that evening to whistle through the trees, everything was still, but Sam's instincts for the bush told him something was wrong.

'Shushh a minute,' he urged the clients, and they immediately quietened down. In the silence, Sam gazed beyond them into the blackness. For a few seconds nothing moved and nobody spoke, and then, like a grey ghost, the huge bulk of the same bull elephant that had eaten the baskets emerged from the night and into the light of the camp.

It came from the bush behind the chairs where the clients were sitting, its long, wrinkled trunk stretched out in front, sampling the new odours of Sam's camp. It was only a matter of a few metres from the clients when it appeared and Sam shouted urgently, 'Everyone, this way towards me, quickly now!!'

Almost as one, each client jumped out of their chairs and dashed across to where Sam was standing. As they looked back at the elephant, its long trunk was snaking around the nearest tent, investigating it. Sam knew it wasn't the smell of meat cooking on the fire that would have attracted it, elephants are herbivores and eat only grass and leaves and roots etc.

'I thought you'd scared it away from the area,' said Hannah, looking decidedly apprehensive.

'Well I wouldn't describe it that way, he just went away on his own really,' replied Sam, 'but he's obviously got a taste for the baskets and is looking for more.'

Whilst there was no chance of the elephant helping itself to some dinner from the barbecue, Sam was fearful that it could still cause terrible damage by treading on chairs or maybe by accidentally putting its foot through the side of a tent as it carried out a thorough investigation of the camp, sampling all manner of different smells, its long flexible trunk acting like a giant, elongated nose.

Sam knew from watching the married couple a few minutes earlier that this old bull would not be scared off by simple arm-waving or shouting, or even the traditional method of clapping hands loudly. He'd seen and heard it all before.

How on earth am I going to do this, he wondered to himself. As he looked over to where the safari Unimog was parked, he suddenly remembered something one of the other company guides had told him when faced with the same circumstances.

He ran over to where the vehicle was parked and fished the key out of his pocket. He had remembered that the guide had told him he'd once scared an elephant away by driving close, but not too close, to the elephant and revving the diesel engine.

'Somehow,' the guide had said, 'they don't like the sound of a diesel engine. Petrol engines are no good, they're too quiet, only diesels work.'

Sam thought it was worth a try, the elephant was now right inside the camp and the clients had had to move even further back. One of tents had been left open in the panic to get away and the old bull was standing outside, with its trunk rummaging around inside.

Fortunately, Sam had disconnected the trailer and had made the camp nice and spacious. He carefully drove the Unimog, which is about the size of a small lorry, towards the elephant, stopped a few metres short and began to rev the engine loudly. It had no effect at first, so he drove a little closer and started to rev the engine again.

This time, the elephant seemed startled by the noise and immediately withdrew its trunk from the tent. It gave a long, hard stare at Sam and then simply lumbered away back into the blackness of the bush.

Sam followed the bull with the vehicle as far as he could, just to make sure it was wandering away. When he was satisfied, he returned to the camp and checked that no-one was injured. Some minor damage had occurred to belongings inside the tent, not much though, and so Sam continued his cooking duties as if nothing had happened. The clients however, thought it was all very exciting! One of them had noticed the two streaks down each side of the elephant's head.

'What are they?' asked Fiona.

'Hmmm,' said Sam to himself, wondering how he might explain this to the group. 'Ok,' he carried on in reply, 'those streaks indicate a certain condition that the elephant is in. It's called being in "musth" and it means that, even at his age, he would be *really* glad if he found a female elephant!' He stared at the group, almost begging for their understanding. 'And if he doesn't, he'll just get very grumpy!'

'Ah,' replied Fiona, 'got it!! Typical male behaviour!' Several other clients nodded their understanding, laughing and grinning!

The following day, Sam used his GPS device to guide him to the location the company had chosen for viewing the eclipse. On the way, they had passed the couple who had camped near them the previous evening.

'We're going to watch it from down the track so we don't interfere with you and the group. Thanks for your help last night, by the way,' said the husband.

'No problem, but look, why don't you come and view it with us? It'll save you having to find a spot, we've got a couple of experts on board here if you have any questions, and we've got loads of tea and coffee. You guys don't mind, do you?' asked Sam, gesturing to his clients sitting behind him. Everyone was happy to have them along.

'Well, that's fantastic, thanks, we'd love to join you. My name's Frikke and this is Avril.'

'Sam, and the crew!!'

It was just 7-30 in the morning and they had at least an hour before the moon would start to block out the light from the sun. By 8 o'clock, Sam had arrived at the exact spot, got a fire going and had the kettle on the griddle.

'Who's for coffee?' The large bush-kettle was soon boiling and Sam brewed up fresh tea and coffee.

The clients meanwhile assembled all manner of camera equipment, set up tripods and checked the batteries of their camcorders. Sam's company, Drifting Ways, had supplied a set of special glasses to the clients so that they could look directly at the sun when the moon started to move across.

As he gave out the glasses, he warned everyone, 'Looking at the eclipse without these special glasses will damage your eyes, make sure you use them please.' Frikke and Avril had obviously thought ahead, and brought their own.

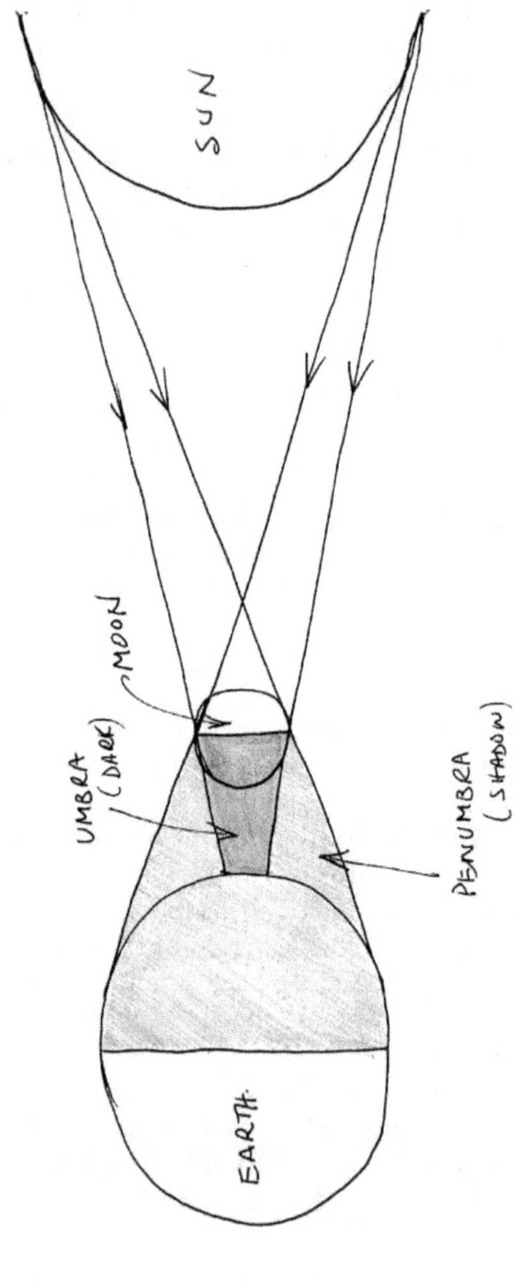

Hamish's sketch describing Umbra and Penumbra

When everything was set up, Sam gathered everyone together and said, 'Look, I've read up on eclipses but I don't know that much.' Turning to Hamish and Fiona, he carried on, 'You two are obviously our experts, how about you explain to us what we're going to see and why.'

'Glad to,' replied Hamish, 'I'm sorry if I talk about things any of you already know, but I'll start at the beginning. You can only get a solar eclipse when the moon is full, or in its "new" phase and it only happens when the sun, earth and moon are in direct alignment. Light from the sun is blocked out by the moon passing between it and the earth, as opposed to a lunar eclipse, where the earth passes between the sun and the moon, causing a shadow on the moon's surface. There are shadows cast on the earth's surface with a solar eclipse and these are called Umbra and Penumbra; let me show you where they occur.' Hamish took a stick and started to draw in the sand.

'Here,' said Sam, passing over a large notebook and pencil, 'use this, it'll be better.'

'This is the sun, this is the moon and here's Earth. Light travels from the sun and gets partially blocked by the moon, causing shadows on the Earth's surface. If you're in this area,' said Fiona, pointing, 'you'll be within the Penumbra and only see what's known as a "Partial Eclipse", but if you're here like we are, in the Umbra shadow, you'll see a "Total Eclipse", that's what we're watching today. It all depends on where you are on the earth's surface.'

'Fiona and I will tell you what's happening at each stage when the eclipse actually starts rather than try to tell you everything now.'

'Good idea, thanks,' said Sam.

'Just make sure your equipment is ok before it starts everyone, you don't want to miss anything, trust me. Some eclipses last quite a long time, but this one will be over in minutes.'

As they were making sure about their cameras etc, Fiona said to her fellow travellers, 'Listen!' Everyone stopped what they were doing and listened to the everyday sounds of the African bush, the bird calls, the rustling sound of a dung-beetle scurrying through dry leaves or the sound of nearby impala ripping browse from branches; sounds that can be heard at any time, but which seem to disappear into the bustle of daily life.

'You'll notice the difference when the darkness comes,' she said.

As the time approached for the eclipse to start, Hamish began to count down the seconds, much like a rocket launch in America. At the exact moment it had been calculated to start, he shouted excitedly, 'Look, here it comes!'

Cameras whirred and clicked as a tiny sliver of black edged into the extreme right-hand side of the sun.

'This is called First Contact,' called out Fiona, 'the moon is starting its journey across the sun. As it moves across almost all the way over, there'll be Second Contact and then Maximum Eclipse when the moon is directly right in front of the sun.'

Sam and the others watched the spectacle wearing their special glasses and gradually, the dark sliver grew larger and larger. Now, as the moon was moving across the sun, blocking out its rays of light, darkness was returning to the land, only a few short hours since it had left at the start of this day.

Animals were again beginning to prepare for what they thought was the night. They stopped eating, or moving about, antelope began to find a comfortable spot to lie in and birds began to roost in the trees.

Once again, Fiona said to the others, 'Ok everyone, *now* listen.' This time, the silence was eerie! There was no sound, nothing was moving, there was no wind and the air was perfectly still. One of the clients said quietly, 'Awesome!'

'Isn't it just, it's all part of the magic of an eclipse,' remarked Hamish.

In the fading light, about 50 metres away, Sam saw the huge, grey bulk of the same elephant he had chased away from the camp. He wondered idly whether the early return of darkness bothered the biggest of all land animals, as he carried on stripping leaves and twigs from branches.

He would find out just a little later!

By this time, the sun had very nearly disappeared and Sam and the others were looking at the moon in shadow. It was totally opposite to the chalky white colour normally seen at night and appeared as a jet black ball.

Eventually, the moon moved directly in front of the sun and the eclipse was complete. Everything had gone dark, but not like the pitch black of night time, there was still a thin circle of light from the sun around the outside edge of the moon where it didn't quite cover the entire fireball. This gave enough light to resemble early dawn or perhaps early evening.

For the few precious seconds that the moon was directly in front of the sun, Hamish called out, 'This is called Maximum Eclipse and that circle of light around the edge of the moon is called the Corona, isn't it fantastic?! Keep watching everyone, the moon will start to move away very shortly in the Third Contact stage.'

Sam watched, completely mesmerised by the circle of light, which appeared to be dancing and flickering around the black ball of the moon. He glanced down at his watch and noticed the time was shortly after 9 o'clock in the morning, which just made the darkness all the more bizzare, the sun should have been blazing out of a cloudless sky.

And then, as the moon continued to move across the sun, a brilliant, pinpoint flash of light suddenly appeared at its extreme right hand side. It was like a flare going off in the sky. This truly was spectacular! For a few short seconds, that single point of light was connected all around the moon by the Corona.

'And there's the Diamond Ring!' cried Fiona, excitedly. Everyone could see just why it had been called this and marvelled at the beauty of this wonderful, natural event. 'I never get tired of seeing this,' she said, quietly.

As the moon continued to move away from in front of the sun, the day became lighter and lighter, effectively telling the animals that yet another "day" had begun. Unfortunately, they would never understand why they had had so little sleep this "night".

When it was all over and the sun once again shone brilliantly, all the clients agreed that it had been well worth travelling to see and the memory of it would remain with them forever.

Sam became a little philosophical and said, 'Just think, solar eclipses like this one have been happening ever since the sun and moon were formed, and they will go on happening for as long as the earth, sun and moon exist.'

'Just on that point,' said Hamish, 'scientists reckon that the sun is about half way through its life of an estimated 10 billion years. So, unless, we humans have discovered how to artificially recreate the sun's energy, all life on earth will cease to exist in about 5 billion years!'

Hamish's statement was greeted with stunned silence. 'Mind you, at the rate we're going,' he continued, 'it won't take us anywhere near that long to completely destroy our planet.'

'We all seem so insignificant compared to what we've just witnessed, thanks for talking us through it all,' muttered Sam.

'Just one question, Hamish' ventured Avril, 'it's nothing to do with the eclipse, but why is it that the moon appears larger in some places and at certain times, than others?'

'That's because the moon doesn't go round the earth in a circular motion, it travels in an elliptical orbit.'

Taking up a stick, Hamish drew the outline of a large egg-shaped diagram in the sand and placed a small stone in the centre. He drew a letter A at the top, B at the left side, C at the bottom and D at the right side. He placed a smaller stone where he had drawn the letter A.

'Now, imagine this stone here in the centre is the Earth and this other one is the moon. If an object, in this case our moon, moves around this shape,' he said, tracing the outline with his stick, 'from A at the top, round to B, on to C at the bottom, round again to D and back to the top at A, it will be closer to the Earth at points A and C than it will at B and D. It will therefore appear larger at A and C than at B and D because it's that much closer to us. Does that explain it?'

'Ok, thanks Hamish, that makes sense now,' said Avril.

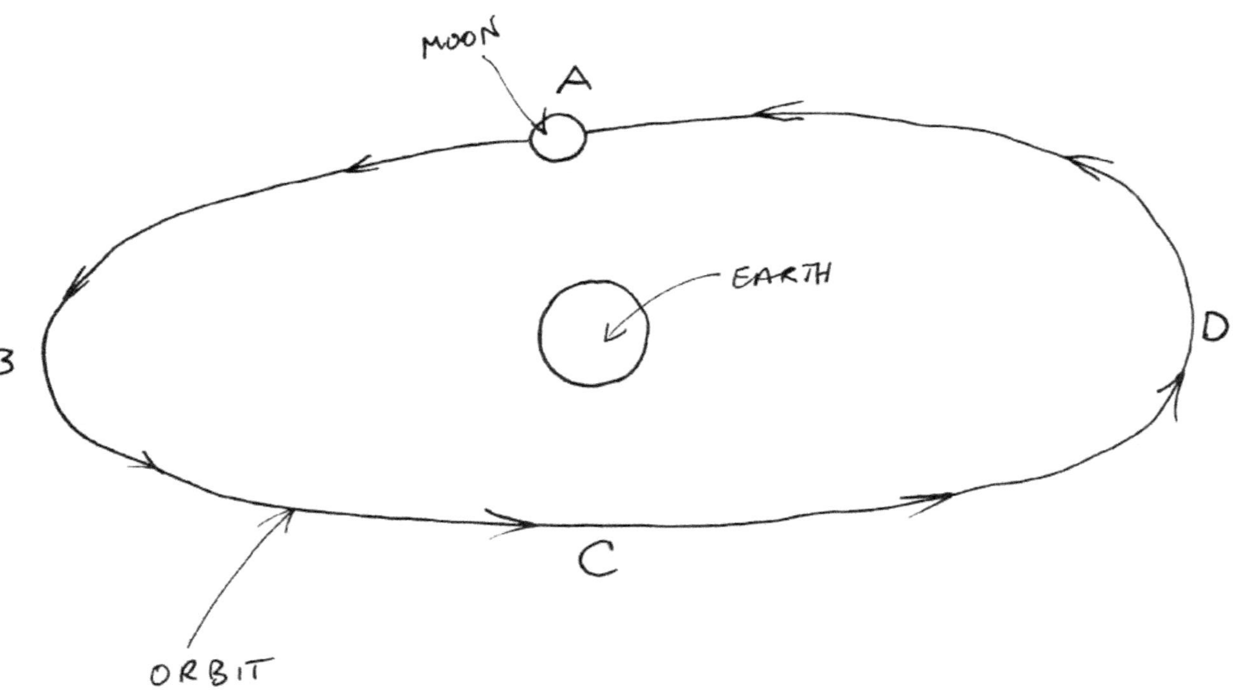

Hamish's sketch of the moon's elliptical orbit.

The eclipse was over, they had watched a fantastic natural event and now, everything had returned to normal. That was not however, the end of this particular adventure for Sam's group!

When the clients had packed away all their camera equipment and Sam had put the fire out, they stood around for a few moments discussing the eclipse and what each thought of it. Everyone said that it had been a privilege to see it and thanked Sam and Drifting Ways for arranging it so well, and of course Fiona and Hamish for their explanations.

At last, Sam said, 'Ok, good, glad you all enjoyed it, but now we have to get going. Frikke, Avril glad you could be with us, go well on your journey and be safe, the rest of you motley crew, on the truck!'

Although it was an instruction to the clients rather than a request, Sam had a neat way of making it sound like fun and all the clients were chuckling as they climbed aboard their vehicle. They waved their farewells to the South African couple and then both parties went their separate ways. Unfortunately, the smiles and laughter of Sam and his group were removed a few short moments later.

The mood on the Unimog was very upbeat as everyone chatted amongst themselves. Sam was joining in but trying to concentrate on his driving at the same time. The track they were on was taking them alongside a heavily wooded thicket on their right. They had only travelled about a kilometre away from their eclipse viewing area, when Sam drove around a sharp bend to the right and was shocked to see the old bull elephant, the same one he had chased away the previous night, standing on the track. He hadn't been able to see it because, as the vehicle was right-hand drive, the trees had blocked out his vision around the corner. At that moment, he was only a few metres away and heading straight for it.

Sam's reactions were immediate, 'Whoa!' he shouted as he yanked the steering wheel to the left. The Unimog bounced violently across the edge of the track and skidded to a stop, narrowly missing the elephant's bulk. The clients were taken completely by surprise and the action of the vehicle bumping over the sand, threw most of them out of their seats in the back, some ending in a heap on the floor of the truck.

As old as he was, the bull elephant was still able to step smartly backwards, out of the way. He was clearly now more than a bit grumpy, angered by this rude interruption in his feeding. His "musth" condition probably didn't help either!! Sam wasn't going fast but it took a deal of skill for him to avoid crashing into the massive bulk.

As soon as the vehicle came to a stop, Sam looked over to where the bull was standing, only a matter of five or six metres away. He'd veered over to the left, so the whole right hand side of the Unimog was being presented, as if on a plate, to the now, really ticked-off elephant. He'd encountered Sam three times now, and each time just made him that bit more angry. Not only that, the size of the Unimog truck was enough to convince the old bull that it could be a danger to him. He'd obviously had enough of Sam and whatever this big white monster was, and decided to do something about it.

The old bull was furious, and just a little frightened at the same time! Sam immediately recognised the danger signals, the elephant's ears began to flap wildly and at the same time, it was shaking its massive head from side to side, causing a cloud of dust and dirt to erupt from its skin. It was so close, Sam could feel the rush of air from its flapping ears. It let out a shrill trumpeting sound as it moved swiftly towards the Unimog and the stranded passengers.

Sam was praying that this would be just a mock charge, something that the elephant would use to tell Sam and the others to go away and leave him alone, finally. This was not, however, going to be a mock charge.

Suddenly, the elephant's intention became all too clear to Sam. 'Look out everyone,' he shouted urgently, 'hold on to something, he's going to hit us!' The bull elephant closed the gap between it and the vehicle within a split second and crashed headlong into the side of the Unimog with a sickening crunch. Sam had seen him coming and tried to throw himself away from the impact, but he was in the driver's seat, his feet were trapped in the well by the pedals. All he could do was lean away across the passenger seat, but it was enough to save himself from serious injury. The immensely thick skull of the elephant had completely trashed the driver's door. Had Sam still been against it when it had hit, he would have taken the full force of the impact.

For a second or two, there was complete silence, no-one moved. Normally skittish birds had long since flown away to watch from a safer distance. The air was silent, as if the bush was holding its breath. Sam looked up at the elephant as it stood triumphantly at the side of the Unimog, towering over it like a grey mountain.

For an instant, he thought that would be the end of the attack. His mind was racing; the Unimog would be too heavy for the elephant to push over and the animal itself was too old and weak to do it anyway, he thought. A lighter truck would have been flipped over onto its side instantly from the force of the collision, but this was a large safari vehicle loaded with equipment and seven people. The elephant had managed only to move it sideways a short distance across the sand.

'Keep still, everyone, I think he's finished with us,' urged Sam. But he was wrong, their ordeal was not over; he underestimated the mood and strength of this old bull. With another shrill trumpet and violent flapping of his ears, the elephant lowered his head again and crashed into the Unimog for a second time, and this time, he seemed more determined than ever.

The clients were understandably crying and screaming as the massive animal used its solid, bony skull to force the heavy Unimog over onto one side, its long curved tusks making contact with the underside of the vehicle, helping to lift the driver's side wheels off the ground. Everything seemed to be happening in slow motion, it was obviously taking all the elephant's strength.

The high-pitched, anger induced trumpeting of the elephant mixed with the terrified screams of the clients, as the vehicle came to rest on its left side. A fine dust of the sandy soil burst from the ground in a blinding cloud as the truck crashed down, throwing everyone and everything into a painful, tangled heap, with all manner of loose articles showering upon them like shrapnel.

The screams of the clients seemed to anger the elephant even more. The stricken Unimog was no longer a threat, but the elephant, not understanding that, carried on pushing against it, forcing it through the sandy surface.

Eventually, satisfied that he was no longer in any danger, the victorious elephant stepped back slightly from the vehicle. It gave one more mighty swish of its huge head, its ears flapping noisily against its body. It raised its trunk high into the air and sounded one more ear-piercing trumpet. One of the clients screamed as she thought there would be yet another attack, but this was a victory trumpet.

Moments later, the elephant seemed to relax, he lowered his head and folded his ears back against his shoulders. He continued to stare at the vehicle for one or two seconds longer, then he just turned and moved swiftly into the dense bush, away from Sam, his clients and the overturned Unimog and trailer.

Sam could hear the moans and groans of everyone in the back. Some were clearly in pain, others were simply sobbing in terror. He couldn't blame them for feeling frightened and it took all his influence to calm them down. Sam knew he and the others were in a bad situation, but he reassured them.

'It's ok,' he said, 'he's gone into the bush now. He won't come back, he's won the argument, but stay here while I check.'

Calmly, Sam pulled himself from the vehicle. He took a good look around before he walked a few metres into the thicket where the elephant had disappeared. He could hear the sound of trees being stripped of leaves well into the distance and was satisfied that the elephant was no longer a danger to them, and had resumed feeding.

Arriving back at the Unimog, he looked over what was a very sorry sight. The vehicle was on its side, possessions and articles had been strewn around and six people, six frightened out of their wits people, were cowering within the body of the truck.

'He's well away from us now and moving on all the time. Let's get you all out and see what injuries we have.' Miraculously, no-one had anything serious, just a couple of bumps and scrapes, a bit of skin missing here and there. Sam took out his first-aid kit and applied plasters and dressings where they were needed.

'Why did it attack us like that?' asked Claudette, her voice trembling.

'Oh, a combination of things really; the size and sudden appearance of the Unimog probably scared him a little; he was more than likely really confused by this morning's eclipse, you know, morning daylight, then darkness and back to daylight all within a few minutes, being chased away last night and the fact that he hasn't found a nice, female elephant he can get friendly with.' He tried to make the atmosphere as jokey as possible and winked at Claudette!

'The elephant is not a naturally aggressive animal,' Sam continued, 'but almost crashing into it like that told him we were a threat to him. He acted that way purely out of self-defence and he just saw us as a means of getting rid of his anger. It was just our bad luck we ran into him on the track.'

He looked around at everyone, 'Ok, is that it, are we all done?' Sam was generally relieved that a few cuts and bruises was all anyone had suffered, it could have been much worse. They would live!!

Now, he turned his attention to the more immediate problem. The Unimog was lying completely useless on its side. He thought quickly and remembered his emergency action in this type of situation. Whether or not they were able to continue their safari, at the very least they would need battery power. The Unimog lying on its side meant there was a real danger of the battery fluid leaking out, making them useless. He swiftly found his tool kit and removed both the heavy-duty batteries from under the front passenger seat.

'Phew,' he exclaimed, 'that's a relief, no leakage,' and placed the batteries under the shade of a nearby bush.

A few minutes later, everyone was staring at the damage the elephant attack had caused, discussing loudly how lucky they had been. That however, was not what Sam was thinking! He was wondering how on earth he was going to get the three tonne Mercedes back onto its four wheels without breaking it anymore than it already was. Both it and the trailer were now lying on their side, the contents of the Unimog having been strewn around the ground by the force of the impact.

'We clearly have a major problem here,' he said to the clients, pointing to their vehicle. 'We have to figure out a way of getting it back the right way up!'

As luck would have it, the area where the elephant had attacked the vehicle was quite clear of trees and bush. However, the track that they had been on was obviously not well-used by other vehicles, there was hardly a trace of tyre marks in the sand. He therefore couldn't rely on anyone else coming along to lend a hand, but suddenly, Sam had an idea!

He gathered the clients around him and said, 'The Unimog is far too heavy for us to lift and push it back upright, I don't even want to try it, someone is bound to injure themselves. So, I propose we use a bit of physics, and digging! I'll explain it as we go along but essentially, we dig a large pit for the Unimog to fall into!' Sam gazed around at the quizzical looks on the clients' faces. Sam himself simply grinned and said, 'Ok, let's get going.'

Firstly, they had to deal with the trailer. If the elephant had merely pushed the Unimog over onto its side and left it, the trailer attached to the vehicle would have stayed more or less upright due to the coupling being able to fully rotate. However, when the elephant continued to attack, it pushed the trailer over as well. This was actually a stroke of luck for Sam because now he could unhook the trailer quite easily, there would be no undue tension in the coupling.

'The first thing we do is take out all the luggage etc to make it lighter and easier to handle, we can re-load it later.' When that was done, the trailer was heaved the right way up, bouncing on its wheels as gravity took over.

'Great," said Sam, 'let's move it out of the way.'

Sam then turned his attention to the Unimog. 'Like we did with the trailer, the first thing we do is get everything movable off the vehicle. We'll clear all the equipment we've got stowed away in the compartments and your personal effects. This will lighten her up a lot. Otto,' said Sam, 'I want you to gather all the water bottles together and keep them in one place. If this doesn't work, we may be stranded here for a while and we'll need to pool all our water.'

'What about all the water in the tank?' asked Otto.

'Well, we've used quite a bit so there shouldn't be much left. I know it makes the Unimog heavier but she's lying on the tap. We can cut a hole in the tank, put a tube in and siphon water out if we need to, but only as a last resort,' replied Sam. Otto nodded in acknowledgement and got to work gathering the water bottles.

Part of the equipment carried on all safari trucks are two shovels, and Sam's was no exception. He threw one of the shovels to Hamish and said, 'Right Hamish, here's what we do. I'll stand here by the crash-bar at the front, you go to where the spare wheel is attached to the back of the truck. Now, Hamish, you take one pace away from the spare wheel and I'll take one pace away from the crash-bar. Then, put the shovels into the sand.'

Sam and Hamish were now standing away from the Unimog, in a direct line with each other and the front and rear wheels.

'Ok, now turn and take three paces forwards, directly away from the wheels so that we form a square with the underside of the truck being one side.'

That done, Sam continued, 'Claudette, grab that big stick over there please and draw a straight line in the sand from the shovels to where Hamish and I are standing, and then from me to Hamish.'

When Claudette had finished, Sam stood back and said, 'Now, this square shape outlined in the sand is roughly the length and width of the Unimog, just slightly larger and this will be the pit the truck will fall into once we've dug out enough sand. Let's go Hamish.'

And with that, both Sam and Hamish began to dig away at the sandy soil. It was easy at first, as the sand was fine and dry, but as they dug deeper, it became more compact, and damp and heavy. Towards the end, it was tough going and all the clients took at least one turn shovelling out the sandy soil.

Eventually, the group had excavated a pit, 3 metres wide, 4 metres long and around a metre deep under the wheels but only half as deep on the opposite side. This was deliberate and Claudette casually wondered to herself why Sam had done this. It reminded her of a swimming pool with a shallow end and a deep end.

'Ok, time out, let's get some water.' Sam then explained the next part of the plan.

'While you all rest, I'm going into the bush to cut two stout poles, each about a metre long. Can anybody figure out why?' asked Sam, teasingly. The blank look on all their faces told him they couldn't.
'The Unimog is lying on its side, the front and rear passenger-side wheels are on the ground. When I come back, I'm going to dig away the sand from directly underneath and between the wheels, backwards away from the pit towards the roof, to about this point.' He put a mark in the sand roughly half way between the wheels and the roof.
'It means that the wheels will not be resting on the sand, they'll be suspended in mid-air. If we don't support each wheel, there'll be nothing to stop the Unimog falling into the pit before we actually want her to.'
'Ah, now I understand,' remarked Fiona, 'you're going to create a fulcrum, or a tipping point.'
'Exactly,' replied Sam, 'the poles will be put under each wheel to support the vehicle while I dig the sand between the wheels. If I can go back far enough…'
'We pull away the poles,' interrupted Hamish, 'gravity takes over, the edge of the pit acts as the fulcrum, she'll tip into the pit on her own and finish the right way up on all four wheels.'
'Correct again,' replied Sam, grinning, 'although I plan not to let her tip until we give her a starting lift. Once we pull the poles away, she may well tip on her own, although I'm hoping we can control it to a certain extent by getting her to tip over the edge just gently lifting around the roof, but we won't know that till the time.'
All the clients now understood the plan and agreed it could indeed work.
'Just for safety, I'm going to attach a rope to the top of the roof frame and I want you Claudette and you Otto, to hold the rope taught to stop her tipping in before time. You must shout if you feel the rope getting tighter because that means she's slipping into the pit, and I'm going to be underneath.'
'No problem,' replied Otto.
Sam walked off into the nearby thicket, making sure that he was always within sight of the camp. Predators such as lion and hyena were always around and the area was just too dangerous to leave the clients

unattended. He hacked away for about 30 minutes, and eventually walked back to the camp carrying two stout tree trunks, each about 15 centimetres in diameter and just over a metre long.

After tying the ropes to the roof frame and positioning Claudette and Otto, he spent the next hour gingerly and carefully digging away the sand from under the two wheels on the ground. When there was nothing left to support either of them, he jammed one of the logs he'd cut, between the bottom of the pit and the wheel, and then dug away the sand from in between the wheels.

'Ok, last part of the plan. Del, pass me those two ropes please. I'm going to tie one end to each pole at the bottom and take the other end straight out, away from the pit. Del, you're going to hold one and Hamish, the other. When I shout, you have to pull hard enough to pull out the poles from under wheels, both together. That's when the fulcrum should work. She may tip on her own, but if she doesn't, the rest of us are going to lift from the roof frame resting on the ground, to see if we can start her tipping in. If we've dug enough sand out, she should simply roll over and land on her four wheels, or at least on two. If that happens, we can probably push her over the rest of the way.'

He had been very careful however, not to dig away too much sand under the body of the vehicle in case there was too much weight being taken by the tree trunks under the wheels. When the props were removed, he wanted to achieve a slow slide into the pit.

Sam then spent the next few minutes examining the pit, the edge of the sand under the Unimog's body, the ropes attached to the poles and the ropes attached to the roof. Satisfied he'd done everything possible to make this plan work, he called all the clients together and said, 'Ok, here we go. Del and Hamish, you have to pull hard. Hopefully, she'll go over on her own, but if not, the rest of us have to lift properly using our legs, not, I repeat not, our backs, I don't want any torn muscles. Right, lets get ready!'

Del and Hamish took the strain on their ropes while Sam, Otto, Claudette, Fiona and Hannah spread themselves along the length of the roof frame.

'Don't take a grip yet, let's see what happens when the poles come away. Del, Hamish,' Sam shouted, 'pull hard when I call, got it!'
'Yup, we're ready,' called Del.
'Right, Del and Hamish, here we go, 1,2,3, NOW!'
The prop attached to Del's rope pulled away from under the wheel quite easily, but the other prop was jammed fast under the other wheel. Sam sprinted across and lent his weight and strength on the end with Hamish. Suddenly, the prop shot out from under the wheel and immediately, the Unimog began to tip. The metal bars of the roof frame lifted off the ground about 30 centimetres, but then stopped. The vehicle was finely balanced on the edge of the pit.
Sam sprinted back to the others. 'Everyone, take a grip on the roof frame and when I say, all lift together and let go when she starts to slide,' said Sam, 'right, now, LIFT!'
Given a helping hand, the heavy vehicle began to roll upright and Sam was surprised at how little help the Unimog needed; he'd obviously judged the edge of the pit to perfection. Sam shouted, 'She's moving, everyone let go and move back!' It was slow to begin with but gravity very quickly took over and the roof suddenly shot up into the air.
As the clients jumped back out of the way of the roof, the Unimog crashed down into the pit with a mighty thump, coming to rest at an angle but with all four wheels in contact with the bottom of the pit.
Claudette said to herself, 'Ah, so that's why!' She had wondered why Sam had made the floor of the pit sloping towards the body of the truck and not completely level. When the vehicle slid off the edge and began to rotate upwards, it didn't have so far to fall back onto its wheels, reducing the danger of structural damage underneath. However, even sitting in the pit at an angle, they had done it, their vehicle was back the right way up.
As one, the seven people around the vehicle shouted and whooped their delight at the plan having worked so well.
'Well done everyone,' said Sam, more than a little relieved,' that's a great job, she looks a bit sorry for herself, but at least she's upright now.'
Sam was referring to the buckled doors and body panels smashed in by the elephant and the windscreen with a huge crack running from

top to bottom. At least the frame of the roof seemed intact so that the rain-cover could be pulled across if needed.

Sam congratulated everyone whilst they laughed with delight at their efforts, but he interrupted their laughter by saying, 'Right, now we need to dig a ramp to drive her out.' After the effort to dig the pit, making this ramp was easy, and they had it done in a matter of minutes.

Sam re-connected the two batteries, jumped into the driver's seat and switched on the lights to check he had a connection.

'Both lights on,' called out Del. Sam looked under the bonnet of the vehicle and could see no reason why the engine wouldn't start. There was no fuel leaking, no oil leaking and the radiator seemed to be intact. He couldn't see any loose wiring or any broken parts. Inwardly, he thanked his lucky stars the Mercedes Benz Unimog was such a strong and well built vehicle.

He switched on the ignition. 'Deep breath everyone, here goes,' he shouted, and turned the starter. The engine spluttered a bit at the first attempt but then died. Sam turned the key again and this time the engine roared into life, albeit with a huge cloud of dark grey smoke belching out of the exhaust.

'That's no problem,' he shouted to the others, 'just a bit of oil burning off inside the engine.' The clients cheered as Sam drove the Unimog out of the pit back onto the track, relieved that everything seemed to be working ok. He checked again for any leaks and found none.

After all their efforts, everyone enjoyed a thoroughly deserved rest and cup of tea at the edge of the track. They were tired from their digging and lifting and pulling, but even so, they all helped to load the trailer after it had been attached once more to the tow-hitch. All the equipment that had been off-loaded or thrown from the vehicle had been re-packed, except for the shovels.

'We can't leave the pit for another vehicle to drive in to, we need to fill it in.'

An hour later, it was done, nobody would know the pit was ever there. Everyone climbed aboard, chatting excitedly amongst themselves.

'What do you have for us next Sam,' asked Otto, laughing, 'a fight with a crocodile maybe?'

'Nope,' replied Sam, 'just a good dinner and a decent night's sleep.'

THE LIUWA PLAINS

Hi, my name is David. I live in England and I want to tell you about my safari to an African wilderness area called The Liuwa Plains National Park, in western Zambia.

'Good morning, ABC Energy Customer Services, David speaking, how may I help you today?'
"ABC Energy" doesn't actually exist of course, I can't name the real company I work for, but essentially, this is how I start every telephone conversation with customers. And I have dozens of conversations, dealing with all sorts of people, polite, rude, obnoxious, confused, young and old, every single, dull and boring day, sorting out their problems and listening to their all-too-familiar complaints. From the moment I sit down at my terminal to start talking, I constantly look at the clock, willing the time to rush by so that I can escape my humdrum existence at the earliest opportunity. After work, myself and the other customer services staff, invariably end up in a pub somewhere, drinking the night and our tedious lives away.
'Is there nothing else for me out there?' I often ask myself.
One day, quite by chance, I was speaking to a customer who told me he had had problems at his house while he'd been on holiday in southern Africa. We got chatting and he told me about some of his adventures driving through the African countryside in an open vehicle with wild animals all around. He described the African plains as being "immense", but he couldn't compare them to anything that I could relate to. He described the smell of Africa, but again, I had nothing to compare it to, and I could only relate to the animals he described by remembering them from visits to the local zoo, or to seeing them on television.
I became more and more fascinated by what he was saying and as soon as I could, started to look at African holiday companies on the internet. The more I looked, the more I knew for certain that I would

go, somehow. I also began to gain a firm idea of just what sort of experience I wanted to have. I started saving my money that very day!

"The Liuwa Plains, a one of a kind adventure", the site said. "not for the faint-hearted."

This sounded like the sort of trip I really wanted to make, a true safari to a totally wild area.

I had read a number of articles in magazines and newspapers written by people who had been "on safari" in Africa. Their descriptions varied between staying at luxury lodges with air conditioning and satellite television, taking game-drives in the morning and evening to view African wildlife, to hiring their own vehicles and heading off to a fenced-in game park with well marked roads and well equipped rest lodges.

All their descriptions seemed to have one thing in common, they all had sizeable chunks of luxury thrown in; a well used swimming pool with sun-chairs all around it, or white-gloved African waiters serving gin and tonics and a la carte food in the evening, or maybe just decent toilet and washing facilities. Is this really what a safari is all about, I had wondered to myself?

The dictionary defines "safari" as a Swahili word meaning a journey. It seemed to me that people had adapted the word to fit practically anything to do with African game-viewing. I had decided to see if there was any company offering a safari which would be more in-keeping with the old fashioned view of such a trip, perhaps a journey into the unknown. My search had led me to a company called Drifting Ways Safaris, based in Maun in Botswana, southern Africa. They seemed to be offering the very thing I wanted to experience, a true safari to a wild part of Africa where very few tourists have ventured before, The Liuwa Plains of Zambia. They described how the grassy plains stretch far off into the distance, to where the horizon meets the sky, the stunning birdlife, the annual migration of thousands of wildebeest from Angola, the predators that follow them and most intriguing of all, the silence that seems to dominate the savannah. I booked immediately!

I then spent the next nine or ten months saving money like crazy and buying suitable clothing. As the time approached for me to leave, I became more and more excited, and maybe just a little apprehensive. I had spent a good part of my savings booking the trip and I was flying further than I had ever gone before, a lot further. In fact, if the truth be known, I had only ever flown to Ibiza a few times before, and I could remember precious little of any of my holidays there, I always got so drunk.

'Not this time,' I said to myself.

Almost a year to the day after first speaking with the man who'd been to southern Africa, I found myself on a flight to my adventure.

I flew down to Johannesburg for the first leg of the journey and then caught a connecting flight to a town in Botswana called Maun, on the edge of the Okavango Delta. At Maun, I boarded a local bus to take me north to another town called Kasane. The ride was long, hot, bumpy and uncomfortable. I shared my seat with a large African woman transporting several very vocal chickens. Every time we went over a bump, these chickens panicked in their cages and showered me with feathers and God knows what other tiny, itchy little creatures! Although our bus was apparently fitted with air conditioning, it had broken down several years previously, a state of repair that, according to the lady sitting next to me, was "normal"!

Several times, the driver had to weave his way around huge potholes in the road and on one occasion, we had to stop while a herd of fifty or so elephants crossed the road in front of us. Some of them looked in our direction, perhaps curious as to who or what we were, but generally, they ignored us. This was my first sight of truly wild animals, and as they passed in front, I could smell their animal odour. I knew immediately what the customer had been trying to describe and why I couldn't understand, it was like nothing I had ever smelt before.

I had arranged to meet my guide in Kasane, at a hotel on the banks of the Chobe River. At the appointed time, a Land Rover safari vehicle arrived. Driving the vehicle was a young man, probably no older than twenty, smartly dressed in shorts and a safari shirt bearing the company logo. He jumped down from the driver's seat and approached us waiting in the foyer.

'Hi,' he said cheerily, 'my name's Gabriel, I'm going to be your guide to the Liuwa Plains.'

I say "us" because over the previous evening, I had met a charming couple in the hotel who would both be coming on the same trip, an American husband and wife from Georgia, Chris and Lynne. It turned out that there would be a total of five of us on the trip; myself, Lynne and Chris from America, Helmut from Germany and Cathy from South Africa; truly, an international safari.

After the brief introductions and an assurance that we would be further briefed on the trip later that evening, we set off back into the town, back to a supermarket.

'You need to stock up with five litres of water each per day. Where we're going, there's no fresh water and nowhere to buy any. You need to get it all here,' Gabriel informed us.

Just then, another young man, also African, approached the Land Rover and greeted us. 'Everyone,' said Gabriel, 'this is Aupo. We run this trip together.'(I learned later that he had the curious surname of Wireless but he liked to be called by his nickname, Aupo, pronounced ow-u-pa). He had been getting the last of the food supplies and when these were loaded into the trailer, Gabriel drove round to a nearby garage to fill up with diesel, something else he said was not available where we were going. This was sounding better and better; no popping down to the shops or to the bar for a casual drink, we would take everything with us!

Before going on to Zambia, we spent the first two nights camping in the bush in the Chobe National Park, Botswana. We took game-drives in the morning and afternoon whilst we were in Chobe and saw many animals, including lions, elephants, hundreds of antelope called Impala, zebra, crocodiles, hippopotamus, buffalo, and the birds we saw were just stunning. There were birds with plumage in colours I had never seen before, shades of green and blue that simply shimmered in the sunlight.

On the day of our departure for the Plains, Gabriel once again stocked up with last minute supplies of water, diesel and food, and then we were off! We crossed through the border with Namibia, drove across the Caprivi Strip and eventually, after some very prolonged and bureaucratic immigration controls, we entered Zambia and took the road to our destination, the Liuwa Plains.

The first few kilometres were tarmac, just like the roads in England and I began to wonder if it would be like that all the way. However, the smooth tar ended and the road became a smooth dirt road, then a slightly less smooth dirt road and then a really rough dirt road with potholes the size of a small family car. The Land Rover lurched from side to side as Gabriel negotiated the holes and plunged into deep depressions filled with water, which sometimes swept up over the bonnet. This was more like it!

The roads seemed to change character every few kilometres and became more and more tough to negotiate, sometimes very stony and rough, at other times deeply rutted with boulders and tree roots everywhere. During the trip, the Land Rover and trailer got four punctures owing to the incredibly tough terrain.

Around lunchtime, we received a sad lesson in how some things work in Africa, or at least in that part of the continent.

'We'll stop here for lunch,' Gabriel said as he stopped the Land Rover under the shade of a large tree at the side of the road. 'David, give Aupo a hand getting the table and chairs set up please, I'll get the food out.'

We then sat down to a lunch of rice salad, cold meats, tomatoes and bread, most of it left over from the previous evening's dinner. As we ate, I noticed a small group of three or four children standing, watching us from around twenty metres away.

'Don't worry about them,' said Gabriel, nonchalantly, 'they're from the local village and they're waiting.'

'Waiting? For what?' asked Lynne.

'Nothing in this land gets wasted. If something breaks or becomes useless, it will eventually be used to make other things work, or be turned into something else. It might take a while but that is what will happen. And so it is with food. If we have anything left over from lunch, and we will, I made sure of that, they'll get the benefit.' Gabriel pointed to the small group.

'Isn't that being arrogant and condescending?' said Lynne, angrily.

'Not at all,' replied Gabriel, calmly. 'It doesn't take a genius to figure out that they don't have much, just look at their clothes. It's a sad fact of life that they have much less than we do. Can you imagine how it would look if we simply threw away good food that we couldn't eat because we'd had enough? If that's what you think we should do Lynne, please go ahead and throw it away, but make sure you let them see you do it.

'This is where I always stop and I always make sure that we can give them something to eat. I know how it sounds, but don't you do more or less the same thing when you donate clothes or toys to a charity?'

Nobody spoke in reply, and Lynne looked at the ground.

'Ok, who's going to volunteer to give it to them?'

'I will', replied Lynne.

'Good, make sure you give it to the girl in the blue dress, she's the eldest and she'll share it out to the others. Copy what she does when you give her the bag, it's a very polite form of thanks.'

I then watched as Lynne approached the young girl, who took the bag from her with one hand, bent one knee very slightly and tapped the top part of her chest lightly with her other hand. Lynne repeated the gesture and the small group ran back towards the village, laughing and skipping.

'Thanks,' said Lynne quietly to Gabriel.

'No problem. This is Africa, it's how it works here. As well as all the animals, this is what you're here to experience, the culture, a different way of life, the poverty but also the happiness; the way local people appreciate and understand their environment. When you all go home, I guarantee, you will have a different set of values.'

That evening, just before sunset, Gabriel chose a spot for us to camp. After driving slowly along the track and gazing into the bush from the side of the road, he suddenly turned off the track and began to force the Land Rover through the undergrowth. Small, slender trees and bushes were being bent under the massive steel crash-bar at the front of the Land Rover.

'Aren't you destroying these trees?' Cathy asked, accusingly.

'No,' replied Gabriel, 'if you look behind where we've driven, you'll see the trees are merely bent over, they don't break, they'll have recovered by tomorrow morning.'

He finally stopped at a nice sandy spot about 200 metres in, and away from prying eyes.

'How did you know this was here?' I asked Gabriel when we got there.

'I could see it from the road,' he replied, winking at me cheekily as he dropped down from the vehicle.

The highlight for this evening was that, after a really dusty and hot journey, being bounced around on the back of a Land Rover, Gabriel had heated some water over the log-fire and Aupo had erected a bush-shower for us. Nothing had ever felt so good before as having a warm water shower in the middle of the African bush, gazing up at the sky turned a vivid pink by the setting sun.

The following day saw us, or rather Gabriel, tackle the infamous "Mango Tree Road".

'This was an old trading route.' explained Gabriel, 'People would bring their goods by ox and cart to local towns such as Kalangola, the town we passed through yesterday, eating mangoes along the way. They threw the pips to the ground and thousands of mango trees grew up all along the route. People would come from as far away as Kalabo, the next town we're heading for. From here, it's only about 70 kilometres and that's how long the "Mango Tree Road" stretches; not that far you might think, but it'll take us most of the day to reach it.'

The road was now a barely discernible track of sand, much finer than any you'd come across on a beach somewhere.

'Make no mistake,' said Gabriel, 'today will be difficult. The sand here is so fine, it tends to build up in front of the vehicle tyres, bogging her down. There'll be a lot of pushing and maybe some digging to do before this day is out.'

Sure enough, the driving was very tough and the Land Rover ground to a halt several times. That was the signal for us all to get off and start pushing. Gabriel had several different strategies for freeing the Land Rover, and they all seemed to work.

As well as powering his way through the sand, Gabriel very often had to negotiate the forest of mango trees which grew all along the track, sometimes blocking it so much that we had to literally squeeze the Land Rover and trailer through some very narrow gaps. Some gaps, we couldn't manage and Gabriel had to reverse the Land Rover and trailer, no mean feat, and find another way around.

We passed through dozens of small villages along the way, from where children would run down the slope to the road to wave at us as we passed. All the villages were set on one side of the road, high up on slopes.

As the Land Rover ground its way along the sandy track, Gabriel explained, 'This area was once a desert and the villages have been built on the sides of what are ancient sand-dunes.'

On the other side of the road was the Zambezi River flood plain, which wisely contained no houses or villages.

'Watch out for the dogs!' Gabriel said, and immediately I saw two scruffy, ugly mongrel-type dogs charging down the slope towards the Land Rover. They were barking furiously, displaying quite vicious looking teeth, stained dark with old meat and scraps. I became quite alarmed as they got nearer and nearer to the wheels. They showed no signs of slowing at all, but suddenly, each of them dug their paws into the sand and came to a skidding halt, centimetres away from death under the wheels.

'Don't ever go near one of those dogs,' warned Gabriel, 'they're not friendly and if they bite, you'll get really sick from all the disease they carry.'

'Nice!' I thought.

After a long and arduous journey, we eventually arrived in the town of Kalabo, on the edge of the Liuwa Plains around 4pm that day. After completing more paperwork at the booking office in the centre of the town, Gabriel drove us back towards the outskirts, but suddenly diverted along a sandy track, down a short incline and stopped the vehicle on the edge of a wide, fast-flowing river.

'What are we doing here?' asked Chris, looking up and down the river. 'This is the Luanginga River and we're going to cross it in the Land Rover,' replied Gabriel.

I looked at the swift current and said, 'You are joking, aren't you?'

'No, not joking,' he replied, 'the Land Rover is designed for this type of work. You can all stay on the vehicle if you want or Aupo will guide you across the river if you want to wade it.'

'I'll stay on,' I said.

'And me,' said Cathy.

'What about crocodiles?' asked Lynne.

'None here,' assured Gabriel. Aupo gathered the others together and led them across to the other side.

'Ok, good, make sure everything is off the floor of the Land Rover and on the seats. I'm just going to check for holes or rocks on the river bottom,' said Gabriel, and with that, he started to wade very carefully across the river. He obviously knew the track that the Land Rover would take because he walked deliberately along one straight line and then returned a few metres to the side, exactly where the wheels would run on the bottom. The water came up to the top of his waist, almost to his chest.

'Isn't it a bit deep?' I asked.

'No, it's ok,' he replied, 'we have a snorkel on the side so the engine can breath without water getting in. We could go a lot deeper than this.'

After a few more preparations, Gabriel slowly drove into the water. The vehicle seemed to be going down, deeper and deeper into the river until the water was actually coming up over the bonnet and splashing up the windscreen. Water was flooding into the vehicle from both sides as Gabriel drove steadily through the current. It was obvious that he was skilled in driving through the African bush. He neither stopped nor hesitated all the way over, just kept the Land Rover and trailer going at a slow, steady speed.

When Gabriel emerged from the river on the other side, he stopped to allow the huge amount of water that had flooded in to drain from the sides. He obviously knew what he was doing, and I was delighted that my adventure was proving to be just that, a true adventure!

We camped that night not far from the river and continued our journey the following day. Eventually, around mid-day, Gabriel stopped and pointed to a sign that marked the start of The Liuwa Plains National Park.

A few kilometres further on, we saw the first of thousands of Blue Wildebeest that we would see over the four days we would be there.
'At this time of year, the wildebeest, along with zebra and other antelope, migrate from Angola, over in that direction,' said Gabriel, pointing generally westwards. 'They come in search of fresh grass, which they know will be here because the rains always come at a precise time of the year. Predators like the cheetah and hyena follow the herds of antelope, and with a bit of luck, we might see some of those as well.'
I thought the wildebeest were comical looking animals, large heads, large bodies and thin, spindly legs that looked as though they may snap at any moment.

Our camp for the next four nights was called Katoyana and it was run by members of the local Lozi tribe. The camp had no fences or boundaries and consisted really of just some flat, sandy places to pitch our tents with some very basic toilet facilities nearby. Our bush-showers however, would prove to be much better than those at Katoyana camp.
After we had pitched our tents, set up the camp and had a nice cup of tea, Gabriel took us out onto the plains. The first thing that struck me was the sheer emptiness of the landscape. As we drove along the barely visible tracks, I looked out towards the horizon and was instantly reminded of the description on the website. In the far distance, there was a line where the blue African sky met the green grasslands and apart from a few trees, there was nothing to get in the way of the view, whichever way I looked.
'Wow,' I said, 'just how big is this park?'
'It has an area of around 3660 square kilometres,' Gabriel explained. 'The only inhabitants are the animals and some Lozi tribe villages,

which are mostly around the perimeter. Other than that, the place is empty, that's why we come here.'

Sometimes, Gabriel stopped and switched off the engine. The only sound was the distant, gentle lowing of the grazing wildebeest herds. And when they weren't around, there was complete silence. Compared to my life back in England, this was bliss.

(When I got home, I did some research and found out that the park is roughly the same size as the county of Kent in the south-east of England!)

We drove past several waterholes where tiny little yellow flowers, creating a carpet of colour, had sprouted on the sloping sides and at one time, we saw four hyena lying amongst the flowers. Gabriel drove the Land Rover as close as he could to the hyena without disturbing them too much.

As we were taking our pictures, he explained, 'They'll stay here for a while yet, probably till it's nearly dark. Then they'll go and either hunt or find a dead animal to feed off.'

'I thought they were just scavengers,' remarked Steve.

'No, not so.' replied Gabriel, "It is true they are the number one scavenger on the plains, if there's a dead animal to feed off they'll find it. But if they can't find a dead one, they will hunt and kill their own food. It's just they prefer others to do the hard work for them!'

Over the next couple of days, we saw many more hyena out on the plains, some even coming close to the Land Rover to investigate us; curious looking dog-like creatures with huge shoulders and head higher than the rump, large efficient-looking ears and powerful jaws. They looked every inch the survivors they are.

We spent that evening watching a fabulous sunset, where once again, the sun dipping below the horizon turned the colour of the few clouds in the sky from grey to bright pink in a matter of minutes. As night fell, we returned to the camp, where Aupo had cooked us a wonderful meal of barbecued lamb chops with rice and salad. I went to my tent that night, very contented.

One day, as we were making our way to the north of the plains, Gabriel stopped the Land Rover and gazed ahead of us with a pair of field glasses.

'Ah' he exclaimed, 'homo sapiens!'

On the far horizon, we could just about make out a line of four or five people walking along. Although not really allowed to drive off the "roads", Gabriel immediately turned us off the track and headed for the little group. They were quite some way off in the distance and we had to get a bit of a wiggle on to catch them.

Eventually, on the horizon, we saw a clump of trees and as we got nearer, it was obvious this was their temporary camp. There were crude shelters of grass and sticks, evidence of cooking fires and most importantly, racks of drying fish. (I remembered that on our way onto the plains on that first day, we had passed a small group of people walking in the direction of Kalabo, about 40 kilometres distant, carrying bundles of dried fish to sell in the market.) On closer inspection of the fish, I could see that they had obviously been there for some days, tiny little maggots were crawling all over the flesh. Everyone took a few photos, well lots of photos actually and then we set off to find the fishermen.

As we breasted a small hillock, we saw a large lake ahead of us and there were our fishermen, five men in total, in the middle of the lake, fishing in a way that had not changed in generation after generation.

'Ah, found you,' muttered Gabriel, quietly to himself. The five men all looked up as we approached the lake in the Land Rover. They stopped what they were doing for a few minutes, watching us intently. Eventually though, they continued with their activities, not paying any more attention to us.

Gabriel stopped the Land Rover about 100 metres away from the lake. He turned round to us and said, 'I've seen this before but you are about to witness something very few visitors get to see, African men fishing in a traditional African way. They've seen we're not going to disturb them so we'll get off the truck, but please, do not go too near them, stay a respectful distance away. If they want to talk, they'll approach you. And whatever you do, don't take off your shoes and socks and go paddling in the lake. Apart from disrupting their fishing, there are lots of little nasties lurking in the shallows that just love nice, white flesh to munch on. They,' he went on, pointing to the fishermen, 'may be barefoot, but they are practically immune to the bugs.'

We all got down from the Land Rover and wandered about around the edge of the lake. Four of the men were in the middle, stretching out a long net, and the fifth was walking around the edge holding what appeared to be three spears. They were long lengths of thin poles with crudely made metal points tied to the ends.

'What are they actually doing?' asked Helmut.

'The four guys with the net are herding the fish into the shallow water at the edge of the lake,' replied Gabriel, 'but watch what the guy with the spears does.' We all looked in the direction of the lone fisherman, walking around the edge of the lake, very slowly, holding his spears high above his head. Suddenly, he stopped and stood absolutely still for a few seconds and then, in one quick movement, he threw all three spears into the water at the same time. He dashed forward to pick them up and one of them had a sizeable fish, flapping and wriggling on the end.

'He uses all three spears at the same time purely because he has more chance of hitting the fish with one of the three than if he just threw one at a time.'

'Pretty obvious I suppose, when you think about it,' I said.

He dropped the fish into a basket he was carrying over his shoulder, retrieved all his spears and carried on wading. After herding what fish they could into the shallows, the other four simply set about spearing them and throwing them into baskets.

Gabriel gathered us all together. 'You might be wondering where all these fish come from,' he remarked, 'there isn't a river or a stream nearby, the lake is only full due to rainwater. Any ideas?' he asked, looking around at each of us shaking our heads. 'Well,' he continued, 'they're a species of catfish. During the wet season, they're active and plentiful, but when the rains finish and the lakes are drying up, they bury themselves in the mud and lie dormant till the next rains come along. We could come back here to this spot in six months' time and not see a drop of water. The fish however, will still be here, buried under our feet, just waiting for rain. They can't last forever down there, but they have adapted themselves to lasting many weeks. It's a dangerous life-cycle, if the rains arrive, they live, if they don't or are late, they will probably die.'

'It's even more dangerous when the locals decide to go fishing,' joked Steve.

We watched and chatted in broken English with the men working the net and spearing the fish for about an hour and then set off back to camp for a brunch.

We spent the rest of the day lazing around the camp, some of us writing, some sleeping. Gabriel and Aupo busied themselves with maintenance on the Land Rover. We had taken a few punctures on the way up and these needed repairing before our return journey.

Although lacking the larger game animals such as giraffe and elephant, the wildlife we encountered on the plains was extensive and exciting, especially the bird-life. Easily the most elegant of all the species of birds we saw was the Southern Crowned Crane; a large, beautifully coloured bird with a gorgeous, bright orange headdress. Taking long strides along the ground, they would beat their wings gently until they were going fast enough to take to the air. Everything they did seemed to be in slow motion.

One morning, we were out exploring the Plains when we, or rather Gabriel spotted a large Snouted Cobra snake hunting down a hole in the sandy track. It was continually burrowing into the hole, around half of its 1.5 metre body length disappearing each time, trying to locate and kill whatever it knew was down there. Whenever it came out, empty-handed so to speak, its head disappeared again a few seconds later. It was a really determined creature.

Suddenly, from another hole close by, we saw a huge toad emerge and hop away pretty smartly from this powerful and deadly predator. The snake eventually gave up and slithered away into the long grass.

The highlight of our game hunting expeditions however, came the following day. It was about 5-30 in the morning, the air was chilly and the sun hadn't risen. I suppose it would be fair to say that a number of us weren't really awake as we drove across the grassy plains, but

Gabriel was his usual bright and breezy self, always looking in every direction, trying to spot anything of interest.

As we motored slowly along the tracks, I saw large herds of wildebeest all around us but too far away for us to be a bother to them. They carried on grazing the fresh grass without even looking up. It was such a peaceful scene.

Then, suddenly, without warning, wildebeest directly in front of us seemed to panic and stampede all in the same direction, away to our left. The peace was shattered by their loud snorts of alarm, warning others of some unseen danger. Gabriel slammed on the brakes and stopped the Land Rover. We were all jolted awake!

'Something has spooked them, they're not just trying to get away from us.' As he said it, we immediately saw why they were panicking.

'Look, look, over there,' shouted Gabriel, excitedly, pointing to our right. Galloping for its life at full speed was a young wildebeest being chased by a female lion. The chase had probably only just started when we came along as the lion was still some twenty metres behind its prey. Clouds of dust and sand were being kicked up by the wildebeest, so much so, I thought the predator must be almost blinded. But it was catching up fast! Nobody spoke as we watched the chase, each of us knowing the eventual outcome. Now we were all awake and our cameras were clicking away furiously!

The wildebeest was running and jinking to its left and right in its desperate attempts to escape. The lion however, matched it move for move, and with every stride, the distance between the two animals reduced. The efforts of the doomed wildebeest seemed futile.

Then, almost as quickly as we had first spotted the chase, it was over. It had lasted only for about ten to fifteen seconds. The young wildebeest was never going to outrun a hungry, fully grown, adult lion and as soon as it was right behind its prey, without breaking its stride, I saw the lion leap and grab the rear end with both of its front legs. The weight of the blow, along with the speed the wildebeest was running at, caused it to stumble off-balance and collapse to the ground. The lioness was on it in a flash, grabbing the stricken animal by the throat and holding on until its struggles stopped. Its death was inevitable!

What we witnessed that morning was something I'll never forget. Wildlife film-makers sometimes wait for weeks or months to film life and death situations on the plains, and here it happened right in front of us.

'Wow,' exclaimed Gabriel, 'you guys are so lucky to have witnessed that. We'll try and get a bit closer but not so much as to disturb the kill.'

Gabriel positioned the Land Rover about twenty to thirty metres away from the feeding lion. We had a perfect view. 'She will feed quickly now, she needs to. Anybody know why?' Gabriel asked as we watched the lion tearing into the wildebeest flesh. Nobody answered, 'Because if she lingers too long, she won't feed enough before hyena chase her off the kill.'

'Surely, a couple of hyena won't be strong enough to chase a fully grown lion away, will they?' asked Helmut.

'Oh, yes, absolutely! First, there won't be just a couple, more like five or six, second, they will be hungry themselves and third, they'll work as a team to scare her away. She'll be no match for the best scavenger on the plains.'

We carried on watching and taking pictures for around the next ten minutes when sure enough, the first hyenas started to arrive.

'Look,' said Gabriel, pointing in the distance, 'there they are, they will have heard the commotion and come searching.' The lion looked around when she heard the distinctive "laughing" cry of the hyena, but carried on feeding.

'Watch what happens now,' whispered Gabriel. 'They'll work as a team to get her off the kill, they'll distract and harass her till she gives up and leaves.' As he spoke, I saw one hyena approach the lion, a bit too close for her liking and she charged at it, snarling. The hyena darted out of the way but then two came in to try, and the same thing happened. This time though, when she wasn't on the carcass, other hyenas ran in and started to tear into the wildebeest flesh. The lion tried her best to scare them all away but in the end, she obviously thought better of it and left.

'She won't starve,' said Gabriel, 'she ate quite a bit before the hyena came and she'll find something else later. She's actually the only lion known to be resident on these plains. It's unusual as lionesses only sometimes live a solitary existence; they usually form groups or "prides" as they are known. We normally find her around this area somewhere because this is her territory. Look at the hyenas now.'

As soon as the lion had left, the scavengers fell on the carcass. They squabbled and fought each other for the best parts, some of them tearing off massive chunks and running off with it to eat in peace.

'There's something I want to ask about the wildebeest,' said Steve, 'why are there so many young amongst the herds and why are the small ones a tan colour?'

'Good question,' replied Gabriel. 'It's a question of survival,' he explained, 'as a species, they have discovered that if they drop their young at roughly the same time each year, that is, now, when there's fresh grass to eat, the youngsters' chances of surviving the predators are greatly increased. A newly born calf is able to run with the herd a few minutes after it first stands, although obviously not as fast. I don't think there's a particular reason for the colour but it could be early camouflage to protect it from predators till it gets older and can run faster. There will always be losses, as we've just seen, but the vast majority will survive. It's a miracle of nature that, supposedly dumb animals, can figure these things out.'

I had to agree, I found it amazing!

Members of the Lozi tribe live in small villages dotted around the edges of the Plains. Our attendant was from such a village and one afternoon, Gabriel returned to the camp and said, 'Badiri has invited us to his village to meet some of the local people. I've been to some of these villages before and I can almost guarantee that the villagers will put on a display of music and dancing in our honour. Do you fancy going?' As one, we all said we would.

'When?' I asked.

'This afternoon,' replied Gabriel, 'but let's eat first.'

We set off for the village just after lunch. At first, we were following a well-defined track through the grass, but this gradually disappeared. Badiri then took over guiding Gabriel through the bush. The terrain became ever more difficult, very large bumps and hollows in the ground hidden from view by the long grass. Eventually Gabriel called a halt a couple of hundred metres from the village.

'I don't want to risk going any further with the vehicle,' he said. 'The ground is really soft and marshy, and the very green grass indicates that water is near. If I take the Land Rover in very much further, there's a real chance she'll get bogged down.' (It always amuses me how vehicles are always "she".) 'We'll turn around and go back to firmer ground. We can walk in from there,' Gabriel continued.

Apparently, one of the golden rules of driving in the bush is that you always follow your own tracks out of an area. The ground was obviously very wet and soggy, I could feel the wheels spinning slightly as Gabriel was attempting to turn the vehicle around to pick up his tracks.

'This is getting decidedly dodgy,' he said as he made the last turn to go back out. He had to make a wide sweep to pick up his track, when suddenly, the Land Rover lurched violently and alarmingly over to the right-hand side. There were a few shouts and screams from us but instinctively, I and the rest of the group lunged for the high side of the vehicle in case she toppled right over. Thankfully, she came to rest at an angle of about 40 degrees over to the driver's side. It was a very scary moment and we all kept shuffling about and shouting.

'Quiet down and keep still,' Gabriel ordered urgently, 'stay up at the high side and don't move till I tell you.' Gabriel was clearly very concerned about the situation and we didn't need to be told twice!

When everything was calm and the Land Rover settled, Gabriel pointed to a seat in the middle and said to me, 'Right David, very carefully lift that seat flap. Take out the length of rope and pass one end to Badiri.' By this time, Badiri had slipped out of the passenger seat and was standing alongside the Land Rover. 'Tie the other end around there,' he said, pointing to a spot on the roof frame. 'Badiri, take your end and walk about ten metres away. Pull on the rope when David has tied it off. David, when you've tied your end, get off the Land Rover carefully and help Badiri to pull on the rope. Everyone else, get as high up as you can to counter the weight loss.'

Gabriel was obviously trying to ensure that when we got off, the vehicle didn't topple over into the swamp. I tied the rope on as instructed and gingerly slipped over the side of the vehicle to join Badiri. The others were only allowed to get off the vehicle one by one with Badiri and I holding onto the end of the rope. The Land Rover didn't tilt any more as the other passengers got off, and Gabriel decided that she was stable enough and not liable to go any further over without our holding on.

Unknown to Gabriel, he had attempted to turn the vehicle around right on the edge of a large, water-filled marshy area, a swamp in other words. Just looking at the terrain, it looked no different to the solid ground we had been on. The tall strands of grass concealed the swamp perfectly, there was no reason for us to suppose it was even there at all.

'Why didn't Badiri warn you,' I asked Gabriel, 'he must have known it was there, he lives here.'

'Well, to be fair to him,' replied Gabriel, 'these swampy areas can get bigger or smaller depending on rainfall. We've had a bit of rain and he didn't realise the swamp had grown to the size it is.'

Gabriel's instinct however, had proved correct. Had we driven any further towards the village, the front of the Land Rover would have gone over the edge into the swamp. As it was, we had come to rest with the two right side wheels over the edge sitting in soft, swampy mud.

Attempts to drive out proved unsuccessful as the wheels had sunk into the mud, which simply filled in the tyre treads as the wheels spun, making it like trying to drive over ice. Within five minutes, all the villagers had come out to watch the spectacle and Gabriel soon had them organised into pulling and pushing parties, again without success.

We dug long trenches into the mud away from the wheels, but again they simply span ineffectively. Grasses and branches were put down without success, cursing and threatening God's wrath didn't help, and the dozens of ideas coming from the villagers didn't help either. When Gabriel had placed the branches under the wheels, they were simply flicked out by the spinning wheels.

Helmut saw this and said to Gabriel, 'How about we put some long poles in front of the wheels lengthwise, sort of making a platform for the wheels.'

'Worth a try,' replied Gabriel, 'Badiri, ask your villagers to bring poles please.' They appeared within minutes and the idea worked a treat, the wheels just caught enough of the wood to get a grip and although the poles were sent spinning away, the Land Rover came out of the mud and onto the level, which just goes to show that the experts don't always have all the answers!

A grinning but very muddy Gabriel simply stated, 'That's safari for you!'

Once we had stowed all the ropes and digging equipment back on the Land Rover, we walked into the village and listened to the villagers making music from a xylophone type instrument. Instead of metal bars, it had various sizes of hollowed out gourds hanging beneath the instrument, producing a range of lovely, soft sounding notes.

We talked with the villagers as best we could and had great fun joining in the dancing around the music makers. Eventually though, it was time to leave and return to camp for a well earned rest and another delicious meal.

It was Helmut's birthday that day and whilst we had been away, Aupo had baked a cake! Miles from anywhere, on an open fire with no oven, Aupo had baked a superb sponge cake! Fantastic!

We spent the last day much as we had spent the previous three, wandering over the plains. In all that time, we saw only one other vehicle and that was way in the distance on the horizon. To all intents and purposes, we were completely alone in that wilderness. We spent our last evening as we had spent the first, drinking wine and watching the sunset; a perfect end to four wonderful days on the open African plains.

We began our return journey early the following morning, crossing the Luanginga River once more. The recent rains had swelled the river and the current was flowing even faster than when we crossed earlier. Gabriel did his usual preparation and then drove the Land Rover down the steep bank and into the current. The water crashed into the side of the vehicle as it went deeper and deeper. The strength of the current forced the water up and over the tops of the doors and into the footwells. It flowed over the top of the bonnet and up the windscreen. I could hear the engine straining to power its way through the water but Gabriel eased the vehicle through and we emerged on the other side, water cascading out from any little gap in the body. It was even more exciting than the first time we crossed.

Gabriel checked us out of the park in the office and we drove straight round to a market on the outskirts of Kalabo. Here, Aupo stocked up with some fresh eggs and tomatoes and Gabriel managed to find some fresh rolls for lunch and charcoal for our camp fires.

The return journey from the plains followed much the same route as our journey there, along the Mango Tree Road, past all the villages, the waving children and the suicidal dogs.

That night, we had a terrific thunderstorm. As we made camp in the evening, Gabriel looked at the ominously black clouds that blanketed the sky and muttered, 'We are in for one massive storm later.'

The clouds had been gathering, building and darkening all day and over dinner, we could see and hear distant rumbles of thunder and flashes of lightning getting ever nearer.

In the end, it became a race to finish eating and get all the loose items stowed away. The thunder was crashing all around us, the darkness being lit by flashes of lightning streaking across the sky, sometimes lasting two or three seconds.

As we scrambled to put everything away, including the chairs, the wind was increasing in strength. I could hear it whistling through the trees. Leaves and small branches were being thrown around everywhere. The gusts of wind became stronger and stronger and then the first few spots of rain fell.

We hadn't managed to get everything away before Gabriel shouted, 'Leave that, everyone, into your tents, now!' The howling din of the wind in the trees virtually drowned out his voice.

Almost immediately, the storm broke right over our camp. The rain came down in torrents. The tents we had were completely waterproof, so we all stayed nice and dry, and safe from lightning strikes.

With the rain pounding down on the tent fabric, the noise was phenomenal but it paled in comparison to the sound of the thunder, so explosive and sudden, it hurt my eardrums. It rumbled on long after the initial clap, gradually fading away, only to be replaced without a break by the next almighty crash, directly overhead.

Through the open air vents under the fly-sheet, I could see the lightning flashes briefly turning pitch darkness into almost piercing brightness. The rain continued to hammer down for what seemed like an eternity. The lightning strikes and thunder claps came as one, time and time again!

The storm slowly built to a crescendo, so violent and continuous it made me shudder. And then, a few minutes later, nothing! It was as if the water tap had been turned off, the lights had been switched off, the wind machine turned off and the thunder-drummer had gone home. There was no sound apart from rainwater dripping off the leaves of the trees. The storm had lasted a little over 30 minutes, but it seemed like hours.

When we emerged from our tents, the camp was in chaos. The equipment we hadn't managed to stow away before the storm, a few chairs and some of the cooking pots was scattered around the camp, picked up by the gusts of wind as though they were feathers. The heavy aluminium camp-table had been blown onto its side and massive puddles of brown, muddy water were dotted all around the camp.

I doubt I'll ever experience a storm so violent again and I'm not sure I want to; it was just a bit scary.

We reached our final destination, Livingstone, two days later. Here, our safari would end. Gabriel told us all the activities we could experience but I wanted to do only one thing, take a microlight flight over Victoria Falls. I was not disappointed! Even though the falls were not as full as they would be later in the season, (it apparently takes around six months for all the swollen river water to make its way downstream), they were still a magnificent sight, especially from the air. I could see the vast expanse of the Zambezi as it approached the falls and watch as millions of litres of water flowed over the edge and into the chasm below.

There is a permanent cloud of spray across the width of the falls, prompting the name the local people had given to Victoria Falls centuries earlier, "Mosi-oa-Tunya", The Smoke That Thunders, and it certainly did!

My final morning was spent packing my now grubby clothes into my battered rucksack ready for the transfer to Livingstone airport, from where I would fly to Johannesburg in South Africa and then home to England.

Before we left the lodge, my fellow travellers and I drank some wine and toasted each other, but mostly, we toasted Gabriel and Aupo. They had worked very hard to give us a wonderful trip and it was obvious that they did it because they enjoyed it. We shook hands and hugged each other warmly when it was time to go.

It had been a superb trip, well organised and lots of fun. I had seen things I would probably never see again and I had done things I would probably never do again. And it didn't matter if I didn't, the memories of this "safari" would not fade in a hurry.

"Not for the faint-hearted." the internet website had stated, and I could now see why!

THE LEOPARD

Sam knew he was in a tight spot!

He had been in dangerous situations many times before in the bush, but now he really was afraid. It wasn't a particularly hot day but Sam could feel the individual beads of sweat popping out on his forehead, slowly running down both sides of his face and eventually dripping off his chin. In contrast, his mouth felt bone-dry, his tongue and lips swollen, he knew that even if he wanted to scream out, he would be unable to. He could feel his heart pounding in his chest, so hard he thought it must show through his sweat-soaked shirt.

He wondered to himself whether his fear would give him away. It's a well known fact that fear is its own communicator, capable of being detected without words or actions. He concentrated hard on remaining absolutely still in the face of this danger he had never experienced before. There was complete silence all around him, a deafening silence, the kind of silence that always comes before an attack. He would have been able to hear a leaf dropping to the ground. And those eyes, cold and cruel! He stared at the eyes that stared back at him, challenging him to make the first move. His nerves were at breaking strain. A quick but expert look at his situation had told him that his only avenue of escape lay beyond the danger, but they would never let him pass. He knew he was trapped! They had won!

The atmosphere around him was electric with anticipation of the attack he knew would come. And still they stared. Then, to his left, out of the corner of his eye, he saw a slight movement and he knew instinctively that this was where the attack would come from. He realised he would have to confront it, and turned fully to face the threat, ready to defend himself in any way he could. If necessary, he would fight for his life. He knew all eyes would be staring at him, watching and anticipating his every movement, enjoying and savouring his fear. There was nothing he could do now, he knew this was the moment. He took a deep breath, steeled himself, and waited for the inevitable.

Suddenly, the threat became a reality, it was upon him.

'Sam,' asked Baeti, still waving his hand in the air, 'how long have you been a safari guide?'

A huge smile crossed Sam's face as he gazed around at the rest of the "threat", the other twenty or so children in the classroom, their eyes fixed on him, waiting expectantly for his answer.

'Oh, about a year and a half now,' he replied, relieved that the first question of what he knew would be many, was such an easy one to answer.

Sam and his best friend Gabriel had both attended this same primary school when they were younger, in fact, Sam was standing in the very same classroom where he and Gabriel had first met and formed their friendship. The head-teacher had asked each of them to come and talk about their experiences in the bush, but Gabriel was away on safari and so Sam had been left to face the "danger" alone.

Having asked the first question, Baeti had unwittingly prompted several other children to raise their hands high in the air, all trying to get Sam's attention and hoping, excitedly that he would point to them. He patiently went round the class, asking each child in turn to stand up and ask their question, and each wanted to know something different.

He spent the next half an hour or so describing his adventures and explaining how safaris work, especially camping in the bush.

'It's not all fun and games,' said Sam, 'sometimes it can be very uncomfortable. It's never a pleasure having to put tents up in the pouring rain or trying to light a fire with damp wood. The lights we have to have in the camp attract so many bugs, small and large. They crawl all over you, get inside your clothing, in your face and down your ears when you're trying to concentrate on cooking a meal. And you always have to be cheerful with the clients, even in the difficult times, and with difficult clients. But,' he went on, 'just being out in the bush, seeing all the animals, birds and trees more than makes up for the difficult times.'

'What sort of vehicle do you drive?' asked Byella.

'Nowadays, we use mainly Land Rovers converted to carry 16 passengers,' replied Sam, 'but we do also use an old Mercedes Benz Unimog truck as a back-up vehicle if there isn't a Landy available. To tell you the truth,' said Sam, lowering his voice, 'the Unimog is my favourite. Whatever we use, we also tow a large trailer with luggage and food supplies. The vehicles don't get stuck too often in mud or sand, but it does happen and then we have to dig trenches in front or behind the wheels to get the vehicle out. Sometimes, we can be stuck for hours, but we'll always get her out in the end.'

One young girl, Dineo, asked, 'What's the most exciting thing you've seen on a safari?'

Sam had to think hard about this question, he had had so many exciting adventures. Eventually, he settled on the incident he was going to describe, but decided he would first talk about some of the different species of animals, birds and reptiles, and their relationship to each other in the bush.

'Snakes!' said Sam, pronouncing the word slowly, trying to sound sinister by emphasising the sss sounds. 'We humans love to hate snakes don't we? But practically all snakes are more afraid of us than we are of them. They get away from us as fast as they can normally, it's only when, or if they feel threatened that they attack. Unfortunately, sometimes we can't help what happens. My best friend's mother was bitten by a Black Mamba they came across on a path through the bush, and she died a few hours later. The mamba didn't want to harm her really, but she stepped in front of Gabriel to protect him and it simply attacked out of fear.'

Sam went on to tell the children about the snakes that live in trees, the arboreal ones and those that live on the ground, the terrestrial ones.

He described the numerous types of antelope, and the various species of monkeys and how mischievous they are. He talked about the larger animals such as the elephant, the rhinoceros or the buffalo, what they eat and the type of areas they are most likely to be found in.

'Talking of elephants, who knows of a connection between an elephant and an insect?' All the children looked around the class to see if anyone knew the answer. No-one!

'Well, there's a particular insect that has a real liking for elephant dung! It collects the droppings by rolling a quantity into a ball, walking backwards on its front legs pushing the ball along with its back legs, finding a suitable place and then burying it. The female lays her egg inside a chamber within the ball underground and leaves. When the young insect hatches, it lives off the dung until it's ready to leave the nest, when it digs its way to the surface to start life. Who can tell me what this insect is called?'

Almost as one, the children all called out, 'A Dung-beetle!'

'That's right!'

'Why elephant dung?' someone called out.

'Because of all the nutrients, it's richer than other animal's dung. The young develop better. They don't use elephant dung all the time, but they do prefer it'

After that, Sam talked about animals that have a social structure in their lives. 'Wild dogs for example,' he said, 'while the rest of the pack goes out hunting, there's always at least one dog that stays at the den to look after the young, a babysitter if you like. They all look after each other's youngsters. Elephants,' he went on, 'will form a solid barrier to protect calves from attack and are always watching out for danger at waterholes. Baboons and other primates such as vervet monkeys,' he continued, 'like nothing else than to groom each other and have all the nits and fleas picked out from their fur. They'll pop it into their mouths if it's a particularly juicy one!'

And he told them about the animals that feed on others, the predators. 'How many of you have ever heard of a lion?' Everyone in the class put up their hand, 'But,' continued Sam, 'how many of you have ever heard of an ant-lion?' The children looked around the class, but no-one had their hand in the air.

'Ah,' said Sam, 'now the ant-lion is a fascinating creature, and a predator. I thought that most of you would have heard of the larger animals such as an elephant or a giraffe, or a lion, but the smaller ones are often neglected. The ant-lion,' he said, 'is an insect about the same size as the nail on your index finger, but it has huge claws and a really bad attitude.'

He waited until the little giggles had stopped, and then carried on, 'It catches other insects by digging out a steep-sided, funnel-shaped trap in dry sand, normally under trees. You've probably seen them but not realised what they are. After it completes the trap, the ant-lion buries itself in the sand at the bottom of the funnel, and waits. Here, let me draw it for you.' He used the class blackboard to show the shape of the funnel and a rather over-sized ant walking along the surface.

'Another insect, usually a normal little ant like this one, trolling along, minding its own business, unfortunately walks too near the edge and falls into the bottom of the trap. It then tries to use all its legs, six-wheel drive if you like, to get out. But the sides are too steep. The ant-lion feels the trapped insect struggling to get out and makes sure it stays in the trap by using its claws to flick sand away from beneath the ant so that it keeps falling down into the bottom. When the ant-lion figures the little ant is too tired to resist, it suddenly shoots out its claws and grabs the body of the ant. It thrashes it from side to side in the bottom of the funnel to kill it or at least stun it, and then drags it under the sand to eat it!' There was complete silence in the classroom.

'One thing you all have to understand,' said Sam, 'is that some animals, such as antelope or warthogs, or indeed ants, are much smaller and far weaker than some others and unfortunately, they form the natural source of food for the more powerful, such as lions or cheetahs, or ant-lions. In their world, it is completely natural for one species to catch and eat another. The animals that hunt others for food are called predators and the ones hunted, the weaker ones, are called prey.'

Sam glanced toward the teacher standing at the back of the class. She nodded approvingly.

'So,' he said, 'I think one of the most exciting things I've seen on safari would have to be the time I saw a leopard, a predator, stalking and catching an antelope, its prey. Would you all like to hear about it?' Not really expecting anyone to say 'No, thanks!,' he carried on.

'I remember,' he said, 'it was around the end of the month of April. The rains had very nearly finished and everything had become lush and green. I was on a safari with 4 clients, Ollie was from Australia, Richard was from South Africa, Jane was an American and Michael came from England. We were in Moremi Game Park, only about forty or fifty kilometres from this school, and we were heading towards Victoria Falls in Zambia. Who can tell me something about Victoria Falls?' he asked.

Silence!

'Anything at all?' asked Sam.

More silence! Then, 'It's wet!' exclaimed a mysterious, unidentified voice from the back of the room!

'Hmm,' murmured Sam, after the giggling had stopped. 'Yes, correct, whoever that was! The falls have of course, been known to the local people for thousands of years. The first white person to see them however, was a man named David Livingstone. He found them in the year 1855 and he named them Victoria Falls after Queen Victoria, who was the Queen of Great Britain at that time.' Even more silence. Sam got the impression the children weren't that interested in the history of a simple "waterfall"!!

He carried on, 'Well anyway, this was our second day in the park and we had had a lot of luck with spotting animals. Earlier that morning, we'd seen a pride of lions feasting on a zebra they had killed only about an hour before and around the end of that afternoon when it had cooled down, we saw a cheetah chasing an antelope across the savannah. Can anyone tell me the difference in appearance between a leopard and a cheetah?' Sam looked around at the dozen or so hands that had shot up into the air.

One in particular caught his eye. Mirika had her hand higher than anyone else, and she continued to try and stretch as high as she could to attract his attention. She was almost half way out of her chair in her efforts to get picked to give the answer. Sam decided he couldn't ignore such enthusiasm and said, 'Yes, young lady, what's your name?'

'Mirika', she replied looking around triumphantly at the others who didn't get picked, her hand still far higher than anyone else's.

'Alright Mirika, you can put your hand down now,' said Sam, 'and tell us what the difference is.'

'Well', she said, 'a leopard has groups of spots, except they're not spots, arranged around its body. They look like small bunches of flowers. And,' she said, 'a cheetah has single spots all over, and they are spots not flowers. And', she went on immediately, without drawing a single breath, 'a cheetah is taller than a leopard but a leopard is heavier. And a cheetah is a faster runner than a leopard.' Sam waited for more information, but it became obvious that Mirika had run out of differences.

'Thank you Mirika', said Sam, 'that's absolutely right, a cheetah has single spots and a leopard has small groups of spots, commonly called rosettes. The cheetah is the fastest land animal in the world and catches its prey by outrunning what it's chasing. The leopard on the other hand, is much more crafty and stealthy. It sneaks up on its prey and sometimes, ambushes it.'

Sam looked at Mirika, who had just about the widest grin ever on her face, obviously enjoying the fact that Sam had chosen her to give the answer.

'After we'd made camp and rested for a few hours, we drove out into the park to see if we could spot some more animals. As I was driving past some long grass, a small movement caught my eye and I stopped the truck to see what it was. I remember, there was no wind to speak of, so the grass wouldn't be swaying in the breeze, it had to be an animal. As I was looking, a young female leopard simply walked out of the grass, into the clearing where we had stopped. I turned the vehicle around so that the clients could get a better look before she disappeared back into the grass and away from us, they're very shy animals.

'But she didn't do that, instead, she wandered up to the truck and sniffed all around. This was something strange for her and she was investigating what it was, trying to identify it by its smell. By now, I had told the clients to sit on the roof of the vehicle to get a better view of her as she walked around. She stayed by us for a good 10 minutes or so, just walking in and out of the grass. Who knows what an impala is?' Sam asked the class.

Mirika was first with her hand in the air again, calling out softly, 'Me, me, I know, I know!' but Sam chose Mululeki to try and answer the question.

'It's an antelope,' he said.

'Quite right,' said Sam, 'they're by far the most common antelope around here and the male impala, known as a ram, has horns he uses to fight with other males.' Sam looked around the class and could see that he had everyone's complete attention, including the teacher's. They were anticipating where the story was going.

'As we were watching the leopard, I saw a male impala with big horns approaching the clearing from our left. It was obvious he hadn't seen the leopard because he just carried on eating grass as he walked along, but she spotted him immediately, and then, simply disappeared back into the grass where she had come from. It was approaching sunset, just the right time for her to start hunting her dinner.

'The impala carried on walking towards our truck, completely ignoring us sitting on the roof looking at him. As I was watching him approach, another movement suddenly caught my eye. The tops of the stalks of grass were moving in a line, as if something on the ground was bending them down. It was further away from where the leopard had disappeared, and the movement appeared to be going in the opposite direction to that of the impala. Then I knew what she was doing. She was taking a wide circle around the antelope to get behind it, a perfect attacking position. I told the clients to be ready with their cameras, this was going to be spectacular.'

'Why didn't the leopard just stay hidden in the grass and jump out when the impala was close enough?' asked Mirika, not bothering with the hand in the air part.

'Good question,' replied Sam. 'You're right, she could have done that, but the leopard hunts and attacks from instinct and ambush. By getting around behind the impala, she would have the best chance possible of attacking the antelope and bringing it down. We all think about wind-direction but predators such as the leopard don't have to think about it, they instinctively know when to move to avoid prey smelling their scent on the breeze. Our leopard may also have been moving around to get down-wind. The breeze would be flowing from the impala to the leopard.' Mirika's face told Sam she was satisfied with his answer, another minor victory for him.

Sam continued his story. 'A few minutes went by and the impala carried on eating and walking towards us, as if he didn't have a care in the world. I could see the stalks moving where the leopard was creeping around and then suddenly, she stuck her head out from the grass and looked over to where the impala was grazing, still completely unaware she was there.

'The leopard crept out of the long grass, about twenty metres or so from the impala, which was just to the right of our truck and in full view. So, imagine it, the leopard is off to the left side, the impala is to the right and we're smack in the middle. We watched the leopard slowly sneak up to an old anthill. She had sunk low to the earth so that all four of her legs were lying almost flat on the ground, and she sort of slithered along like a snake.'

Sam hunched his shoulders and bent over slightly to give the impression of the leopard creeping.

'The impala was still completely unaware of her presence as she hid from his view behind the thick column of dirt. Now, the leopard was watching him intently, waiting patiently to make her next move. She stayed absolutely still for about two minutes, afraid that any slight movement she made would give her away and cause the impala to bolt for safety. She was waiting for the perfect opportunity to attack. Antelope such as the impala, know the dangers that hide amongst long grass and behind termite mounds and anthills, and are very wary.

'Sitting on top of the truck, we all watched and waited to see what would happen. The impala then turned slightly away from the leopard. That was it, that was her chance. Still keeping very low to the ground, she sneaked quickly along to hide behind some old tree branches on the ground, nearer to the impala. She then lay completely flat, perfectly still, but watching the impala intently; she never once took her eyes off it.

'Her camouflaged fur was no good to her out in the open like she was, she had to rely on being hidden from the impala's view. She was now only a matter of a few metres away.

'Suddenly, the impala stopped eating, looked up and sniffed the air. He hadn't seen the leopard, but he had sensed something. There was absolutely no sound coming from anywhere, it was deathly quiet and the tension was really strong. I can't speak for the others, but I was barely breathing, it was so exciting. An attack by the leopard was imminent, but still she watched, and waited. She knew things still weren't quite right and she was determined to wait for exactly the right moment to launch her attack.'

Sam looked around the classroom. Every child in the room had their eyes firmly fixed on him, leaning forward on their desks, their mouths slightly open, as they waited to hear the outcome of the story.

'The impala stayed very still for a long time, not at all sure everything was safe, but eventually, he decided all was well and went back to grazing on the grass. Not one of us on the roof of the truck moved a muscle, not one of us made a sound.' Sam had lowered his voice to almost a whisper and the children leaned forwards even more to hear what he was saying.

'Suddenly', he cried out, making some of the children jump with fright, 'the leopard shifted her feet slightly, getting a good grip on the sandy ground, a sure sign she was going to attack, and then she burst out from behind the logs, running at full speed and within a few short seconds, she was almost up on the impala. When she was just centimetres away, the leopard launched herself from the ground, her front paws outstretched to get a firm hold of the impala.

'But he was old for an impala and very wise. At the very last split-second, he had seen her and at the moment the leopard was leaping for him, he twisted his body away and although she landed fully onto his back, the twisting motion caused her to lose her grip and she fell to the side, her claws ripping into his flesh as she struggled to hold on.

'The impala snorted loudly, giving the alarm signal. He backed off a few paces and we could see the bloody scratch marks the leopard had made on his body, but he didn't immediately bolt for safety. Instead, he put his head down, showing the leopard his horns and almost inviting her to try again.

'Now, the element of surprise, essential for a leopard to hunt successfully, had gone, and the impala was ready to defend himself with his horns. The act of being thrown off the back of the impala had caused the leopard to hit the ground hard and she was a little shaken that she hadn't managed to get a firm grip of her prey.

'She and the impala stared at each other for a few seconds and then the antelope charged forward, back towards the leopard. He still had his head down and he was thrashing his horns from side to side hoping to catch the big cat on one of the sharp ends.'

Sam imitated the movement with his own head, shaking it first one way, then the other.

'The leopard was dancing around desperately trying to avoid the horns. When she had the chance, she darted forward with one of her paws outstretched, to try and grab a hold somewhere. But the gutsy old antelope kept forcing her away with his horns. Once or twice though, the leopard almost got her claws into him and eventually he obviously thought better of fighting with an adult leopard. He probably knew he was going to lose and figured his best chance was to run off.

'The tragedy is children, that if he'd kept his head down and carried on fighting, he would more than likely have been ok, but he turned as if to run off. That was the chance the leopard had been waiting for and she sprang on to the impala's back once more. This time though, he couldn't shake her off. Almost in one motion, she had taken a firm hold of the antelope with her claws and at the same time, reached around the front of the impala and gripped its throat in her jaws.

'The poor old impala couldn't go anywhere with the weight of the leopard on its back. It stood absolutely still, its head held to one side with the leopard's jaws clamped tight on its throat.' Sam demonstrated by wrapping his own fingers around his throat.

'They stayed like that for what seemed like ages but really was only about a minute. Suddenly, the impala started to sway and then its legs simply gave way and it collapsed. The leopard still held on to its throat as the impala fell to the ground. It struggled to get back on to its feet for several seconds, kicking its legs frantically. Slowly though, the struggling began to stop. The impala was getting weaker all the time, but the leopard still held on to its throat. After several minutes, the impala was dead. The leopard had effectively strangled it with its jaws being clamped around the impala's wind-pipe, cutting off its air supply.'

Sam looked around, not a child was stirring and each of them was staring at him, completely absorbed by his story.

'So,' said Sam, 'what do you think the leopard did next?' He waited for someone to put up their hand, but no-one moved, not even Mirika.

'Well,' he said, 'leopards often have their prey taken from them by lions or hyenas which are much stronger than they are. So they take their meal somewhere most other predators don't go, where do you think that is?'

Again, silence.

'They take it up into a tree!' Sam said and heard one or two class members whisper, 'Wow!'

'The leopard dragged the dead impala across the open ground to a large tree and then started the long climb up the trunk with the impala still in her jaws. I know it sounds incredible,' he said, 'but it's absolutely true. The leopard's legs and jaws are amazingly strong, strong enough to allow her to drag the animal into the tree.

'Using her claws to grip the tree bark, she climbed up to the first branch and then lay the carcass across it, wedged against the trunk. Despite her immense strength, the fight with the impala and then dragging the carcass up the tree meant she was exhausted. She simply lay next to the dead antelope, panting for breath. She would eat her meal later, in peace.' Sam looked at Dineo, who had asked the question, and said, 'That was probably one of the most exciting things I've seen.'

Dineo, along with the other children, said nothing, she and they simply stared, open-mouthed at Sam.

Although he had described a rather gruesome scene, Sam knew that as they grew older and more mature, the children in the classroom would understand completely the reason why these things happened in the bush. They might not like it, but they would understand. They were after all children of Africa!

For the next 20 minutes or so, Sam answered all sorts of questions the children asked, from how many different types of animal he thought existed, to whether or not he had a girlfriend! He answered all of them without hesitation, explaining things where necessary.

They would have carried on forever if the teacher hadn't eventually stepped in. 'Stop now children,' she said gently but firmly, 'it's 10 minutes past the time you should go home and we should let Sam go home as well. Say a great big thank you to him for coming in and spending the afternoon with us.' The children held another impromptu competition to see who could shout 'Thank you Sam' the loudest.

Although he was relieved that his ordeal was finally over, Sam had secretly enjoyed his experience. It wasn't every day that he could describe his adventures to such an enthusiastic audience. He had been in dangerous situations many times before, but he would remember this adventure in the classroom, facing that most frightening of all groups, a 'herd' of inquisitive school-children, for a long time to come.

THE POACHERS

There was a sickening thud as the powerful trap snapped shut on her leg. She was in agony, but Libuku would not have cared. To him, it meant money, a lot of money!

As a young boy, Libuku had realised that his future lay only in his village with his family, milking the cows and growing the maize corn that would help feed them throughout the year. He knew nothing of life beyond the village where they lived in a round shaped hut with dried cow dung as a floor and grasses on the roof.

His day started in the freezing cold of dawn, when he walked about a kilometre from his home and brought in the family's three cows for milking from the bush kraal where they, and cows belonging to others in his village, had spent the night being watched over by a boy from another family.

All the cows in the kraal were thin and scrawny from a lack of lush grass. They didn't move quickly at the best of times, but if he saw his cattle were walking too slowly, Libuku flicked them with the herd-boy's whip he had inherited from his grandfather. It was made from long thin strips of cowhide leather, plaited together to form one continuous length, tapering at the end to a single strand and attached at the other to a stout length of hardwood about a metre long. Even at the age of 12, Libuku prided himself on his expertise with the whip. He could snap the head off a stalk of elephant grass at several metres.

When the cattle had been brought in, Libuku then spent the next hour sitting on a crudely made stool, teasing the milk by hand from the cows' udders into a bucket. He would be lucky to get four or five litres altogether, such was their poor state of health.

Once they had been milked, one of Libuku's younger brothers would take them back into the bush to watch over them whilst they foraged for whatever grazing they could find, before returning to the kraal overnight.

By the time the milking had finished, the sun had risen and warmed Libuku's thin but strong body. When he had completed all his duties at home, he gathered up his books and began the five kilometre walk to his school. He had no shoes on his feet, but there again, he had never owned a pair of shoes. He had been barefoot all his life and consequently, the soles of his feet were as tough as leather. He felt no pain as he walked over stones and branches on the track.

Libuku stayed at school until around midday. The education he was receiving was basic at its best but his parents insisted he attend every day. His father was adamant that educating his children would bring his family out of the appalling poverty they suffered.

Released from school, Libuku walked the five kilometres home and then spent the rest of the afternoon working in the fields. He cleared land by chopping down trees, sometimes taking days over one tree and its roots. With a large hoe, he dug trenches for planting maize. The hoe was probably the most important tool the family possessed. It was nothing more than a square shaped, slightly rounded piece of metal, sharp along the bottom edge and attached to a long length of wood. As crudely made as it was, it was remarkably efficient.

When the maize was growing, he weeded the rows, trying to allow them the best chance of producing a good crop. At the right time, Libuku gathered the large stalks of corn and took them to his village where his sisters and other females from the village, pounded them into a fine flour in the bowls hollowed out from tree trunks. This flour would be cooked with water to make nshima, a food which looks like mashed potato.

Libuku's day ended only when the sun dipped below the horizon. He returned to his village, ate the meagre evening meal of nshima and some vegetables; his family could rarely afford meat. In the dusky light before night fell, he would chat with his friends and join in the music and dancing around the fires, and then lay gratefully on his sleeping-mat.

Dawn the next day came much too quickly for Libuku.

Occasionally, Libuku's grandfather would tell him stories about his adventures as a young man, walking for days through the bush, trapping and hunting animals for their meat and skins.

'One day,' the old man said, 'I heard that rich men in big cities paid a small fortune for the ivory tusks of elephants. I knew my bow and arrows were not enough to bring down one of those beasts, so I made myself a gun, a muzzle-loading rifle. My father, your great grandfather used one and he showed me how to make it.'

Libuku was fascinated, 'Tell me how grandfather,' he said enthusiastically.

'You must first carve a piece of wood to…'

'That's enough, Libuku, go to bed,' said his father Thapelo, sternly. When Libuku had closed the door to their hut, Thapelo turned to his father and said, 'Don't fill the boy's head with stupid ideas of hunting and guns, his place is here with the family, working in the fields.'

The grandfather felt sorry that his grandson's life would be so narrow and turned his head away from Thapelo to hide the sadness he felt sure would show in his eyes.

Early the next morning, as Libuku was just leaving to fetch the cattle for milking, his grandfather took him aside and said, 'Tonight, after we eat, come with me and I'll show you my rifle.' He winked at Libuku and held his finger to his lips. 'Not a word!'

Libuku was beside himself with excitement all day. Eventually, after the evening meal, both of them wandered away from prying eyes, especially Thapelo's, to where the old rifle lay hidden in the branches of a tall tree. Libuku's eyes went wide with excitement as he held the crudely fashioned gun. It was obviously an old relic, the wood of the stock was grey and dry and the barrel rusty from years of lying around. However, it was the first time he had ever handled any form of firearm, or even seen one for that matter.

'How did you make this grandfather and does it still work?'

'Yes, it would work, with a bit of cleaning. First,' explained the old man, pointing 'you have to carve the stock from a strong piece of wood, thick enough for your shoulder here, thin enough to hold in your hand here and long enough for the barrel to sit on along here.'

Looking at it, Libuku could see that the barrel itself was just a long piece of hollow metal piping, about a centimetre in diameter. It had been bound in place on top of the wood with lengths of wire.

'See this, I hammered the end of the barrel nearest me closed and welded it so that the gunpowder wouldn't explode backwards into my face.'

Libuku nodded and without looking up asked, 'How does it fire?'

'Gunpowder alone isn't enough to fire the bullet with any power, so we burn some branches from the chitonto tree and mix the ash, gunpowder and water to make a paste. Normally, a bullet is fired out of a metal cartridge, and this paste acts like that cartridge. When it's dry, we ram it down to the bottom of the barrel. We make the bullets from melting old lead battery terminals and ram one of these down too. We have to stop the bullet from falling out so we just roll some grass into a ball and lightly push that down against the bullet.'

'What are these holes for?' asked Libuku, pointing to two holes that had been drilled in the barrel near to the welded end, one on the side and the other just above it on top.

'We have to light the charge-paste to fire the bullet, so we put a little bit of gunpowder on the stock next to the bottom hole in the side here, see the scorch marks?' Libuku nodded. 'We cut down matches and then ram the ends into this hole above it. Then we make a trigger and a striker out of one piece of metal and nail it loosely to the side of the stock. The trigger is tensioned with a thin strip of rubber from an old tyre innertube and when it's released, it strikes the matches and the sparks then light the gunpowder at the lower hole. That then ignites the charge in the barrel, firing the bullet.'

The grandfather's excitement nearly matched Libuku's as he carried on explaining, 'See here on top, these little saw marks tell me how much charge-paste to put down the barrel depending on what I'm shooting at, elephant, buffalo, or just a small antelope.'

Libuku's grandfather's eyes misted over a little as he remembered his youth. 'There were two or three of us in our village with these old muzzle-loading rifles. We went into the bush for days or sometimes weeks on end hunting whatever we could. Whatever we shot though, we always cut up the meat for the village but if we shot an elephant, we had to hide the tusks high up in a tree, out of the way of Rangers' eyes, till we could sell them to the rich men from the cities. They paid us handsomely for the ivory, but we always managed to spend it easily.' Even at his tender age, Libuku knew exactly what his hard-drinking grandfather would have spent the money on.

He passed the old rifle to Libuku, whose eyes went wide as he held the lethal weapon in his hands. 'Can I fire it someday, grandfather, please?' 'Well, maybe one day, when you're a bit older and we've cleaned it up a little.' He didn't want to anger Libuku's father too much, and in truth, he wasn't entirely sure the gun wouldn't explode in his grandson's face!

In the months that followed, Libuku and his grandfather spent all their spare time, usually in the evenings, wandering in the bush, trapping and snaring animals of all descriptions. Libuku's grandfather had always been disappointed that Thapelo had not wanted to learn the ways of the bush and was only too pleased to pass on his knowledge to his grandson.

Sometimes, other boys from the village would go with them and Libuku rapidly gained an enviable reputation amongst them all, and the surrounding villages, as someone who understood the behaviour patterns of animals and especially how to trap and skin them for meat.

One day, when Libuku had just turned 14, a stranger approached him as he walked home from school.

'I've heard you are a good hunter and an expert trapper,' the stranger said, 'do you want to earn some money hunting for me?'

Libuku studied the man's thin, honey-coloured face and guessed he was from a different region of Africa, perhaps further north, near the great desert of Sahara.

'I don't know you, which village are you from?' said Libuku, suspiciously.

'My name is Ahmed and where I'm from is not important. Are you interested in earning some money?'

'How much?'

'First I need to know you can do it and do it well. If you lay this trap for me and catch what I need, there will be others and then we can talk about the money.'

Libuku remembered the hunting stories his grandfather had told him and agreed immediately, thinking he could earn lots of money for his family and impress the old hunter at the same time. If he could boast to his grandfather about the animals he had trapped alone, maybe he would let him use the rifle sooner.

'That's all you have to do,' explained Ahmed, 'just tell me where the trap is, other men from another village will deal with whatever it catches, but I want you to lay this one where you know of rhinoceros, perhaps near a waterhole or a rhino midden.'

Ahmed noticed Libuku's quizzical look. 'A midden,' he explained, 'is where an animal does his or her toilet, always in the same place.'

He handed over a heavy metal object with a strong chain attached to it. Libuku could see that two parts of the trap, joined together at the bottom with metal pins and each with vicious looking sharp metal spikes would be prised apart and then held down by clips. There was a flat metal plate in the centre, beneath the two folded arms.

'When these two are flat and clipped down, a rhino steps on this plate here,' said Ahmed, pointing to a flat surface in the centre, 'that releases these two spring-loaded arms, trapping the leg.' Although he didn't know it, Libuku was looking at what is commonly known as a "mantrap".

Nothing will escape from this, thought Libuku.

'I'll need someone to help me,' he remarked, struggling to push the two arms apart.

'Take a friend if you must then, but you share the money and he mustn't say anything, understand?' Libuku recognised the threat in Ahmed's voice but said nothing, he was thinking only of the money.

He and his good friend Kamwi could hardly contain their excitement as, a few days later, they arrived at the spot Libuku had chosen. School had finished for the day and both boys had walked there on their way home. Kamwi lived in a different village but attended the same school as Libuku. There weren't that many to choose from!

'Where will we lay the trap?' asked Kamwi.

'Come, I will show you.' Libuku led his friend through the bush along a track barely visible to the naked eye. A few minutes later, they stood at the edge of a small waterhole.

'I've seen a female rhinoceros with a calf in this area, and this is where she comes to drink, now follow me,' and Libuku walked back along the track. 2-300 hundred metres away from the waterhole, the bush opened out to a large clearing, in the middle of which, lay a large pile of rotting dung.

'And when she's in this area, this is where she does her toilet, always here.'

'Always?' asked Kamwi.

'Yes, all rhinoceroses do it, they will use one place as a toilet. She wanders over quite a large area and there will be other dung heaps she uses, but round here, this is where she toilets. We have no word for it in our language but in English, it's called a midden. If we lay the trap here beside the midden we're almost bound to catch her.' Kamwi's eyes lit up as his mind instantly went to the money he would earn for helping Libuku.

They walked around the dung heap until they found a suitable spot near a large tree. Libuku placed the trap on the ground where it would lay hidden under the sand and then he and Kamwi had to use all their strength and weight to prise open the evil looking jaws and lock them into place. When it was ready, they covered the area with a few twigs and seed pods, just to make it look as natural as possible, attached the chain to the base of a tree and buried it too under the sand.

The trap was set.

They walked home to Libuku's village, Korodziba, on the eastern edge of Hwange National Park in Zimbabwe, laughing to themselves about all the money they were going to earn and how they were going to spend it. Neither of them had any idea that some people in faraway places would pay far, far more than they were going to get for the two horns on the front of the rhino's head.

Nor did either of them give any thought as to the pain and suffering they were about to cause. Even if they had, neither of them would have cared, the money was all they could think about.

The trap lay dormant under the sand for a number of days. Late one evening, a female Hook-lipped or Black rhinoceros and her male calf wandered into the clearing towards the midden. She took her last fateful step and suddenly the two metal arms exploded out of the sand.

She had unwittingly placed her right front foot onto the metal plate, hidden just below the surface and her weight triggered the release of the two spring-loaded metal arms, which gripped and dug into the flesh on both sides of her leg, just above her foot. The short, sharpened spikes, like small daggers on the inside of the two arms, tore at the flesh as she struggled to escape. She wasn't going to!

The stout metal chain anchoring the trap erupted out of the sand as she fought desperately to free herself. Her efforts to escape became ever more frantic; she pulled this way and that, all the time bellowing in panic. The more she struggled, the deeper the arms of the trap ripped her flesh, inflicting terrible wounds on her leg. Her eyes were wide with fear.

There wasn't much she was afraid of but this had never happened to her before and now she was very afraid, for herself and her calf, which watched her desperate efforts to escape. He knew something was wrong, but not understanding what was happening, he would not be able to help his mother. He simply stood there and watched.

After what seemed like an eternity, the female rhinoceros stopped struggling, the pain was just too much to bear. She lay down on the ground, waiting for whatever fate was going to do with her and looked at her beloved calf, which was more confused than afraid.

'We want you to go over to Hwange Park and check out some campsites this week.' Gabriel's boss Heiko said to him. 'These are the coordinates of the ones we want you to look at specifically, but we want you to travel around a bit as well to look at the area and assess how much game there is, what the roads are like, that sort of thing.'

Heiko handed Gabriel a small hand-held GPS unit, about the same size as a Smartphone. He had an excellent sense of direction, but Gabriel was not afraid to use modern technology to help him and he would need this piece of equipment because although he had been born in the area, Gabriel had never before been to Hwange National Park although he knew exactly where it was. Safari companies based in neighbouring Botswana and South Africa, such as Drifting Ways Safaris had stopped visiting the park some years earlier because of the ever increasing large amounts of money demanded by the Zimbabwe government. These companies had decided that there were other parks to visit in southern Africa, where the governments didn't try to squeeze so much money out of them.

Over the previous few years however, the situation had eased a lot and the Zimbabwe administration had realised that excessive charges to visit the park had driven away the very companies that provided them with the income. Safari companies from all over southern Africa were now welcomed into Hwange with its upgraded facilities for international clients. Even so, Heiko wanted Gabriel to visit the campsites and report back on their suitability; he didn't entirely trust the new enthusiasm of the Zimbabwe government.

'Would you like to earn 25 dollars?' Ahmed had caught up with Libuku as he walked home from school. It was Thursday, Libuku's last day before the school broke up for holidays. 25 dollars was a large sum of money for the schoolboy and he was keen to earn it.

'Yes, yes, what do I have to do?'

'Do you know where this is?' asked Ahmed, pointing to a spot on a crudely drawn map.

'Yes, I know it, it's about a half day's walk from here. There's a big rocky hill, grandfather and I have camped there many times, and there's a large river close to it.'

'That's right,' replied Ahmed, 'and at the foot of that hill is a wide patch of open dirt. Have you seen that?'

'Yes, but it's only a dirt patch. I've seen some elephants eating something off the ground, but there's nothing else there.'

'Never mind about that, all you have to do is sprinkle this around the dirt patch when no elephants or other animals are there, it's only something to stop them eating the earth. Can you do that?'

Libuku took the jar from Ahmed and whilst still examining the contents, retorted, 'Of course I can!' He rather resented the implication from Ahmed that he wasn't capable of undertaking a task as simple as this.

He could see that the jar was full of very small crystals, a bit like sugar. If he was honest with himself, although he didn't know what it was for, he suspected that Ahmed was not really telling the truth and was asking him to do something not quite right. But he was not about to appear afraid in front of his new friend. Besides, he thought to himself, just think what I can buy with 25 dollars!

He'd laid the metal trap in the sand just a few days previously, and now he would get even more money when Ahmed paid him for this little task. He would, of course, share the money with Kamwi, although not on an equal basis.

'Alright, go there on Saturday and be careful you don't get any on your hands. And if you help me on Sunday as well, I'll give you another 10 dollars on top,' offered Ahmed. Libuku couldn't say yes fast enough, although he immediately regretted his impulsiveness, thinking about how he would have to deal with his father. Sunday was a special day in Libuku's family. It was always dedicated to attending church twice during the day and then meeting with family and friends around the campfire in the evening.

'Good, where will you be Sunday morning?'

Libuku's mind raced ahead. On his way to the rocky hill, he knew he would pass near to where his friend Kamwi lived, a village called Sekolela. He could stay with Kamwi for the night and meet Ahmed just outside the village.

Even though he wasn't at all sure, Libuku tried to sound confident, 'I'll wait for you by the three baobab trees outside Sekolela,' he said, pointing roughly in the direction of the village.

'Ok, I know those, be there at sunrise,' ordered Ahmed.

Libuku did not know that the crystals were cyanide, an incredibly dangerous and powerful poison. Neither did he know that the area he was being asked to spread them was a "salt lick". There used to be a large termite mound at this place, in amongst some smaller ones. The tiny insects unwittingly brought minerals such as lime and salt to the surface when constructing their home, but over the years, elephants had gradually destroyed it, spreading the rich soil around to form the lick. Many animals living purely off grass and plants, herbivores, eat the dirt to gain the valuable nutrients they need to supplement their diet. Ahmed however, was interested only in one animal.

Unwittingly, Libuku was about to kill his first elephant as a poacher. Even if he knew that that animal, as large as it is, would probably die in agony, he wouldn't have cared.

That same Thursday when Libuku broke up from school for the holidays, Gabriel and Diteko, his colleague from Drifting Ways set out from Maun in one of the company's converted Land Rover Defenders loaded with camping equipment, food and water.

Diteko had only returned from a five day safari the previous evening and knew nothing of the plans. 'Where exactly are we going?' he had asked.

'We'll be heading out for Nata and then turning left at the junction to head for Kasane. When we get to Mpandamatenga, we're going to turn right and head into Zimbabwe and then into Hwange. We're checking out the park and some camps for Heiko. Get some sleep tonight and tomorrow we'll study the map for a route.'

Early the next morning, Thursday, Gabriel and Diteko had looked over a large scale map of the entire park.

'I don't think it matters which way we go round, what do you think?' Gabriel said to his friend.

'I think if we head down the western side first, through Tsamahole and Shakawangi Wild Areas and then head north-east for a while, that will give us a good look at the game around there. We should then be able to cut the road here at Jambile and get back up to Main Camp,' said Diteko, pointing, 'and then we can have an easy drive past the camping areas, back to Robins Camp and out to Mpandamatenga.'

'Good plan, I agree,' said Gabriel. 'It's going to be tough going, we'll be doing at least 3-400 kilometres in the park, and counting getting back to Maun, we'll be covering about 1500 kilometres all told, maybe more.' Diteko looked at Gabriel as if to say, what's new!!

'Ok, let's go.'

Hwange Park is spread over about 15000 square kilometres and if the camps they were going to were that far away, he also knew the roads, or tracks mostly, would be rough and very bumpy. Both Diteko and Gabriel were used to driving long distances along these bad roads during their normal safari trips.

About 6 hours later, they arrived at the entrance gate to Hwange Park, generally regarded as one of Africa's greatest national parks. Gabriel spent the next hour or so filling out lots of forms and then paid the entrance and camping fees for himself and Diteko. They finally set out for their first camp, in the late afternoon. Gabriel checked the GPS, just to make sure it was recording the track they were on, and then a few hours later, they pitched their tent for the night at a small clearing just off the road. He and Diteko slept very well after a tiring day driving hundreds of kilometres from Maun.

Over the following two days, the two guides explored the wilderness areas along the western edge of the Park. Gabriel did the majority of the driving but both made extensive notes on the quantity and type of game they encountered, the suitability of wild-camp areas where it was allowed, the roads or tracks where they existed. Finally, on Saturday evening, they made camp in the Shakawangi region. The next day they would explore the Dzivanini wild area in the south of the park before heading north for Main Camp and then east to return to Mpadamatenga.

After agreeing to meet Ahmed on the road, Libuku approached his father. 'Can I go and visit Kamwi on Saturday and Sunday, please father?'

'No, you know there's work to be done in the fields and we have church on Sunday, you know that.'

Thapelo's family took their religious faith very seriously, and the service on that day would be special. It would last several hours over the morning and early afternoon, with lots of praise-singing and dancing by the congregation. The rest of the day would be taken up with group discussion and activities.

'But father, the rest of the boys are going to collect honey from the bush on Sunday, can't I miss church just this once and go with them, please,' Libuku pleaded.

After a long silence, Thapelo said, 'Alright, just this once but there are weeds to be dug from the maize rows and there's a tree stump I want to get out, it's stopping me from planting new maize.'

'Thank you, father, I can do that next week.' Libuku felt bad about lying to his parents, but those thoughts evaporated quickly when he reminded himself of the money he was going to earn.

He spent all day Friday working feverishly hard in the fields, cramming in two or three day's worth of effort. He felt an enormous amount of guilt, not for spreading the crystals, which he suspected was to kill animals, but for lying to his father and his younger brother, whom he had persuaded to milk the cows for him on both of the days he would be away. Heavy toil, digging and tending the crops would be his self imposed punishment.

It took him longer than he thought to hike to the site of the mineral-lick, it was further away than he remembered and he arrived tired and worn out in the middle of Saturday afternoon. It was only the thought of the money that had kept him going.

The sun had beaten down on the parched earth all day, driving most animals to find whatever shade they could. Consequently, the salt lick was deserted when he arrived. It was a large area, circular in shape, about 200 paces around. Libuku could see the remains of at least three old termitaria, small stumps showing where the large stacks had once been. The light brown coloured dried mud from which they'd been made, distinguished the actual salt lick from the surrounding ground.

Libuku sprinkled the colourless crystals from the jar as evenly as he could over the entire area. He noticed a sweet, pleasant odour. 'Hmm,' he muttered to himself, 'if they smell so nice, maybe they can't be all that bad.' Although he tried to convince himself that everything was ok, he didn't really believe it.

When he'd finished, he sighed heavily at the thought of the long walk he had ahead of him to Kamwi's village. He arrived at his friend's house late that evening, exhausted from the trek.

'You have to keep this secret Kamwi,' whispered Libuku to his friend, 'if anyone asks, especially my family, I spent Sunday with you and we went into the bush to collect honey but we didn't find a bee's nest, ok?'

'Alright, but what are you doing?' asked Kamwi.

Libuku hesitated! He thought to himself, why am I afraid to tell Kamwi? And then he realised that he knew that what he was doing for Ahmed was wrong. But once again, the money he would get rode roughshod over his suspicions and he pushed them to the back of his mind.

'I'm just going to help a friend, that's all. I'll explain everything later but for now please just say what I want you to say,' he replied, unconvincingly. He disliked deceiving his parents and now, having involved his friend in his conspiracy, he felt even worse.

Early the following morning, Libuku waited impatiently at the side of the road by the old baobab trees. At last, he thought as Ahmed stopped the open-backed pickup truck alongside him.

'Jump aboard,' he called cheerily, and Libuku found a place to squat amongst four other men sitting in the back. There was a second light skinned African man sitting in the front seat alongside Ahmed. Libuku would learn later that this second man's name was Salim.

The bush track was very rough with a barely visible route. They had to divert several times around fallen trees and large marshy areas. The journey took several hours and they eventually arrived at the salt lick near lunch time, around noon.

Libuku went wide-eyed and gasped at the scene that greeted them. Ahmed had obviously chosen the spot well. Animals would generally come across the salt lick on their way to drink from the nearby river, and wouldn't pass up a chance to stock up on minerals.

A massive bull elephant lay on his side in the middle of the mineral-lick. He was dead. He had been around 70 years old when he took some of the poisoned dirt into his stomach, but Ahmed was interested only in the gigantic tusks, well over 2 metres long and as thick as a man's thigh, that stuck out from the animal's jaw.

Away from the elephant, there were carcasses of other animals lying around, obviously dead. Vultures, marabou storks, jackals and hyenas squabbled noisily for the best positions and were already picking and tearing the flesh from the bones. They in turn would die from eating the poisoned meat.

'Take your spears and spread out,' shouted Ahmed to his men. 'There'll be other elephants around in the bush, find them, you know what to do.' Each of the other four men picked up a short handled spear with a vicious looking, double-edged blade.

Over the next two or three hours, two other elephants were discovered, still alive. Each was lying on its side, uttering feeble grunts. As soon as they were found, two men went to each of the animals and plunged their spears deep into the massive chests, piercing the heart and killing them, finally.

Libuku stared at the blood-covered spears as the men returned to the vehicle.

'Ok,' shouted Salim, 'get the axes and start on the tusks.' He and Ahmed were clearly running the operation together.

Libuku finally realised the awfulness of what he had done. He had caused this slaughter merely so that Ahmed and his helpers could hack out the valuable ivory. He watched and listened as the men, singing in harmony as only African men can, swung their axes in time to the rhythm. One by one, the tusks from all three elephants were chopped away from the dead animals and loaded onto the pick-up. The largest ones from the dead bull at the mineral-lick were so long, they stuck out over the side, and the ends of the tusks, where they had been embedded in the jaws were wet with blood, some of which dribbled down the side of the vehicle.

Libuku helped with the carrying and loading and with every step he took, his hands full of blood-smeared ivory, his heart became heavier with guilt. Although he kept up the appearance of someone not caring about the animals that had been slaughtered for money, inwardly, he was dying.

As he worked, he remembered talking with his father as they walked through the bush. They had stopped to watch a herd of grazing impala and Thapelo's words came back to him.

'Libuku,' he'd said, 'we live alongside these animals, we are not their masters. There is a delicate balance between us and them, it's called the environment. And it's ours to protect at all costs. If that balance is destroyed by our actions, mankind will probably survive, but our world will be a much sadder place, and our children of the future will despise us for what we took from them; the chance to experience nature in its raw state. It is our environment to protect, not to do with as we please. Remember that when you go with your grandfather and his old gun.'

Suddenly, remembering his father's words, he knew he no longer wanted to shoot his grandfather's old muzzle-loading rifle, it spelled only death.

All the time they had been there, there was a sense of urgency. Ahmed continually shouted at the men to, 'get the job done,' and 'quickly now, let's get out of here.' He was obviously afraid of prying eyes, probably armed Game Rangers. He would have no desire to get into a fight with those guys.

It was the middle of the afternoon when everything was done and the ivory loaded into the back of the pick-up.

'Libuku, cover the tusks with that tarpaulin and wipe the blood off the side of the truck. Then lets get out of here,' ordered Ahmed. Nobody really watched what Libuku did, and consequently, nobody noticed that he neglected to wipe away the smears of blood.

Ahmed spun the tyres of the pick-up in his haste to get away from the area. Sitting in the back, his helpers opened some cans of beer and began to drink to their good fortune. Libuku took a can, but didn't drink.

Ahmed drove away as fast as he dared. His plan was to leave Hwange Park south of Libuku's village, Korodziba, and drive to a spot where he would rendezvous with a helicopter in a remote area. Ahmed would then pay the men, including Libuku and leave them to get back home as best they could. He and Salim would then take the ivory and head for where they would sell it on to dealers. From them, the ivory would be smuggled to various parts of the globe, wherever the price was the highest.

Libuku didn't know it but the buying and selling of ivory is illegal in practically every country in the world. The fact that elephants are poached for their tusks only increases the price of the ivory, resulting in huge profits for the poachers and smugglers, but not for those local villagers like Libuku, who readily slaughter the animals for just a few dollars.

For the first time, Libuku thought not about the money he was about to be paid. He thought about the agony he had brought about and how he had done it. He realised that he was now involved with criminals. He began to feel afraid. Ahmed was a professional poacher, and the helpers with him, including himself, were simple village men working for the promise of what to them, was a large amount of money. For that reason, no matter who they were, Libuku knew that not one of the laughing, drinking, jovial men sitting with him in the back of the truck, would hesitate to kill him if they thought he might give them away to the Rangers.

To keep up the appearance of enjoying his gruesome work, he pretended to drink from the beer can he'd been thrown and joined in the banter and joking as they made their way along the track.

Suddenly, there was chaos!! The pick-up lurched violently to one side, cans of beer were sent flying, the liquid contents spraying around everywhere. In an instant, bodies and elephant tusks were thrown together in the centre of the cargo space as Ahmed had to swerve urgently off the track to avoid a head-on collision with another vehicle coming from the opposite direction.

The men were more than a little drunk by this stage and despite the painful knocks, they thought it was hugely funny and roared with laughter as the other vehicle, a big Land Rover, came to a sudden stop in some trees.

That same Sunday morning, Gabriel and Diteko finished exploring Dzivanini area. They had made their notes, discussed what they had seen and then finally set out north back towards the tourist road that would eventually lead them past Main Camp and on to Robins Camp where they would leave Hwange and drive back to Maun. They were on the same track that Ahmed would later drive along, from the opposite direction.

They chatted endlessly as they bounced and bumped along the rough track. Diteko kept a careful watch on the GPS, not wanting to miss anywhere they should turn. On and on they drove, pitching from side to side over the rough track, right through lunch and on into the late afternoon. The track wound its way through dense areas of bush, across wide open stretches of savannah, around large rocky outcrops.

'This really is a beautiful park,' remarked Gabriel. Diteko grunted a reply. He was hot and getting very tired.

They passed an unoccupied camping site named on the map as Liputi and Gabriel stopped the Land Rover as Diteko entered the coordinates of the camp, just for future reference, should they or anyone else need it. They would shortly be glad they did.

At that point, they were about 50 kilometres away from the main road out of the park and Gabriel knew they wouldn't make it that night. They pressed on for another 20 kilometres or so.

'I don't think there's been one straight stretch more than a hundred metres long on this track,' remarked Gabriel. 'Pass me the water bottle please, nkosi.' Gabriel used the local Setswana term for "friend".

Pressing the end of the bottle to his lips, he took a long swig of the cool, sweet water and at the same time, watched the track with one eye. It was a technique he had perfected over the time he had been driving in the bush. Or, at least, he thought he had perfected it.

As he started to negotiate a sharp right hand corner in the track, Diteko suddenly shouted, 'Watch out!' as Ahmed's pick-up careered round the bend from the other direction, heading directly for their Land Rover.

The track ran round the outside of a large clump of trees, effectively making it a blind bend, and neither vehicle was going particularly slowly. Most vehicles in this part of southern Africa are right-hand drive, and sitting in the passenger seat, Diteko had seen the pick-up truck coming the other way fractionally before Gabriel.

He dropped the water bottle and yanked the steering wheel over to the right to take emergency avoiding action. The Land Rover swerved sharply off the track and crashed into small trees on the edge of the thicket. The pick-up swerved off the track to the other side, bouncing heavily over the rough ground, but didn't stop. As it careered past, both Gabriel and Diteko heard the laughter of several men sitting on the back of the vehicle, they obviously thought it was a huge joke.

Cursing the other driver, Gabriel reversed back onto the track, but before driving on, he gazed straight ahead of him and was silent for some time before he turned to Diteko and asked, 'Did you notice anything odd about that pick-up?'

'Yes I did, it looked like it had smears of blood on the side. I was wondering whether you'd seen that as well. I only got a glimpse as it passed but it definitely looked like blood.'

'Exactly,' said Gabriel, 'and I think there was a tarpaulin covering something in the back.' Both men looked knowingly at each other.

'Are you thinking what I'm thinking?' whispered Gabriel.

'Poachers,' replied Diteko, almost spitting the word out. They both knew that these were men who would not think twice about slaughtering an elephant or a rhinoceros purely for the tusks or horn.

'They're not interested in the ivory or the horn, it's no good to them,' muttered Gabriel, 'it's the dollars they can get by selling it on, and they're simply not bothered about how many they have to kill to get that money.' Gabriel's voice betrayed the disgust he felt at this awful practise. He knew there were enormous amounts of money to be made from this despicable and illegal trade, and local men would be used by the criminal gangs, who were often from neighbouring countries, to shoot, trap or somehow kill these animals.

'They can probably sell ivory on to the Chinese or Arab dealers for about US$200 per kilo, maybe more. A big bull can have tusks weighing 20-25 kilos each, easily. That's around $10,000 for one elephant!!'

'Do you think they were an organised gang?' asked Diteko.

'Organised yes, but not a gang. I think the ones in the back of the pick-up were local men, paid a pittance to do the dirty work by Janjaweed guys, who'll probably be waiting for them somewhere else. They'll take the ivory or horn, whatever they've got, on to where the international dealers will buy it off them.'

'Janja who?' queried Diteko.

'Janjaweed, they're a bunch of armed militia-men from the north, around Sudan who just fight wars. But there's so much money to be made in poaching, they've come south and started to raid the parks down here for elephant and rhino. They're really nasty, armed to the teeth and utterly ruthless. They sometimes use attack helicopters with large calibre machine guns. They'll mow down an entire herd in the blink of an eye but where the bush is dense, like around here, they'll employ the local men and pay them to kill the animals and bring the ivory or horns to them.'

'What do you think we should do?' asked Diteko.

'Well, we sure as hell aren't going to let them get away with it if they are poachers,' Gabriel replied. They talked about it for a while and eventually agreed on a course of action.

'They were heading south and I don't think they can reach the edge of the park before darkness. I figure they'll camp somewhere first and set out again tomorrow at dawn. If we can find their camp, we can sneak in and look in the back of the truck. If it is ivory, we can call the anti-poaching unit on the satellite phone,' ventured Gabriel.

By this time, the poachers were about 15 minutes ahead of them. Gabriel turned the Land Rover around and began to go after them.

'If we start from the point where the pick-up swerved, we can identify their tyre tracks and follow them,' said Diteko. He was much better at tracking than Gabriel, and sure enough, he picked out the tyre tracks almost immediately.

'They're very distinctive,' Diteko said, 'the tyres are so old, you can see where there's no tread at all in places. We should have no trouble following them.'

Sometimes the tyre tracks disappeared into the grass, but Diteko searched for them using the tried and tested method of walking back and forth across the front of the Land Rover and always managed to pick up the trail.

'Sunset is around 6 o'clock tonight,' said Gabriel, 'I reckon they'll push on until dark and then make camp, probably around 6-30.' He was taking into account the fact that night comes very quickly in Africa once the sun has sunk below the horizon.

A short time later, as daylight was fading, Gabriel pulled off the track and hid the Land Rover in thick bush.

'I'm sure they'll have made camp not far ahead from here. If we go on with the Land Rover, either the engine or the headlights will give us away.'

Before they left, he entered the coordinates into his GPS unit. Diteko looked at him quizzically, 'Not that I don't trust your tracking skills old friend,' said Gabriel, 'it's just easier.' Diteko wasn't so sure, but he said nothing.

Their plan now was to follow the tracks on foot to where, hopefully, the poachers had decided to stop for the night. Gabriel had agonised over whether the gang would drive on in the night, to wherever they were to meet the guys who would take the goods from them. In the end, he and Diteko both agreed that because they were in such a remote part of the park, there was no urgency to drive during darkness. The area is thickly wooded and has virtually no human habitation, nearly crashing into Gabriel and Diteko had been a chance in a million.

'That old pick-up probably doesn't have lights anyway,' muttered Diteko. They both realised however, that their plan was a gamble.

It was very nearly dark and they had been following the tyre tracks using their head-torches for around 30 minutes, when Diteko suddenly stopped. 'Look here Gabriel,' he whispered, 'one of the tyres is punctured.' Gabriel could see how the track had been chewed and scuffed by the flat tyre. 'And listen!'

Sure enough, Gabriel heard faint sounds coming out of the darkness in the distance.

'Voices!' exclaimed Diteko, 'It must be them, we are close.'

Twenty minutes later, they had crept close to the poachers' camp and were hidden from view in thick bush. They had chosen the position well; a flat, open area concealed from prying eyes by some large trees and several old termite mounds and anthills. Even though the area was remote and devoid of humans, Ahmed and Salim's military training dictated they should still take precautions.

Gabriel could see the vehicle off to the side. They had travelled only about 10 kilometres from where they had nearly crashed, the puncture causing them to halt probably sooner than they would have liked.

'You stay here,' he whispered to Diteko, 'I'm going to take a look in the back of that pick-up.' Moving silently across the sandy earth, taking extreme care not to step on fallen twigs, Gabriel finally crept up to the side of the vehicle. He peeped over the top and could see the poachers all sitting around the campfire, some chatting and some arguing. He very carefully lifted the tarpaulin in the back and a quick glance at the cargo confirmed their suspicions.

Suddenly, out of the darkness, a figure, silhouetted against the firelight, wearing combat fatigues with an automatic pistol strapped to his leg, approached the truck. Luckily for Gabriel, the glow from the fire didn't quite reach the pick-up and he was able to remain in almost complete darkness. Swiftly, but very carefully, he ducked down behind the side of the vehicle and lay perfectly still on the ground while the poacher rummaged around for something in the open back. Gabriel hardly dared to breathe in case he gave himself away.

Eventually, the man found what he'd been looking for, Gabriel heard the characteristic fizzing sound of a beer can being opened. He waited a few moments before he peeped over the side of the pick-up. To his relief, the poacher had returned to the others sitting around the fire. Replacing the cover, he crept back to where Diteko was waiting.

'Definitely poachers,' he whispered, 'let's go.' Before they went however, Gabriel remembered to enter the coordinates of the camp into his GPS.

Going away from the poachers' camp, they made much better time back to their vehicle in the bush.

'So, what did you find?' asked Diteko.

'Just what we thought; I counted six tusks, big ones too, a couple at least two metres. They probably came from old, solitary bulls. The blood wasn't quite dry, so they must have hacked them off today. Goodness knows where the elephants are, just hope they had the decency to shoot them and not let them suffer.' He knew it was unlikely; bullets are expensive for local villagers!

'How many poachers did you count?' asked Diteko.

'Seven,' replied Gabriel. 'and one of them is a young boy, probably only about 13 years old. I had a near miss when one of them came to get a can of beer from the back of the truck. He was definitely military, so probably a Janjaweed scout.' They hurried back to their Land Rover to carry out the next part of their plan.

In another part of the vast park, the female rhinoceros could feel herself getting weaker. It had only been a night and a day since her leg became trapped, but already she was exhausted through lack of food and water and her efforts to break free. Her normally great strength was draining away with her ever more feeble attempts to escape. Her calf continually walked around where his mother lay, snuffling against her, encouraging her to get up.

The predators and scavengers of the bush had been gathering slowly, waiting their chance. They had no idea what a "mantrap" was but they instinctively knew that she was in trouble and getting weaker. Even so, they dared not approach. Crippled as she was, the rhinoceros could still be a great danger to them if they tried to attack her now. And the calf would defend its mother at all costs. Waiting was their only option.

Discovering the poacher's camp and viewing the contents of the pick-up had been the first part of Gabriel and Diteko's plan. For the next part, Gabriel got out his satellite phone and dialled his boss Heiko's home number in Maun.

'Heiko, listen, we're still in Hwange and we've come across poachers in the south east part of the park. We've got the location of their camp, but I don't have the Rangers' number at Main Camp, can you find it for me please.'

'Stand by,' replied Heiko, 'I'll call you back.' Ten minutes later, Heiko called Gabriel on the sat-phone and gave him the number of the Anti-Poaching Unit, a specially trained, heavily armed group, dedicated to catching animal poachers. Gabriel gave Heiko a very brief outline of what had happened and that he and Diteko would help the Rangers if they could.

'Ok, good luck and be careful.' Gabriel thought the last piece of advice was a bit unnecessary.

Fifteen minutes later, Gabriel had relayed to the Anti-Poaching Unit all the information he had about the poachers, what they had in the truck, how many there were and the exact GPS coordinates of where their camp was situated .

The Ranger on the other end said, 'Don't stay where you are, you're too exposed. Look on your map and find Somalisa, south east of Main Camp.'

'Got it,' replied Gabriel.

'Good, now look for Korodziba village, south of Somalisa and then find Liputi camp to the east of Korodziba.'

'Yep, got Liputi, we came past there earlier, it's an abandoned camp but I put the coordinates into my GPS for reference anyway.'

'Good work, we will come down via Somalisa and Korodziba and meet you at Liputi. That will give us plenty of room to skirt around where you say the poachers are camped.'

'We'll be there.' Gabriel hung up. 'Let's go, we have to get back to Liputi camp.'

'What time is it now?' asked Diteko.

'Just after 8 o'clock.'

Both men looked at their map and estimated the distance the Rangers had to travel was about 120 kilometres over rough, sand roads.

'By the time they get geared up, loaded and on the road, I reckon on at least 6 hours before they get to us, say between 2 and 3am.'

'Let's go then,' said Gabriel, reversing the Land Rover back onto the track. He knew that Diteko's estimate wouldn't be that far off correct. These Rangers were experts at driving on sand roads, whatever the weather, day or night. He and Diteko could at least get a few hours sleep before they arrived.

At 2-15 the following morning, Diteko woke Gabriel and whispered, 'They are here!'

A few minutes later, 5 Rangers wearing camouflage clothing and heavily armed with M16 automatic rifles and Glock pistols, jumped down from a large vehicle, which Gabriel immediately recognised as a

SAMil, which was an abbreviation for South African Military. They had been developed by the South African Defence Force during the bush-war with Angola. Big, imposing, brutes of vehicles and extremely reliable, they were a favourite of all neighbouring countries for this type of work.

A sixth Ranger, obviously the man in charge, pulled up sharply behind the truck in a Toyota Land Cruiser. Gabriel introduced Diteko and shook hands with all the Rangers.

After listening intently to what Gabriel and Diteko told them, the leader of the unit, a huge muscular man dressed in army fatigues named Ranger Sergeant Rodwill outlined their plan to capture the poachers.

'The first thing to stress,' said Sergeant Rodwill, 'is that we will make every attempt to capture them, put them in prison and recover the ivory. Neither Gabriel nor Diteko have seen any automatic rifles, there were none in the pick-up, is that right Gabriel?'

'None that I saw in the back, I didn't look in the cab, but the one guy I caught a glimpse of was definitely military.'

'Exactly, so that does not mean that they haven't got any, they could be sleeping with them under their blankets, it's what I would do in their shoes. If Gabriel's right and these are Janjaweed militiamen, they will definitely have weapons; we know that from past experience. Gabriel and Diteko will take us back to where they originally left their vehicle; that should give us plenty of distance not to be heard. We will then approach the camp on foot and find whatever cover we can. The element of surprise must be on our side, so absolutely no noise. Check your weapons before we set off for the camp.'

Gabriel was impressed with Sergeant Rodwill's professional manner, he obviously knew what he was doing. He had drawn a plan as best he could of how the poachers were camped, and Rodwill spread it out on the Land Rover bonnet. He began to point to individual positions.

'According to Gabriel, there's plenty of cover, so, David, I want you here on this left side, Simeon here next to David and Evens here next to me. Lesedi and Gideon, spread out to the right, I'll be here,' he said, pointing to a spot in the middle of where his Rangers were positioned.

'Gabriel and Diteko, you will stay out of the way up here, especially if there's gunplay, understand?'

They both nodded but Gabriel said, 'What if they make a dash for the bush away from your line?'

'We obviously can't encircle the camp, we might end up firing at each other. But we're placed in a rough semi-circle and if someone does make a bolt for the bush, the two guys at each end, that's David and Gideon will *deal with them*!!' Ranger Rodwill stared hard at Gabriel, trying to convey his meaning. Gabriel and Diteko both understood.

'We'll stay out of the way,' whispered Diteko. They weren't about to argue, not with a man like Sergeant Rodwill.

'Gabriel,' said the Sergeant, 'when you went to the camp, could you make out what language they were talking?'

'The two guys in combat gear spoke to each other in a language I didn't understand but when they spoke to the others, they used English.'

'That's excellent, thanks. I plan that we get to the camp before they have risen, so we need to be there before first light. Hopefully, we can take them by surprise and they'll be sleep-fuddled. Under other circumstances, we might have used stun-grenades to disorientate them, but I need them to understand what I say, so I will call on them to surrender. ***But,*** ' and he emphasised the word, 'if they don't and start shooting, we will shoot back and we will shoot to kill. These men know the penalties for poaching and they won't hesitate to kill any one of us to get away. Are you clear?' Everyone nodded, they had no desire for a fire-fight, but at the same time, they were hardened Rangers and would return fire ferociously and lethally if fired upon.

By 3-30am, they had arrived at the spot where Gabriel and Diteko had left their Land Rover earlier the previous evening. From here, they would proceed on foot.

'Everyone, check your equipment,' ordered Sergeant Rodwill before leaving, 'I don't want any foul-ups with empty magazines. Those of you with lights, test them now.'

Two of the Rangers carried large rucksacks containing battery packs for the very powerful hand held spotlights. They would be positioned either side of Ranger Rodwill, in the centre of the Rangers' line. It was a tried and tested method to disorientate the poachers without the use of grenades. At a given signal, the Rangers would turn them on and anyone looking directly into the lights, even for the briefest of seconds, would be temporarily blinded.

Using his GPS, Gabriel guided the Rangers back to within a few hundred metres of the poachers' camp. Ranger Rodwill called a halt and gathered his unit around him 'Gabriel, give me your GPS.' Handing it to David, he carried on, 'David, take your night vision goggles and Gabriel's GPS. Go to the camp and scout the area, look for cover and try to see where everyone is sleeping. Go!'
David was back with the group within 20 minutes. 'Most of the poachers are lying around the fire, I counted five. There's a pick-up truck to one side, but still close to the fire and two guys are sleeping alongside it, on the camp side. I couldn't see anyone behind the pick-up. There's plenty of cover to the side we'll approach from, logs and trees etc and there are several old insect mounds and stacks behind the truck and heavy bush beyond that. We'll have to be careful no-one makes a bolt for the trees. They're obviously not expecting a visit; they haven't posted any guards, or if they have, it hasn't worked, everyone's asleep.'
'Excellent work, thanks David. Seven poachers, is that how many you counted Gabriel?'
'At least', he replied, 'and one of them looked to be just a young boy about 13-14 years old.'
Ranger Rodwill nodded an acknowledgment and then looked again at the crude map drawn by Gabriel. 'David, point to where the truck is please.'
'Here,' replied the Ranger, 'and the stacks and trees are here and here.' Armed with that better information, Rodwill added some features to the map and altered David and Gideon's positions slightly to cover any attempt to escape into the bush.

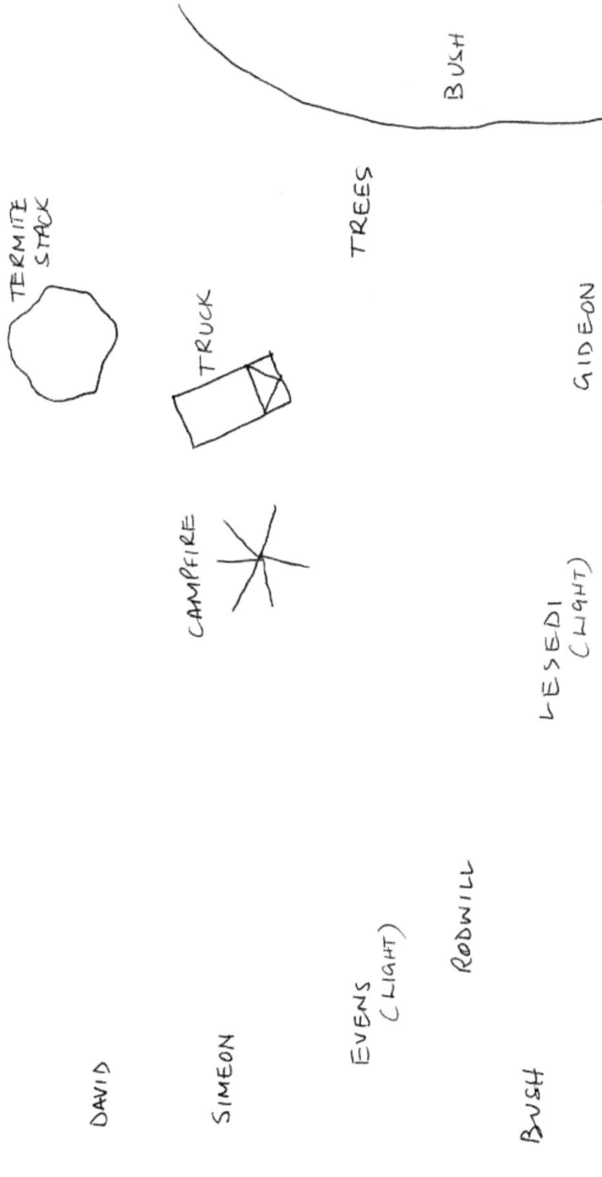

Sergeant Rodwill's plan of the camp and his Rangers' positions.

Making no sound at all, the group approached the outside of the camp and by 4-10am, everyone was in position, concealed behind whatever solid cover they could find, fallen trees, large rocks, anthills etc. Having had several gun battles with poachers in the past, Ranger Rodwill would take no chances that any of his men would be caught in the open with no cover and vulnerable to automatic rifle fire. He listened to the snores coming from the camp, and waited.

Slowly, the dawn changed the light from inky black to dark grey as it crept onto the horizon, but Ranger Rodwill continued to be patient. He was waiting for that moment when it would still be dark enough for the lights to be effective, but light enough that he and the Rangers could see the poachers.

The time was now around 4-30 in the morning, the time when experts say that the human body and mind are at their least effective. It was getting lighter by the second and a quick check told Ranger Rodwill that there were five bodies lying around the now dead campfire and two by the truck. Scanning the area with his night vision goggles, he could see no movement. Everyone was still asleep.

This was the moment.

Knowing that they would be completely bewildered and confused by sudden noise and activity, Ranger Rodwill fired his automatic pistol twice into the air. The stillness of the African night amplified the sound of the shots so that they sounded like cannon shells exploding, but they lacked the deafening effect that stun-grenades would create.

From behind his cover of a large anthill, he shouted at the top of his booming voice, 'This is the Zimbabwe Parks Authority Anti-Poaching Unit. We are armed and your camp is surrounded. Show yourselves and surrender and you will not be harmed. Resist and we will shoot.'

There was immediate panic and chaos in the camp. Bodies that at one instant were sound asleep around the remains of the campfire were suddenly awake, on their feet, confused as to where the commanding voice had come from. They began to run around, bumping into one another in their confusion, just as Ranger Rodwill had planned.

However, as quickly as the local men had risen, Ahmed and Salim were up and out of their blankets before any of the others had left the ground. It was the kind of response highly trained military personnel make; awake and alert in an instant, ready to deal with almost any threat.

'Get behind the pick-up,' shouted Ahmed to Salim as both men picked up their automatic weapons.

'Lights!' shouted Ranger Rodwill, knowing the poachers would be taken completely by surprise. Instantly, the two powerful spotlights lit up the scene brighter than any daylight. At least two of the poachers in the middle of the camp suddenly held their hands up to their eyes, screamed and turned their heads away. They immediately threw themselves back to the ground, face down, arms and legs outstretched. The spotlights continued to illuminate the camp.

Ranger Rodwill shouted again, 'Give yourselves up, do not resist, we are armed! Raise your hands and lie on the gr………!'

The first volley of gunshots came from the area of the pick-up truck. There was a distinct thud as one of the lead bullets buried itself into the trunk of the tree Ranger David was behind. From their distinctive metallic sound, every Ranger there knew at that point that they were facing ruthless poachers armed with Soviet made AK47 assault rifles, the favoured weapon of militias from the north of Africa. These men would be well trained and fearless, unlike the men without guns lying on the ground.

'Two men behind the truck,' shouted David, immediately returning fire. The sound of bullets ricocheting off the metal of the pick-up filled the air.

With his automatic weapon against his shoulder in the ready-to-fire position, Ranger Rodwill stuck his head out from behind the anthill. As he did so, Salim made a break from the cover of the pick-up truck, firing his automatic rifle from his hip as he went. He ducked behind a substantial tree just as Gideon and Lesedi opened fire on him.

'He's making a break for the bush,' shouted Ranger Rodwill. Sure enough, a second later, Salim broke cover again and started running for the bush still firing wildly at the shadows. Ranger Rodwill ignored the bullets whizzing around him and took a quick but accurate aim. Instinctively "leading" his target Salim, he fired a short burst of five or six rounds, over the heads of the terrified poachers lying on the ground.

Salim stumbled as the first of the shots took him in his legs and hips, breaking bones. An instant later, shots from Gideon and Lesedi tore through his lower abdomen and stomach. He was dead as he hit the ground, his body twitching in its death spasm.

'I'm out,' shouted Gideon, as he ducked back behind the cover of a fallen leadwood tree to reload another magazine.

Hearing Gideon's shout, one of the poachers lying on the ground near to Gideon's position decided to seize his chance. Realising the Ranger would take only a few seconds to reload, he jumped up from where he had been lying on the ground, carrying a machete. He ran straight towards Gideon's cover, holding the large knife aloft and screaming as he went.

Libuku looked up from where he was lying, saw what was happening and in an instant, jumped to his feet and ran to intercept the poacher. He crashed into the side of Gideon's would-be attacker and both man and boy fell to the ground, not more than a few metres from the Ranger.

Libuku was much the weaker of the two and after fighting bravely, he was soon overpowered by the larger man. The poacher pinned the side of Libuku's head to the earth with one immensely strong hand, and with the other, he raised the machete, ready to strike down at his neck.

'Take him Lesedi, *now!*' shouted Sergeant Rodwill.

Lesedi already had the back of the poacher's head clearly in his sights. The single bullet found its deadly mark and the poacher pitched forwards, the machete falling out of his grip. Libuku was covered in blood, brains and bone as the poacher's head and face exploded in a red mist.

Up to that point, the Rangers had been firing short bursts at the pick-up truck, hoping to flush out the men with the guns. It had worked with Salim, but Ahmed was proving to be more stubborn. He was firing single shots from behind the pick-up, hoping to conserve his ammunition. When Salim had been shot dead, Ahmed had taken advantage of the temporary confusion to dart behind an old termite stack, closer to the bush and escape. He knew however, that David would have his dash for freedom covered from his position and realised he would have to choose his moment to break cover carefully. He also knew that as soon as the Rangers heard the click of the empty magazine, they would rush his position. He still had his pistol, but that would be completely out-matched by the M16 rifles of the Rangers. He knew he was in an impossible position but was ready to fight it out, to the death if necessary. He had no desire to be locked up in a prison cell for most of the rest of his life.

Gabriel and Diteko meanwhile, had done what Ranger Rodwill had told them and stayed out of the way, so far. From where they had taken cover however, behind a small rocky outcrop, they could clearly see Ahmed crouching down beside the termite column.

'Wait here, nkosi,' whispered Diteko and crawled quickly along the ground to where David was squatting behind his tree.

'We can see the guy from where we are and I don't think he knows we're there. If you come over to us, you might be able to get a shot at him.'

David cradled his rifle in his arms as he crawled back to the rocks with Diteko. Ahmed's senses were now at their most acute however, and David's rapid movement caught his eye. He turned to where the Ranger was still on the ground and fired a burst from his AK47, one of the bullets passing straight through the soft calf muscle of David's right leg. He wanted to scream out but instead, his training took over and he raised himself onto one knee. In the same movement, he brought his M16 rifle up to his hip and returned Ahmed's fire. The poacher was hit in the shoulder, but it was only a glancing shot.

Recovering from reeling backwards with the force of the bullet strike, Ahmed tried to raise his weapon again.

'Drop it, drop it!' shouted David as he took more careful aim at Ahmed's body.

Ahmed took one last look at his position and tossed his gun away towards David's position. It landed in the dirt about a metre and a half in front of the stack. 'Don't shoot, please don't shoot,' he pleaded, 'I'm hit, I'm dying.'

Trying to make out he was more wounded than he actually was, Ahmed stumbled forward away from his cover and fell to his knees, his AK47 crucially just in front of him, centimetres away.

David's training should have told him to make Ahmed throw the rifle to one side and then lay on the ground, arms and legs outstretched, preventing any sudden movement or attempt at action. But he didn't and it was a mistake that nearly cost him his life.

As he struggled to get to his feet, David closed his eyes momentarily, trying to deal mentally with the pain in his leg. Ahmed saw this and took advantage of the Ranger's lack of concentration. With hatred in his eyes and a snarl on his lips, he reached down to his AK47. He wrapped his finger around the trigger and began to bring the weapon up off the ground, level with his target, David.

David's pain-racked eyes watched Ahmed as if he was acting in slow motion. Even so, he felt powerless to prevent what was about to happen.

Ahmed was milliseconds away from being in a position to shoot the helpless Ranger from a range of only a few metres, when the air was filled with the sound of a burst of automatic fire. David watched as Ahmed was suddenly lifted off his feet and thrown backwards with such force, he was airborne as his bullet-riddled body slammed against the steep side of the termite stack that had been his cover.

Ahmed's poaching days ended with him sitting on the ground in a pool of his own blood with his legs out in front and his head hanging limply down to one side. He was dead.

Spinning round, David saw that Simeon still had his M16 tucked into his shoulder in the ready-to-fire position, a faint wisp of smoke curling its way out of the end of the barrel.

'Thanks,' David called to Simeon, who simply nodded his head in acknowledgment.

For a few glorious seconds, there was complete silence. The shooting had stopped, as had the shouting of orders and the din of battle.

Suddenly, the same booming voice that had started the melee called out, 'You men in the middle of the camp, lie on your stomachs with your arms and legs outstretched to the side. I know you can understand me; do as I say and you will not be harmed. If anyone tries to escape or do something stupid, we will shoot to kill.'

As all four, including Libuku speedily lay on their stomachs and stretched their arms and legs as wide as they could, Ranger Rodwill could see he had their complete surrender. The spotlights were switched off.

'Check him out, carefully,' he ordered, pointing to Ahmed. Simeon and Evens approached the still body of the poacher. David kicked the AK47 to one side and examined his blood soaked body. He made a show of trying to find a jugular pulse, but he knew it was pointless, Ahmed was dead. The other Rangers checked Salim and the local man shot by Lesedi for any sign of life. Finding none, they collected the AK47 rifles and automatic pistols from Ahmed and Salim and along with the villager's machete, brought them back to Ranger Rodwill.

The fire-fight was over, it had been short, but deadly. Three of the seven poachers had been killed and David wounded. Ranger Rodwill was satisfied that he had tried everything to avoid any shooting and he was sorry that wives of the dead men would now be without husbands and children would be without fathers, but that was the decision these men had made. He could live with it, his job was done.

Away from the fire-fight, the life of the black rhinoceros was ebbing away. Every time she tried to move, the cruel spikes of the trap sank ever deeper into her torn flesh. As she rested her huge head on the sand and looked up at her calf, she noticed some scavengers of the savannah, the jackals and vultures, skulking in the distance, just waiting for her to die. Other, larger predators and scavengers wouldn't be far away. It would not be long now before they attacked, whether she was dead or alive.

When the bodies of the dead men had been laid out and covered, Ranger Rodwill turned his attention to the four survivors of the gun battle. They were now made to kneel down in front of him. He gazed at each one individually and then spat in the dust, to show his contempt.

'How did you kill the elephants and where are they?' No-one answered. Ranger Rodwill approached one of the poachers completely at random and was about to aim a kick into the man's stomach when the man kneeling next to Libuku shouted, 'Stop, please, we've had enough,' and inclined his head towards the boy, to indicate to the Ranger where his answer might come from. Ranger Rodwill moved position and stood in front of Libuku.

'Where are the elephants, and how did you kill them?' Ranger Rodwill repeated. The youngster was clearly frightened out of his wits, he was shaking with fear, but initially said nothing. He looked around with wide eyes at the other Rangers, who clearly wanted him dead, or so he thought. Rodwill and the other Rangers simply continued to stare at Libuku. One or two of them made a show of chambering ammunition in their automatic weapons.

Libuku gave in and in a desperate attempt to win favour from the burly Ranger towering over where he was kneeling, his hands in metal handcuffs, the young poacher blurted out, 'Please don't kill me. I will take you to the elephants but I'm not sure where it is from here. '

'How were they killed?'

'That man over there,' said Libuku, indicating to where Ahmed lay, 'he gave me something to spread over the earth where the animals eat the dirt. I don't know what it was, the place is back along the road.' Libuku inclined his head backwards to show Rodwill the direction.

Obviously hoping to win some favour from the Rangers, one of the captured poachers suddenly blurted out, 'I know where it is, I can show you, sir!'

Ranger Rodwill turned to his colleagues and almost whispered, 'It must be a salt lick, he poisoned a salt lick. David, get on the radio back to base and get some men and digging equipment standing by. When we find it, we'll have to dig it out and neutralise it.'

Turning back to Libuku, 'What else have you done, what else have you killed?' Ranger Rodwill demanded.

'Nothing,' Libuku whimpered.

'Tell him about the trap or I'll kill you myself,' shouted one of the other poachers.

Ranger Rodwill stared down at the boy, who could not look into the big Rangers' eyes.

'I set a trap in the sand a few days ago, one with two arms and big springs. It's in a place not far from my village.'

Recognising the description Libuku gave of the vicious mantrap, Ranger Rodwill's face turned red with anger, he knew what pain and suffering such a device caused. He listened to Libuku but he wasn't convinced about his honesty. He slowly lowered his rifle to encourage the poacher to have a better memory. When it was aimed directly at his chest, Libuku suddenly blurted out, 'I can take you, I can take you, please don't shoot me.'

Ranger Rodwill had no intention of shooting the young man but he wasn't about to be lied to by him either. 'What's your name?' he demanded.

'Libuku,'

'How old are you?'

'16,' he replied, hoping he wouldn't be caught in the lie.

'Well Libuku,' said Ranger Rodwill, 'I know this park very well, give me some better information, a special tree or a waterhole maybe, near where you set this trap, I need to know you're not lying.'

Libuku thought for a moment, 'A baobab,' he almost shouted, 'there's a big baobab with the middle of the tree missing.'

Rodwill knew of this ancient tree with the hollow trunk, but he wanted more. 'And what is next to this baobab?' the Ranger asked, suspiciously.

'A smaller baobab, a baby one. The rhino trap is not far from there, maybe an hour's walk.'

Despite attending school, Libuku was not well educated and had no idea of distance except in how long it would take to walk. Ranger Rodwill was satisfied with this answer as he knew where Libuku was talking about. The baobab tree was only about 25 kilometres away.

'When did you set the trap?'

'Four or five days ago, near a toilet midden.'

Ranger Rodwill knew the poachers' methods. An organised gang, such as the Janjaweed would kill the rhino there and then, but local poachers employed by the gang would rather save the ammunition and let the rhino die over several days. Not knowing if the trap had sprung or when, he knew this could turn into a race against time.

'Right,' he said to the other Rangers, 'here's what we do. Gideon, run back and bring up the SAMil. In the meantime, these guys,' indicating the poachers, 'will put the spare wheel on the pick-up. When Gideon gets back, we'll clear up this camp, load the bodies, ivory and prisoners onto the truck and then we all go back to where we left the Land Rover and the Toyota. David, are you ok to guard the prisoners in the back of the SAMil with Simeon?'

'No problem, boss'

'Good, Evens, you drive the pick-up when the spare has been put on. Lesedi, you're with me.'

An hour later, everyone was back at the place Gabriel had left his Land Rover and Ranger Rodwill issued a fresh set of instructions.

'Lesedi, you stay with David in the back of the SAMil, Gideon, you drive. Simeon, you come with me in the Toyota, we may need your medic skills. We'll take this Libuku with us to find the trap and see if it's been sprung.' There was a distinct note of disgust as Ranger Rodwill almost spat out Libuku's name.

'Gabriel and Diteko, please follow me in your vehicle.' He pointed to the last of the Rangers, 'Evens, you follow the SAMil to the station in the pick-up. If my guess is right, you should be heading more or less in the direction of where the salt lick is and this man can show you where it is, right.' The captured poacher realised Ranger Rodwill wasn't asking, he was telling him he would. The poacher nodded his agreement eagerly.

'I'll radio ahead to tell them you're coming in with the bodies and at the same time, ask for a helicopter unit to help us with the search. When you get back Gideon, start organising the men to dig out the lick. Ok, everyone clear? Let's go.'

The calf continually walked around his mother, calling to her to get to her feet and walk with him into the bush. He simply could not understand why his mother kept lying there, her head on the ground looking for all the world as though she was taking a midday nap. He did not appreciate she was dying.

They arrived at the baobab tree around lunchtime and immediately heard the clatter of helicopter rotor blades in the distance. There was nowhere for the helicopter to land because the bush was far too dense, so Ranger Rodwill spoke to the pilot over his radio. 'The task is simple,' he said, 'we need to find either the trap or whatever is caught in it. From what Libuku has told us, we're looking for a clearing with a midden, it's probably within a five kilometre radius of this baobab!!'

By this time, Ranger Rodwill had relented a little and removed the handcuffs from Libuku's wrists.

'I'm trusting you not to run away, now which direction is the trap?' he said. Libuku immediately pointed away from the Baobab and the helicopter flew off high above the bush.

Not five minutes later, the pilot called Ranger Rodwill on the radio and shouted, 'We see it, we see it, a female rhino and a calf. The adult is down, I can see a trap caught around the front leg, there's lots of blood staining in the earth from the wound on her leg, she looks in a bad way.'

Gabriel saw the helicopter hovering about a kilometre away and headed straight for it, or as straight as he could through the dense undergrowth. He knew instantly that the calf was going to be a problem for them. It would defend its mother at all costs, despite its relatively small size.

Fortunately, the helicopter found a clear space to land in not far from the rhino. They had brought with them emergency medical equipment, including a tranquiliser gun and darts. As part of his training, Ranger Rodwill had become skilled at basic veterinary practise and was an excellent shot.

The question for Rodwill now however was this; would the female rhino recover from the tranquilising drug in her severely weakened condition?

'I have to tranquilise the rhino to remove the trap. She's obviously weak, but I don't see we have a choice. She may not recover from the drug, but I can't just let her die without at least trying.' Ranger Rodwill was talking as much to himself as to the others. 'Let's see to the calf first.'

Dealing with the rhino calf was easy. From the back of the Land Rover, Diteko slipped a rope over its head and pulled the slip knot tight. It immediately started to struggle but the Land Rover towed him away and Diteko fastened the other end of the rope to a nearby tree, effectively tethering the calf.

'We also have to deal with those,' said Ranger Rodwill, indicating the army of scavengers, not far enough away. 'They could become a little too bold, especially the hyena and we'll have real problems if lions pitch up.' The sergeant was silent for a second or two. 'Wait here and watch him,' he commanded, pointing to Libuku, and disappeared into the bush. A few minutes later, the sound of a single rifle shot split the air.

'He's shot something to get them all away,' said Diteko, and immediately, the waiting scavengers began to drift towards where the shot had come from.

'That should take care of it,' said Rodwill as he returned to the group, 'I shot an old impala a couple of hundred metres away and slit its throat to get the scent of blood into the air. It was a female with a large abscess on her hind quarters. It wouldn't have been too long before the hyena took her anyway. It's a pity, but it had to be done, it wasn't safe otherwise; should keep them busy for hours, listen!' In the distance everyone could hear the yapping and squawking of animals and birds fighting each other for the best bits of the carcass.

They could now assess the situation of the mother. 'She's very weak,' said Ranger Rodwill, 'but the blood seems fresh. I don't think she's been in the trap for too long, maybe a day or even just last night.' Looking at the red staining in the sand, he carried on, 'She has lost a lot of blood but hopefully not too much. It's her struggling that's weakened her if anything.' Whilst he was talking, the rhinoceros had her head on the ground, as if accepting she was going to die.

Ranger Rodwill realised straight away just how bad the situation was for her.

He looked directly at Libuku. 'Do you see what you've done, can you possibly understand the pain you've caused here?'

Libuku could not look Ranger Rodwill in the eye and simply gazed down at his feet. After a few seconds, the young boy did look up and the Ranger saw that tears were streaming down his face. He made a decision. 'Libuku,' he said, 'you can go. I saw what you did to stop the attack on Gideon back at the camp. It was a brave thing to do, I appreciate it and so does Gideon. Go back to your village, don't ever get involved with this sort of thing again, do you hear me?'

'Thank you, thank you,' said Libuku, gratefully. He went to run off into the bush, but stopped after only about ten metres and looked behind him at the tragic scene he had helped to create. He was racked with guilt and walked slowly back to Ranger Rodwill.

'I have caused all this and I'm sorry and ashamed. I want to help,' he whispered. Ranger Rodwill put his hand on his shoulder, looked at him and smiled, but said nothing. He didn't have to.

From a distance of about 5 metres, Ranger Rodwill fired the dart containing the tranquiliser drug into the immensely tough hide of the rhinoceros. He had reduced the quantity of drug, hoping that it would be enough to keep her sedated but not too much that she would not recover from it. The drug took only minutes to take effect.

Gabriel and Diteko immediately grabbed hold of the two arms of the trap and it took all their strength to force them apart. They gasped as the vicious spikes came away from her flesh with a soft sucking noise.

With great difficulty, they held the arms apart, the spring mechanism was so strong, and Libuku lifted her leg away from the trap. After allowing the two arms to close back together gently, Gabriel removed the anchor chain from the tree and was about to carry it all to the waiting helicopter.

'Give that to Libuku,' ordered Ranger Rodwill, 'he laid it, he can carry it.'

Rodwill, Gabriel and Diteko then got to work on her injuries. If the circumstances were different, a specialist medical team would work on her but on this occasion, there was no time, they would have to do their best. They were trying to save her life.

After cleaning the dried blood away from her leg, Rodwill handed Gabriel two or three water containers with a nozzle. 'Squeeze the bottle and force as much water into each of the holes as you can while I prepare the dressing.'

'What will you do with the injuries to her leg?' enquired Libuku.

Although the flesh was torn through her struggling to get free, mercifully, no major arteries had been severed.

'All I can do really is clean up the wounded areas, get all the dirt out I can and then pack the puncture holes and cuts in her leg with antiseptic ointment, bandage the whole area and secure it firmly with duct tape.'

He knew the bandage and tape would eventually be torn away by the sharp spikes on some of the bushes she would brush against, but he figured it would only have to stay on long enough for the blood to clot and scabs to form over the injured parts. He would have to take that chance.

The others watched the rhino for signs that the anaesthetic was wearing off as Ranger Rodwill worked quickly to apply the bandage.

'Gabriel, pass me that tape please.'

Ranger Rodwill covered the bandage with layer after layer of the grey coloured tape, covering most of her lower leg.

'If I put a lot on, it might last for just that bit longer and allow the wounds to heal.'

The last thing he did was to inject a dose of antibiotics. Now, they could only wait. After an agonising five or six minutes, she began to recover from the drug.

With her leg freed from the trap at last, the relief from the pain must have been immense for her. Even so, she was so weak and confused; she struggled for a long time to raise herself from the side she had been lying on. Time after time, she tried to roll over onto her stomach, without success. Everyone there knew that if she couldn't get to her feet, she would die right there.

'This doesn't look good,' muttered Ranger Rodwill.

Knowing he had caused this tragic scene, Libuku stood aside from the others in the group, desperately hoping the rhinoceros would recover. Looking round, he had a sudden flash of inspiration.

'Why don't we release the calf,' he said, 'he may encourage her to get up.'

'Good idea,' said Gabriel, looking towards Ranger Rodwill.

'Yes, go!' said the Ranger.

Gabriel and Diteko ran to where the calf had been tethered. Diteko carefully slipped the noose from around its neck and, once free, he ran straight to his mother and began nuzzling her face and neck.

Minutes ticked by slowly and still the group watched and waited. It had become a fine balancing act. Instinctively, she knew she must get to her feet and get away from this place. Equally, if she lay still for longer, she would regain more strength, but would be vulnerable to the predators and scavengers. She had no idea Ranger Rodwill and the others were there to protect her.

Eventually, the will to live won out and after 30 minutes or so of struggling, she finally stood up on all four legs. She looked dazed and uncertain at first, but at least she was standing.

'She's obviously still in pain, see how she lifts her front leg,' said Sergeant Rodwill, 'but at least she's up.' Everyone breathed a huge sigh of relief.

The last the group saw of either of them was when the rhinoceros calf followed its mother, limping, away into the relative safety of the bush.

'Well done everyone,' said Ranger Rodwill, shaking Gabriel and Diteko's hands. 'Libuku, I expect you to finish your schooling. I know you're not 16, but when you are old enough, maybe you'll consider joining our unit and help us to protect our environment.'

The young man's chest swelled a little at the compliment he was being paid.

Libuku returned to his village. He had been away for a lot longer than he should have been and his family were out of their minds with worry. He had wondered just what he would tell his parents, but in the end, he chose to tell the truth. The whole episode had been a very sobering experience for him and he felt he had matured as a result.

Although initially angry, Thapelo relented, gratified that, in telling the truth, the awful truth, his eldest son had become more of a man than a boy.

Later that evening, Libuku left the chatter from around the campfire and walked to where his grandfather's old rifle lay hidden in the branches. Taking hold of the end of the barrel, Libuku swung the gun hard against the tree trunk, shattering the shoulder stock and bending the pipe forming the barrel almost in half. Nobody would fire that gun again!

Gabriel and Diteko abandoned their trip to look over further potential campsites, they would barely have enough time to return to the Ranger station, fill out the many forms that the Rangers' actions would demand and get back to Maun before their next safari started.

They were silent as Gabriel drove the Land Rover back along the track heading towards Botswana. Each knew that the other was thinking about poaching and the effect it was having on the wildlife of their land, Africa.

Although he knew that poaching elephants for their ivory and rhinoceros for their horn earned vast quantities of money for the men involved, he simply couldn't understand the level of cruelty that could be inflicted.

Diteko looked at Gabriel and asked the question, 'Why?'

THE BUFFALO

The four of them lay perfectly still behind the grass-covered hide constructed in the branches of a large tree. They watched excitedly, barely daring to breathe as, twenty metres away, the adult male leopard nervously approached the base of the nearby tree and began to sniff the air.

'He can smell the bait,' murmured Stephen, the professional hunter, 'he knows it's there somewhere.' Turning to his client, he said quietly, 'Make sure you have a round in the chamber and your safety is off.'

With his hand over the mechanism to deaden the noise, Dimitri worked the bolt-action of his hunting rifle as carefully as he could, aware that the slightest disturbance might scare away his prize. He winced slightly at the characteristic metallic sound as a large calibre bullet was rammed into the breech. Dimitri looked anxiously through the slit in the grass screen and froze as he watched the leopard looking all around the surrounding bush. He'd obviously heard the rifle being loaded and not recognising the sound, was wary that danger was lurking.

Dimitri and his friend Pavel had travelled all the way from Moscow in Russia, specifically to hunt and shoot dead two particular predatory cats in this part of Zambia. That would be all Dimitri's licence allowed him. Pavel took no active part in the hunt, he didn't really care for the killing of animals for sport, but went along with his friend, for whom it was a passion. Dimitri had already shot a male lion the day before and now he was about to fulfil the second part of his allowance, and his lifelong ambition of shooting that most cautious of animals, the shy and cunning leopard.

After remaining perfectly still for nearly half a minute, the big cat circled the tree several times before eventually looking up into the lower branches. He might have suspected something wasn't quite right, but whatever it was he'd heard, it was instantly disregarded as he finally discovered the huge lump of fresh meat Stephen's tracker, Mugudi had lodged there. Dimitri lifted his rifle and held it into his shoulder.

'Not yet,' whispered Stephen, 'wait till he's up in the tree and on the bait, I'll tell you when to shoot.'

With his dagger-sharp claws digging into the bark, the leopard leapt onto the trunk of the tree and within a few, short, graceful bounds, had climbed to the first stout branch where the bait had been tied down. Cautiously, he approached the meat, sniffing all the time, testing for danger.

Mugudi had chosen his spot well, the branch was high enough to deter other predators from climbing but low enough for the foliage not to shield the leopard from the hunter's view.

As he arrived at the bait, the leopard presented a perfect target for Dimitri. He watched him through the powerful telescopic sight, the cross-hairs remaining constantly on his target's body. The shot could only be a matter of seconds away now and Dimitri struggled to control his breathing. He could feel his heart pounding and glanced down at the cuffs on his hunting jacket, they were shaking in time with the trembling in his fingers and hands.

He had shot animals many times in his native Russia but this was the first time he had hunted animals that could kill him with a single bite or slash of a paw. He revelled in the raw emotion that he was experiencing, and he swore a silent oath to himself that from that moment on, he would hunt only game animals that could give him the excitement he was feeling at that precise time.

Watching his prey, knowing it was completely unaware of his presence, Dimitri waited for Stephen's signal to shoot. He had never felt so alive, and in so feeling, completely missed the irony of the slaughter he was about to inflict.

Finally and fatefully, the leopard decided that there was nothing to fear and began to feast on the soft flesh of the bait-meat. At that exact moment, a whispered 'Now' and a light tap on Dimitri's shoulder, ended the life of one of the most elegant of big cats.

Two days later, and much earlier than they expected, Dimitri and Pavel found themselves on a local bus heading back towards Lusaka, and from there, they would journey on to Johannesburg for their flight back to Moscow.

Gabriel meanwhile, was on safari with 5 clients. They had travelled from Livingstone in Zambia, after visiting the magnificent Victoria Falls, crossing the river border at Kazangula and then driving down through the game parks of Chobe and Moremi in Botswana. They had now arrived in Maun, a frontier town in Botswana on the outskirts of the beautiful Okavango Delta.

The last stage of this particular safari would be for Gabriel and his clients to spend three days exploring the Delta. It was July and the previous months of heavy rains had turned the dry and arid areas into a vast expanse of green and lush vegetation, where animals and birds of all species could feed on the rich grassland and drink the cool, sweet water in the thousands of channels and pools spread out over the Delta.

Gabriel had been contacted by his company and he'd been asked to pick up two extra clients from a camp known as Crocodile Camp, situated just outside Maun.

'They're two Russian guys,' said Stefan, one of the owners of Drifting Ways Safaris, 'they've been in Zambia for about a week, but they got fed up and decided to go back to Moscow early. They heard about our trip into the Delta and as they had some days to spare, asked if they could join. They're waiting for you at Crocodile. Their names are Dimitri and Pavel.'

'Okay,' said Gabriel, 'but what were they doing in Zambia?'

'Dunno,' replied Stefan, testily, 'sightseeing I suppose. Just pick them up and take them into the Delta!'

Gabriel did wonder initially why they had got so fed up in Zambia, it was after all, a beautiful country, but eventually simply dismissed the thought. 'And why *not* come into the Delta,' he'd said to himself, 'better than waiting for days in Johannesburg.' Gabriel was not a fan of cities!

He arrived at Crocodile Camp to pick up the two men, who both spoke excellent English. They loaded their luggage into the Land Rover's trailer and then Gabriel introduced them to the other clients on the trip.

'Ok everyone, this is Pavel and Dimitri, they'll be joining us for our trip into the Delta. We're going to drive to a village called Ditchipi, where we'll meet some local people who'll take us in. We'll be travelling by mokorro, a sort of dug-out canoe made from a solid tree trunk, a mokwa tree, and pushed along by a man or woman standing at the back planting a pole on the riverbed. They'll take us along some of the hundreds of water-filled channels criss-crossing the area we're going to explore.'

Gabriel had used a mokorro several times before and he never ceased to wonder at the skill needed to balance and push the unstable craft through the water. Although he was completely at ease sitting in a mokorro, Gabriel knew that the clients, unused to such crude forms of transport, would be very nervous about the mokorros turning over, and them being pitched into the Delta water. Oh well, he thought to himself, that's part of the experience! He also knew it was extremely unlikely, such was the skill level of the local polers.

By the late afternoon of the first day in the Delta, Gabriel and his clients had reached the area where they would make camp for that night. There was nothing to suggest to anyone not used to the Delta, that the area was anything other than part of the bush, but to Gabriel and the polers, it was ideal. Water flowed from the main stream into a narrow, shallow side channel, where equipment and luggage could be unloaded on a small beach. From the water's edge, everything would be taken around 100 metres away to a nice flat, sandy area on the edge of a thick clump of trees, ideal for pitching tents and sitting around the campfire.

Watching Dimitri and Pavel unloading their luggage from the mokorro, Gabriel noticed that each man carried a large rucksack in camouflage colours of green and brown that matched the style of clothing they wore. He was initially curious about this as neither man appeared to be the outdoors type, but he decided that they could obviously use whatever rucksacks they liked and dress how they like. Maybe they simply enjoy the macho, Rambo type image, he thought. He also didn't take any notice of the fact that they pitched the spare tent they had been given, away from the others with the door flap facing the bush rather than into the camp, which would have been more normal. Gabriel would reflect on these thoughts later, with more than a little regret.

As soon as all the tents had been erected and the kettle was on the fire for some tea and coffee, Gabriel gathered all the clients together, sitting around the campfire and gave them some instructions. Amongst other things, he told them about keeping the area clean and litter free, about always keeping their tents zipped shut when they weren't in them, what to do if they had to get up during the night and then he explained the use of the toilet tent.

After that, he said, 'And finally, and perhaps most importantly, you have to understand we are all in a wild area, there are no fences. The animals here have priority, we are visitors in their gardens and we must respect that. There are dangerous animals such as lion, leopard and buffalo around here and as you can see, they're free to come and go as they please. Therefore,' he continued, 'it is imperative that you obey this instruction; during daylight hours *do not* go out of sight and hearing of this camp. You can go for a walk around this spot, but you must keep the camp in sight at all times and you must not go so far that you cannot shout for help and be heard, should you need it. After darkness falls, *do not* wander away from the camp for *any* reason. Do you all understand and accept that?' Everyone, including the two Russians nodded their heads, gravely.

Later, they all enjoyed a super dinner of pork chops barbecued over the open fire, pasta and grilled vegetables, followed by some beers and laughing around the fire. Gabriel took the opportunity to point out some star constellations including the Southern Cross in the night sky, after which, everyone trooped off to bed, thoroughly satisfied with their adventure so far.

Dimitri looked at the luminous dial on his watch. It was 2-30 in the morning, time to go. He opened his rucksack and assembled the Holland and Holland hunting rifle from the parts he had hidden away in his luggage. He had hunted many times in his native Russia and was experienced enough to have left the telescopic sight fixed onto the barrel of the rifle. That way, he wouldn't have to re-sight it before taking any shot. He took out six copper-jacketed cartridges, inspected them for any damage whatsoever that might spoil the flight of the slug and slipped these into his jacket pocket. Next, he picked up his Garmin E-Trex satellite navigation device and entered the position of the camp as a "way point". He would need this to find his way back later in the morning.

'Dimitri, are you sure about this, it doesn't seem right,' whispered Pavel. 'You heard what Gabriel said about leaving the camp, it's dangerous with so many big predators around!'

'You worry too much,' his friend snapped, 'I'll be back before you know it. Watch out for me.'

Satisfied he was ready to leave, he took an age to carefully unzip his tent, step outside into the darkness and then zip it shut again. The last thing he needed was to make any noise at that time in the morning.

As soon as he had zipped his tent shut, Dimitri walked quickly to a small group of trees about 10 metres away. He had to make sure no-one saw him leave the camp and used the cover of the trees to conceal himself. Waiting just a couple of seconds, listening for any sound of someone else's presence but not hearing anything, he made his way out onto the open savannah.

When he was well clear of the camp, he ejected the rifle's magazine, reached into his pocket and fully loaded it with three of the six cartridges. The other three, he slipped into the separate compartments of a fabric pouch he'd attached to the side of the rifle stock. Looking like a small ammunition belt, its purpose was all about speedy reloading if it became necessary. It was the typical shortcut of a hunter.

Dimitri was tingling with excitement at what he was about to do. He switched on the powerful torch he had with him to light his way, and swung it around slowly from side to side, checking to see if any danger lurked nearby. Seeing nothing, he switched it off and waited several minutes for his eyes to adjust to the darkness before setting off on his hunt. The only sound he heard was the occasional, distant "laugh" of a hyena. Other than that, the bush was eerily silent and he could feel the atmosphere around him and the inky blackness of the African night sharpening his senses to a pin-point.

He had left the camp with the sole intention of hunting and shooting a large game animal. Secretly, he hoped for a buffalo, but whatever he found, he would need to be at his most alert if he was to succeed.

The rest of the camp slept on as Dimitri strode out onto the savannah. His eyes had become used to the night and he could now make out shapes such as trees and large anthills in front of him.

He had been walking for almost 2 hours when suddenly, he heard a faint noise in the distance. He recognised it immediately as the unmistakeable sound of grass being ripped from the ground by a grazing animal. Crouching down to avoid any silhouette he might make against the dark sky, he carefully worked the bolt of the rifle to load a bullet into the firing chamber. Staying low to the ground, he walked slowly and deliberately towards the sound, holding the rifle ready to take whatever shot he could make, or perhaps, that he *needed* to make.

By this time, the very first signs of dawn were appearing on the horizon, and the light was growing stronger with every passing minute. Dimitri crept forward, being very careful where he placed his feet on the ground until eventually, he could make out the shape of a grazing buffalo, a few hundred metres straight ahead of him.

At that moment, Dimitri felt every hair on the back of his neck stand on end. He was a hunter who revelled in the thrill of the man versus beast scenario. This buffalo was just the animal he had been hoping to encounter; stalking it silently and efficiently until he was ready to take a shot would test his expertise, his nerve, courage and determination to the full.

He dropped down onto his haunches and sampled the breeze. It was coming over his right shoulder and from very slightly behind him. He knew that any slight shift in the wrong direction, the breeze would take his scent to the buffalo and ruin his chance of a shot. He had to move swiftly if he was to avoid the animal detecting his presence.

Keeping his profile close to the ground and beneath the lightening skyline, Dimitri made his way off to his left. He made barely a sound as he laboriously crept around the buffalo in a wide arc. Every so often, he stopped to check the wind, and then continued to creep round until he could feel it full into his face, carrying with it the unique bovine odour of his prey.

Crouching as low as he could in the grass, he was still around a hundred metres or so from the grazing buffalo, but now he knew he was downwind and his position was very unlikely to be given away by any sudden change in the direction of the early morning breeze.

The animal remained unaware of the danger approaching it. The strengthening light now enabled Dimitri to see that it was a lone, magnificent bull with thick, curving horns ending in dagger-sharp points. Admiring the bull's muscle-packed limbs and shoulders, he thought it the very essence of raw, physical power, an adversary worthy of his self proclaimed prowess as a hunter. He had never missed an opportunity to boast to his friends about his exploits, now he would prove it to everyone by stalking and shooting dead this most dangerous of animals.

He crept slowly and stealthily towards his prey, to a spot where taller grass on the savannah concealed his presence better than ever. He was now only a matter of forty or fifty metres away. Not taking his eyes off the buffalo for a second, he carefully slipped off the safety catch. Normally, the very slight metallic click of the little lever would be lost in the noises of the day, but in the still air of the early morning, it sounded much louder, too loud.

Suddenly, disturbed by the faint, unfamiliar sound, the massive head of the buffalo came up from where it was feeding and looked towards where Dimitri was crouching. Raising its snout into the air, it sniffed the morning breeze to try and detect any scent of danger. Frozen to the spot, Dimitri didn't move a muscle for what seemed like an age.

Finally, satisfied there was nothing to fear, the bull buffalo lowered its head again and carried on grazing the grass. Slowly and deliberately, Dimitri raised the powerful rifle and nestled it into his shoulder. He had to make sure it was in tight against his body because when he pulled the trigger, the kick-back the rifle made as the bullet was fired could dislocate his shoulder if it wasn't in the correct position.

Breathing gently with his right index finger resting lightly against the trigger, he waited. The buffalo had shifted its position slightly and was now facing head-on towards Dimitri, making any attempt to take a shot to the head far too difficult. He knew he had to aim just behind the bull's shoulder, shooting it through its rib-cage and into the heart. The rock-hard "boss" where the bull's horns met in the centre of its head, would deflect any bullet. He had to go for the heart.

Patiently, Dimitri waited for his prey to turn ever so slightly to the side for the best opportunity. The seconds ticked by, the light grew ever stronger, and Dimitri remained motionless, waiting!

Then, as the buffalo continued to graze on the dewy grass, it fatefully moved around, presenting its entire left side to Dimitri. This was the chance the hunter had been hoping for.

'Da, spaceeba moi tovarich', (Yes, thanks my friend) whispered Dimitri to himself in his native Russian. Exhaling slowly and calmly, he sighted the buffalo through the powerful telescopic lens, picking a spot just behind the top of its front leg, held his breath and began to squeeze the trigger.

Gabriel was suddenly awake. He knew it was just after dawn, the daylight he could see through one of the open flaps in his tent hadn't lost its early morning tinge of grey. He was convinced he had heard a single, sharp but faint sound, a bit like the snapping of a twig. It wasn't loud but as a light sleeper, the sound had woken him. His first thought was that it sounded like a rifle shot, but he dismissed this almost immediately. There was no hunting allowed where they were and the area was very well patrolled by anti-poaching units of the Botswana Defence Force. He strained his ears for more noise but hearing nothing, he convinced himself it was just an animal outside, or a dream maybe, although it did trouble him that he couldn't remember anything else about this 'dream'.

He'd told the clients the previous evening that this day would not be as tough as the last and that they could sleep in for a few hours before breakfast, which would be around 8am. He went back to sleep.

The bullet slammed into the side of the buffalo, knocking it off balance. It fell briefly to the ground but was soon back on its feet. It bellowed with alarm, pain and anger and immediately galloped off away from where Dimitri had fired, in the direction of a small clump of trees, around half a kilometre away.

At the instant of firing, the buffalo was still moving slightly, causing Dimitri to miss the spot he was aiming at by a matter of only a few centimetres, but the damage the bullet had done to the internal organs of the stricken buffalo meant that it would die eventually from its wound. It would however, be a slow, agonising death.

Dimitri was not concerned with its pain and suffering. Watching the buffalo gallop away, he decided instantly that he would carry on tracking it until either the buffalo fell dead from the injury or preferably, he could take another shot, finally killing it. He was not going to be denied the opportunity to take a photograph of his triumph. Along with the pictures Pavel had already taken of him with his lion and leopard kills, it would prove what a great hunter he always thought himself to be.

It was to be one of the last decisions he ever made!

Breaking into a slow trot, Dimitri ran towards the trees he had seen the wounded buffalo head for. He knew it was severely injured and couldn't live much longer, but he underestimated the strength and sheer cunning of a wounded buffalo, especially one as big as the one he had just shot.

He was under the mistaken belief that the "Big Five" many people talk about refers to the five favourite animals tourists want to see on an African safari; lion, leopard, elephant, rhinoceros and buffalo. In fact, the "Big Five" refers to the same animals but only because they are the most dangerous animals to hunt, especially when wounded. And the most dangerous of them all, is the buffalo! It will turn and look for a chance to attack the hunter without hesitation.

Dimitri crept along for the last ten metres or so, right up to the edge of the trees. Through the leaves and branches he could make out the unmistakable bulk of the buffalo standing very still in a clearing in the centre. Its head was hanging low, as if it was looking at the ground. He could hear the rough breathing of the wounded animal and he could see the steam being snorted out rapidly through its gaping nostrils. There was a faint spray of pink blood every time the animal breathed out. From this, Dimitri knew he had shot it through the lungs. The bull appeared pathetic to Dimitri; once mighty and powerful, now just a weak and forlorn animal waiting to die.

Before setting off in pursuit, he had worked the bolt of the rifle once more to eject the empty cartridge and load another, leaving just one cartridge in the magazine.

'You are mine,' he whispered to himself.

He strode arrogantly through the thorn bushes and stood just 2 metres in front of his prize. He stared triumphantly at the buffalo for a few seconds, as if in salute to a worthy but inferior adversary, then he raised the rifle once more to his shoulder to finally complete his hunt. He concentrated on aiming at a point on the buffalo's head, just below the massive "boss" of the horns, but in doing so, failed to notice the fury and hatred that blazed in the dying animal's eyes. Unfortunately for Dimitri, it was to be the buffalo that would triumph!

His finger was about to squeeze the trigger when, without warning, the buffalo suddenly lunged forward and was upon Dimitri in a split second, far too quickly for him to get out of the way. It was as if it knew what this hunter was about to do.

As the massive, black head crashed into his feeble body, the buffalo hooked one of its curved horns into Dimitri's stomach, burying it deep inside and yanking him high into the air. Yelling in pain and surprise, the hunter threw up his arms and the rifle went spinning out of his grip, landing in the dirt just a few metres away.

With his stomach ripped open and his guts spilling out, Dimitri crashed to the ground just in front of the enraged buffalo, which then continued to pound his body with its heavy hooves. It rammed its horns again and again into Dimitri's now limp and torn body, pushing it deeper and deeper under the thorn bushes.

Finally, the buffalo collapsed on the ground, exhausted from its efforts to kill its tormentor and from the internal injuries it had suffered from the bullet wound. It would die, but not immediately. Dimitri however, had not survived the animal's wrath, he was already dead.

It was fully light, around 6-30am when Gabriel emerged from his tent and started to prepare breakfast. One by one, the clients joined him with cups of steaming tea or coffee, savouring the sight and smell of bacon and eggs cooking on the fire. By 8am, the camp was bustling with people packing up, drinking coffee and chatting to each other, or taking photographs of Gabriel cooking, the camp itself and the surrounding bush.

At one stage, Gabriel let his eyes wander around the camp. He counted only 6 of the 7 clients and then realised that he'd only seen one of the two Russian men all morning, Pavel. He searched amongst the clients and then saw him standing at the edge of the camp, staring out over the savannah. He appeared to be looking for something, or someone!

Gabriel's intuition immediately told him that something was wrong. He walked over to the Russian and said, 'Pavel, where is Dimitri?' He said it in such a stern fashion that Pavel was in no doubt that Gabriel suspected something.

Pavel knew he would not get away with a lie, 'He went out this morning and hasn't come back,' he muttered, looking down at his feet. In that instant, Gabriel felt a crawling sensation in the pit of his stomach. He remembered his first thoughts about the two camouflage rucksacks he'd seen with both men and then what he thought had been the sound of a rifle in his 'dream'.

'What time did he leave?' demanded Gabriel.

'I think around 2-30 this morning,' replied Pavel, continuing to stare out into the bush. Without being asked, he went on, 'We've been hunting in the Lower Zambezi area, in Zambia. Dimitri had paid thousands of dollars to shoot a leopard and a lion. We were supposed to be there for 10 days but he killed his lion on the first day, and the leopard on the second, so he'd shot his trophies with days to spare. Dimitri decided to try and get Stephen, the professional hunter to let him shoot something else as well. Anything would have done, as long as it was big, but he didn't have enough money to buy another licence. The hunter wouldn't let him without the licence, obviously, but as he'd shot the leopard and the lion quickly, Dimitri kept on and on about the days we would be wasting.'

Other clients, overhearing what Pavel was saying had now begun to gather behind Gabriel.

'There was lots of large game around and he couldn't understand why Stephen kept saying no. Then, when he tried to bribe him with what extra cash he had, Stephen reported us to the Wildlife Rangers and they threw us out of the camp. It took us days to get back to Lusaka by bus.'

'How did you end up here then?'

'On our way to Lusaka, Dimitri had this idea to come down to Maun and try and join onto a safari into thick bush for a few days, anywhere would have been ok, it just happened to be you going into the Delta. If we could sneak on to a proper safari, he figured no-one would know what we were doing.'

Gabriel began to fear the worst.

'Dimitri thought that if we joined a safari, we, or rather he could slip away in the early morning to try and shoot something. If he went out early enough, nobody would know and he could sneak back to camp before breakfast. That's why we pitched our tent with the flap facing the bush. I tried to stop him from going, but he insisted and left really early this morning, well before dawn. I heard a rifle shot earlier but he hasn't come back. Something has happened to him, I know it.'

By now, everyone was listening to Pavel's story. Gabriel was appalled, not only because he and the company had been deceived but also because he strongly disagreed with shooting animals, especially the animals of *his* beloved Africa, for sport. He heard at least one of the other clients mutter, 'Serves him right if he is injured, leave him out there!'

Gabriel could not of course do that, he had to do something to try and find Dimitri. He'd been gone nearly six hours at that stage and Gabriel figured that he would have returned long ago, if he could.

He immediately gathered the five local village people, the polers, around him. 'Ok,' he started, 'if you didn't hear what Pavel told us, we have a client missing. Apparently, he's gone out of the camp on his own before daylight this morning to try and hunt and shoot an animal of some description, we don't know what.'
The polers all frowned at what Gabriel told them, they took the preservation of the wildlife of the Okavango Delta, which they regarded as theirs, very seriously.
'And he hasn't come back. We need to find him.'
The leader of the polers, an older man named Jackson said, 'Ah, I heard a noise this morning that sounded like a rifle shot.'
'Yeah, I heard it too,' replied Gabriel, 'you're all expert trackers, so I need all of you to look for his trail out of the camp and then we have to go after him.' He turned to the head-poler, 'Jackson, please choose your most experienced tracker and after we find the trail, get the others to remain in the camp to look after the clients while we're gone. That will leave three of us to go after Dimitri.' Jackson chose a young man named Rodric to track Dimitri once they had found his footprints.

As soon as they knew what they had to do, Jackson and the other polers/trackers immediately ran out of the camp to find Dimitri's trail. They worked in a very specific manner, criss-crossing all the places where Dimitri might have walked into the bush. Luckily, the area was very sandy with not too much vegetation, but Jackson and the others still had to look very hard for footprints, or "spoor" as they called it, that were not just people walking around camp, or just outside.
Suddenly, Rodric shouted, 'Gabriel, I have it, here, look.' Gabriel and Jackson both ran to where Rodric was crouching over a footprint in the sandy soil, beyond the trees where Dimitri had stood after leaving his tent, and pointing away to the bush. 'See, there's another, the same

shoe sole and another there, look. They go out in that direction,' said the young tracker, proudly pointing the way.

'That's it, well done Rodric,' said Gabriel clapping him on the shoulder, 'let's go!'

They had followed the trail carefully for nearly two hours, stopping regularly to keep their bearings on where the camp lay, when Rodric suddenly stopped and examined the spoor more carefully than usual.

'Look here Gabriel,' he said excitedly and pointed to what Gabriel thought were the same footprints in the sandy soil. 'He stopped here for something, see how the spoor is scuffed around the edges. He was shifting his position slightly and either watching something or listening to some sort of sound, probably ahead of him.'

Gabriel missed all these details. He thought that Jackson had chosen well.

All three set off once more in pursuit of Dimitri. They had gone only a few hundred metres further on when suddenly Rodric called a second halt and peered down at Dimitri's trail. This time, Gabriel could clearly see what both Rodric and Jackson were looking at.

'The tracks go off over there,' said Gabriel, pointing away to his left. He had an idea of why Dimitri had moved, but he kept his thoughts to himself, preferring to let the two trackers figure it out.

Using all his experience and skill, Rodric said, 'I think he had already spotted something ahead of him, maybe a buffalo or a large antelope such as a kudu. From where his prints are pointing, I think he felt the wind over his right shoulder and moved off over to his left to get down-wind of whatever he was looking at.'

Both Gabriel and Jackson agreed with Rodric, he wasn't wrong about these things very often. They set off again with Rodric in the lead, following Dimitri's wide arc he had taken around the buffalo. Gabriel sensed they were closing in.

Rodric eventually found where Dimitri had stopped circling the buffalo. Following Dimitri's spoor, a short distance further on, Gabriel's thoughts were confirmed. A shiny object, lying in the sand caught Jackson's eye. He picked it up and immediately called out, 'Gabriel, come and look.'

'That's a shell casing from a .375 calibre cartridge, good for hunting large game. We're close!'

Now that they had found the spot where Dimitri had fired, Jackson said, 'Gabriel, we know he fired the rifle here. There are no scavengers around, so we know he didn't kill it. What we need to know now is what he shot at, did he hit it and if so, how badly the animal might be wounded.'

Rodric studied the ground carefully and then announced, pointing to spot ahead of where they were, 'His footprints tell me he fired in that direction.' Gabriel also looked at Dimitri's footprints in the sand, but couldn't for the life of him tell which way Dimitri had fired. He was impressed with Rodric's knowledge and understanding of spoor.

'How do you know that?' he asked.

'Look at the front footprint, it's facing in that direction,' replied Rodric, pointing. 'Now look at the slight indentation in the ground just behind it, that's where his right knee was placed on the ground, and here,' he continued, showing Gabriel a small scuff in the sand behind the other two marks, 'this is where the toe of his right shoe dug into the sand. He's kneeling on his right knee with the left foot planted on the ground. He's got the rifle into his right shoulder, and everything is pointing over there.'

Gabriel prayed silently to himself that whatever it was, it had now died and that Dimitri would be found very soon making his way back to camp. In his heart though, he knew this was unlikely, the absence of vultures circling in the skies for miles around told a different story. If, as seemed likely, the animal had only been wounded, they could be facing a dangerous situation and needed all the information they could find.

'Let us look for the killing spot,' said Jackson, and they followed Dimitri's footprints.

'See how he's now running,' said Rodric pointing to the scuffed up tracks.

Fifty or so metres ahead, Jackson spotted some other spoor and called the others over. They all looked down at another track, or rather a set of tracks in the sandy soil. Rodric pointed first to one and said, 'See here look, this is the track of a large, adult male buffalo, and look here,' he continued, 'you can see where it was grazing earlier this morning.'

'How do you know it's a buffalo?' asked Gabriel, 'I know tracks and these could easily be an adult eland.'

'Ah yes, you're right,' replied Rodric, patiently pointing to the tracks, 'it could but look here, do you see how the rear print is slightly smaller than the front, and the shape tells me this has to be a buffalo, a big one too.' Gabriel stared down at the hoof prints in the sand, seeing for the first time the slight difference in size between the front and rear.

'I can see that now, good man Rodric. The deep indents in the sand indicate the buffalo stood still while it ate, yes?'

'Exactly,' replied Rodric, kindly.

Rodric was now right into his tracking expertise. He knew he would find some other clue within a few metres of where he was and began to walk around in ever increasing circles. At last, he found what he was looking for.

'Gabriel, Jackson, over here. Look, here's where the bull went down, the prints are very muddled and you can see the grass has been flattened. This is where it was shot but obviously not killed.' Rodric carried on looking, 'And here,' he shouted excitedly, 'it's up again and running off, in that direction. Dimitri is following it, see his footprints.'

Rodric pointed away from where they were. The buffalo had obviously galloped away from where it had been hit and its spoor was heading directly towards a large thicket, or group of trees and bushes, exactly where a wounded buffalo would go to hide from someone trying to kill it!

'It's probably in that thicket in the distance, I'm sure that's where we'll find it.'

Gabriel knew that older, mature male buffalos, bulls, often wandered off on their own, away from the herd and led a solitary existence. He also knew they are one of the most dangerous animals in Africa, especially when provoked or injured. And Dimitri had wounded, and was now tracking and trying to kill, this most dangerous of animals.

Even as they spoke, Gabriel noted one or two large birds had begun circling over the thicket.

They set off once more at a quick trot in the direction of the trees, but only a few metres further along the track, Jackson found several large spots of fresh blood in the sand.

'Lung shot,' claimed Gabriel immediately.

'How do you know that?' asked Jackson.

'The colour of the spots, they're more pink than red, it's blood mixed with fluid. And look how the spots are spread over a wide area. When the buffalo has breathed out, the blood has been sprayed around in a mist! We've got some bone fragments here too, probably from a rib. This animal is seriously wounded, we need to be very careful from here on,' warned Gabriel. He began to fear the worst for Dimitri.

Gabriel and the trackers were now six or seven kilometres away from the camp. Rodric had followed the spoor of the wounded buffalo easily. Even without tracks, the tiny spatters of blood on the grass stalks would tell where it had gone. The tracks led right into the thicket. They carried no weapons for their protection, so as they approached, Gabriel called a halt.

'I'm going to try and get as close as I can to see what's in there, you two stay here.'

'No,' replied Rodric, 'you approach from the front and we'll spread out at the back of the thicket. If anything goes wrong, we may be able to distract the bull. If he charges us, there are plenty of trees over there to climb. You should not do this alone.'

Gabriel immediately realised that Rodric was right, he couldn't do this on his own. He knew that both men had past experience as hunters, tracking for professional hunts and trapping game animals for meat for their villages. He bowed to their greater experience.

Gabriel watched as the other two walked silently and slowly in a wide circle around the side of the thicket towards the back. When he heard a low whistle, he knew they were in place and he began to approach from the front. Treading as softly as he could, he crept along the ground very slowly. If the buffalo was anywhere near, as seemed likely, he didn't want to risk scaring the animal any more than it already was. Gabriel struggled to control his breathing, he thought it was so loud, whatever was in there must surely hear him.

He managed to creep up to the very edge of the trees to a spot from where he could see right into the middle. The trees and bushes surrounded an open space, and towards the front of this space, perhaps only a matter of ten metres away, he saw the crumpled and bloodied body of Dimitri lying under the tangle of thorny branches with the massive bulk of the bull buffalo lying very close by.

Gabriel realised that lying under the thorns had saved Dimitri from the vultures and marabou storks that had been gathering and circling overhead. It wouldn't be too much longer however, before the larger and more determined scavengers, the hyenas and jackals, began to arrive.

Even from where Gabriel was looking, it was obvious to him that Dimitri had tracked the wounded buffalo into the thicket, where the animal had been waiting. He imagined that Dimitri had been arrogant enough to think that the bull was too injured to defend itself, and gave no thought to the fact that this is when an animal such as a wounded buffalo is at its most dangerous and will attack without fear.

It appeared to Gabriel that Dimitri, in trying to get as near as possible, had gone too close and the animal had charged him. Gabriel could see that with nowhere to run to, Dimitri would have been unable to escape the buffalo charging directly at him. From the position of the body, he could see that Dimitri had been gored in the stomach and then crushed under its massive hooves. His body was so broken and covered in blood, he could barely recognise him. In the sandy undergrowth, a few metres from the body lay a large, bolt-action rifle with a telescopic sight; a typical hunter's rifle.

Gabriel continued to stare into the centre of the thicket, looking for signs of life from the buffalo, hoping beyond hope he would see none. Suddenly however, a tiny movement caught his eye. There it was again! The right ear of the buffalo flicked away a fly and then Gabriel looked closer. He could see the huge chest rising and falling very slowly. It was still alive, and then he heard the slight rasping sound of the animal's breathing. Gabriel kept absolutely still, not moving a muscle, trying hard not to provoke the desperately wounded buffalo any more.

He and the trackers were now in a very dangerous situation. They had no idea of the extent of the buffalo's injuries although Gabriel could see blood trickling down the animal's belly from the lung-shot. It was breathing so slightly that no spray was coming from its wound. Gabriel knew it was weak, but he also knew that at any time, the wounded animal could recover sufficient strength to get up onto its feet and charge him, as it had done to Dimitri. From the moment he and the others had left the camp in search of Dimitri, Gabriel had known that this moment may arrive. He knew what he had to do.

The rifle was the key. He had to recover it, make sure it was loaded, avoid the enraged animal if it charged at him and then, if he managed to do all that, he had to get himself into a position to shoot the buffalo dead, not only to end its suffering, but also to eliminate the risk to himself and his trackers. Dimitri had obviously not realised the danger he was in, Gabriel would not repeat that mistake. But how was he going to recover the rifle without possibly scaring the buffalo into attacking?

Although thickly wooded, there were gaps between the trees and he could see that Jackson and Rodric had taken up positions at the rear of the thicket. Slowly, Gabriel withdrew from the position he was in and made his way quietly round to where Rodric and Jackson lay hidden.

'Dimitri is dead,' Gabriel announced quietly, 'we can do nothing for him. The buffalo is still alive, but in a bad way. The lung shot it's suffered means it will die sooner or later but I don't want to take the risk that it will be later, that's too long; it may stay alive for hours yet, and in a lot of pain. I'm going to try and get hold of the rifle and.....'

'What about ammunition,' interrupted Jackson.

'I'll just have to hope that Dimitri loaded it fully and didn't use them all, or at least had spare ammo with him. I'll get hold of the rifle and get myself into a position where I can take a kill-shot. Hopefully, the bull will stay down, but if it doesn't, you two will have to try and distract it. Make sure you're near a tree you can climb quickly if it comes in your direction. That might give me time to take the shot. Not sure how this'll work, but keep alert.'

Softly and quietly, Gabriel inched back along the ground on his hands and knees through the thick grass near the base of the trees. He made a mental note of a large termite stack near to the thicket he could climb if he needed to avoid the charging bull. The sharp thorns of a small bush scratched the bare flesh of his arms as he crept along. He neither flinched with pain nor, as he inched nearer and nearer, took his eyes off the wounded animal.

At one stage, he froze! The buffalo heard something and weakly turned its head to look in his direction. Although the bull didn't move from its position, Gabriel stayed perfectly still for several minutes before he thought it was safe to continue.

Eventually, after pushing himself through the thorny bushes near the ground, he got himself to a position where he was a matter of only a metre from where the rifle lay. He stretched out his hand and fingers to try and reach it. It was only centimetres away, but it was just too far. Gabriel pushed himself forward through the thorns one last time and reached out for the weapon. He prayed that Dimitri had loaded it with a full magazine.

He managed to take hold of the rifle stock with just his fingertips and began to pull it towards him, very carefully. Suddenly, the buffalo once more turned its head towards Gabriel. This time however, it looked as though it had regained a little strength and worryingly, began to snort loudly, spraying blood and spittle into the morning air. The bull bellowed from deep within its chest and then lurched onto its feet, determined to make one last Herculean effort to drive away its tormentors.

Gabriel's life was now in mortal danger, the wounded buffalo would attack anything and everything that moved, and the nearest target, the nearest danger to it, was Gabriel. He knew he had only seconds before the buffalo would be on him. He began tearing frantically at the branches and twigs of the bush, trying to get himself out, but the thorns held him where he lay and wouldn't allow him a quick exit.

Unless he could get out, he knew that he would die as Dimitri had, trampled and gored to death.

Jackson and Rodric meanwhile, had crept around the other side of the thicket. Seeing the bull get to its feet, both men began to shout as loudly as they could and throw stones into the bushes, hoping to distract the buffalo long enough for Gabriel to grab the rifle properly. (Gabriel would remember later that he heard Jackson and Rodric shouting. At that moment though, nothing registered with him, his entire being was concentrated on surviving the next few seconds!)
The massive head of the bull swivelled around to where they were standing, shouting and waving their arms wildly. In its confused mind, the buffalo saw Jackson and Rodric as the greater threat and instantly charged out of the thicket towards them.
Both men were astounded at the speed of the injured bull, covering the twenty metres or so between it and the men in a matter of two or three heartbeats and they only just managed to scramble up into the low branches of a nearby tree before it reached them, stamping its front hooves in anger and frustration.
Gabriel seized his chance! Grabbing the rifle by the barrel, he pulled it towards him and then painfully dragged himself away from the thorns.
He stepped quickly to Dimitri's body, reached through and patted the side pockets of the dead man's jacket.
'Oh, no, no', he said to himself, slightly panicked at not finding spare cartridges. His mind was racing but he never once hesitated, he knew exactly what he was doing and that he had to end the suffering of the buffalo, he would just have to make each shot count.
Picking up the rifle, Gabriel felt some fabric attached to the right-hand side of the rifle stock and breathing a sigh of relief, realised that Dimitri had fashioned a makeshift pouch to hold the three spare cartridges.
Time was desperately short for Gabriel at this point and he had no time to remove the magazine and check the number of cartridges. He slid back the bolt of the rifle and a live round ejected itself. He caught it in mid-air and then looked down at the open breech. He saw that another round of ammunition was ready to be pushed into the barrel

and he slid the bolt forwards, closing the breech and automatically loading the rifle. He had at least one bullet ready to fire and if necessary, he could remove more from the pouch and load the rifle far quicker than trying to load the magazine, especially if the buffalo was charging at him. He slipped the spare cartridge into his pocket.

Having rammed the last bullet in the magazine into the barrel, he checked the safety catch was set to "off". He was now ready to face the enraged buffalo. His actions had taken seconds, the same amount of time as the bull had taken to reach Jackson and Rodric, but Gabriel had also taken stock of his surroundings. His instincts told him he would have a better chance of a clean shot if he met the buffalo on open ground and immediately ran to the edge of the bushes, towards where Jackson and Rodric had taken refuge.

The buffalo however had already been distracted by the sound of the rifle being loaded and instantly began to charge back towards Gabriel, giving him no chance to get out of the thicket.

The speed at which the buffalo had begun its terrifying charge back towards Gabriel, took him completely by surprise. Without thinking, he instinctively and swiftly swung the rifle up into his right shoulder and fired at the buffalo's chest area, trying to bring it down.

It was a panicky action, a snap-shot and he couldn't hold the gun steady enough to take an accurate aim. Rather than squeezing the trigger gently, he snatched at it roughly and in so doing pulled the end of the barrel downwards and to the right. Over the top of the barrel, Gabriel saw the bullet rip into the flesh at the top of the bull's left leg.

The already severely wounded animal stumbled for just a second before continuing its charge towards Gabriel, but something was different. It was slower and the left leg seemed to be an odd shape. Gabriel realised that the bullet had actually broken the leg bone, or he had at least shot away a major part of it, almost crippling the buffalo. It must have been in severe pain, unbearable pain, but still it charged on towards its tormentor.

It was now so close, Gabriel could feel the thump of the animal's hooves pounding the earth as it careered towards him, only metres away. He had a split second to react and crouching down, he managed to twist his body out of the path of the buffalo and shelter behind a small tree on the very edge of the thicket. The thorns tore at the flesh on his legs, and he felt the smooth, short-haired hide of the buffalo brush the skin of his arm briefly, as it crashed through the undergrowth and out to the other side.

Ordinarily, the buffalo would turn sharply and continue to attack, giving Gabriel no chance to escape. But this animal was mortally wounded, confused and in great pain from its shattered left leg. With every step it took, its strength was draining away and it wasn't acting normally.

Gabriel realised this would be his one chance to get the buffalo out onto open ground. If he could get to the tree where Jackson and Rodric were sheltering, he would be able to use the trunk not only as a shield but also as a support for his rifle, allowing him take a clear, composed aim. Cursing himself for his stupidity in firing in panic, he slid the rifle bolt back, quickly removed a cartridge from the pouch on the rifle stock and dropped it into the empty breech.

Gabriel jumped up from his position on the ground, ignoring the spikey thorns and ran towards the tree. As he raced along, he could hear the buffalo charging back towards him. He felt the earth shuddering as the heavy hooves came nearer and nearer and he knew instantly he would not reach the shelter of the tree in time.

'Look out, look out, he's coming at you again,' 'Dive away, get out of the way', Jackson and Rodric shouted wildly at Gabriel as the buffalo lowered its head and horns into the killing position. Even running as fast as he could, Gabriel managed to steal a glance over his shoulder and saw the buffalo only a metre and a half away. Its massive bulk seemed to fill his entire vision.

He made a split-second decision and dived away to his left. He kept a tight grip on the rifle with his right hand as his left shoulder rammed into the hard but sandy ground. As it thundered past, the buffalo took a huge swipe with its head at its tormentor, hoping to impale him on its sharp horns.

In one fluid motion, Gabriel did a forward-roll off his shoulder and came up onto his right knee, planting his left foot squarely and firmly on the ground. The effort of charging at its enemies was clearly weakening the enormously strong animal.

Its terrifying charge eventually slowed and it only stopped around ten metres away from Gabriel. He could see the effort was sapping its strength. Everything seemed to be happening now in slow motion as he watched the bull laboriously begin to turn towards him. It was a pitiful sight, the once magnificent buffalo hung its head low, breathing heavily and furiously snorting blood and spittle from its nostrils. The forgotten pain of the charge at Gabriel now returned as it limped pathetically around, barely able to plant its left leg on the ground.

Gabriel knew this would be his chance of taking an accurate shot. It would be his only chance, and he so desperately wanted to end its suffering.

He knew from experience that it was useless to try and kill a charging buffalo with a shot to the brain through the front of the head. Apart from it being a moving target, it was too small a spot to aim at. There were other areas he could aim for, but in these circumstances, this was too risky. He knew where he had to shoot.

Before the buffalo had slowed enough to turn itself around, Gabriel had raised the rifle to his right shoulder. He held it there as firmly as his shaking hands would allow, waiting for the buffalo to turn. And then, as the animal was side on to Gabriel, he aimed for the area just behind the front shoulder, between the top of its leg and the tummy. Here, he knew the bullet would pass through flesh, unimpeded by large bones, enter the animal's heart and bring it down. The telescopic sight was useless at this close range, Gabriel simply pointed the weapon and held his breath.

He squeezed the trigger and the recoil of the rifle forced his entire body backwards, the explosion of sound filling his ears. It should have hurt, but Gabriel felt nothing, adrenaline was racing through his body and he was watching the buffalo too intently to feel pain.

The copper-jacketed bullet slammed into the barrel-like chest of the buffalo for a second time and Gabriel saw a tiny spurt of blood erupt as it entered its body, exactly where he had aimed. A split second later, the right front leg, unable to support the animal's bulk on its own, gave way and the bull crashed head first to the ground in a cloud of dust, its rump now sticking up into the air. It stayed in that ungainly position for about two seconds, its hind quarters being supported by its two back legs before they too gave way and it rolled over and lay on its side, blood, steam and spittle spraying out from its nostrils. All four legs were jerking, as its life ebbed away.

Still wary of the danger the severely wounded and dying buffalo presented, Gabriel ran around and approached it carefully from behind. He could hear its rasping breathing and could see a fine mist of blood spitting out of its chest from the first lung-shot. Although he knew it would now surely die very soon from his heart-shot, Gabriel was not going to allow it to suffer any more.

He reloaded the rifle with the spare cartridge from his pocket and took careful aim at a point just behind the buffalo's ear. At point-blank range, he fired for the last time and the bullet penetrated the skull and brain of the doomed animal. It died in that instant.

Gabriel stood over the now lifeless body of the buffalo. As a man of Africa, he mourned its death but he had been pitched into a battle not of his making and his survival had depended on him overcoming one of the most powerful animals on the savannah. There was however, nothing more he could do for the dead buffalo, he would leave it for the scavengers of the plains, the vultures, the hyenas, the jackals and the many others; they would feast well for many days!

The exhausting effort of tracking Dimitri, surviving two murderous charges and shooting dead the buffalo, suddenly caught up with Gabriel and his legs buckled beneath him. Jackson and Rodric had joined him and held him gently as they lay him down on the savannah to rest for a while. The adrenaline coursing through his body caused him to shake uncontrollably for several minutes before he felt sufficiently calm to sit up.

'We need to move, look, they're here already!' Gabriel pointed to a group of vultures that had landed nearby. 'Let's get Dimitri out of the bushes and onto the other side, we should get as far away from here as soon as we can.'

'I agree,' said Jackson, 'there'll be a feeding frenzy here in no time, we don't want to be anywhere near that.'

The two trackers and Gabriel pulled Dimitri gently from the thicket and Jackson lifted his body onto his shoulders. It was a rather undignified way to treat a dead person, but there was no choice. They had no means of covering the body or of cutting poles from the bush to form a crude stretcher. It would be far too dangerous to leave anyone there with the body whilst someone went for help, hyena and other predators would gather within minutes.

As they made their way across the savannah towards camp, the two trackers Rodric and Jackson constantly asked Gabriel to relive various parts of the experience, especially when the buffalo was charging him. At several points, they chanted 'Rra bula nare'. Gabriel realised there and then that this would now be how he would be known to villagers all around Maun. He was being given a title, the ultimate expression of praise by local Tswana people.

"Rra bula nare" means 'The one who kills the buffalo'. He knew that referring to him as "Rra", Rodric and Jackson were giving him the highest possible term of respect.

'This is far enough,' remarked Gabriel, looking back at the distant cloud of dust being kicked into the air by dozens of predators around the body of the buffalo, all squabbling for the best positions to feed at. It had been an hour of back-breaking effort to walk only around one kilometre away from the thicket. 'You two wait here with the body, I'll go ahead and fetch the Land Rover.'

'You go for the truck and Jackson and I will walk on with the body. You come and meet us,' replied Rodric

'Fair enough,' said Gabriel, immediately breaking into an easy, loping stride run towards the camp.

Another hour later, Gabriel, Jackson and Rodric had wrapped Dimitri's body into a tarpaulin and laid him gently across one of the bench seats of the Land Rover. Gabriel did not want the other clients to see his broken and bloodied torso.

Later, back at the camp, when everything possible had been done for Dimitri, Gabriel told the clients what had happened and how he had

had to shoot the buffalo. One of the other clients, an Australian man asked him, 'Did you know where to shoot it or did you just get lucky?' Gabriel noticed the sneering grin on the man's face, as if he expected him to agree he had been lucky.

'I knew what I was doing,' he explained. 'I was taught how to shoot and kill quickly when I went with my father on government-sanctioned animal culls in Moremi Game Park. He was the Senior Warden and occasionally, we had to control the animal numbers to preserve the bush for everything and everyone else. It was usually elephant and buffalo we had to shoot. I never liked it but I know it will always have to be done as long as we live alongside the wildlife.'

Ignoring what Gabriel said, the Australian carried on, 'I've heard that a buffalo is probably the most dangerous animal around here when it's wounded. Why's that?' he asked, 'After all, it's just like a big cow really, and they're pretty stupid.'

Gabriel stared silently at the client for several seconds, not because he had nothing to say, but because he was biting his tongue to keep control of his temper, which he could feel rising very quickly. Eventually, he lowered his head and looked at the ground.

Earlier that day, he had faced a life or death situation, *his* life or death. Although the adrenaline had ceased to rage through his body, he still felt his senses were at extraordinarily high levels. He could still feel his heart racing in his chest, his eyes darting around everywhere, unable to be still and his mind, pinprick sharp. At any other time, a question such as this would have prompted a casual but firm reply from Gabriel.

After a long pause, when he felt able to be calm, he raised his head and looked directly and coldly at the client, who was beginning to regret his question, and his attitude.

'The buffalo, that "stupid cow", as you call it' Gabriel said, calmly, '*is the* most dangerous animal on the savannah when wounded because of its cunning. Other animals in the Big Five, such as the leopard will not hesitate to attack a hunter, but the buffalo is different. If it's only wounded, it will obviously charge away from where it's been shot, but eventually, providing it's still on its feet, it will actively look for an opportunity to attack the hunter. Even then, the buffalo doesn't just attack. It can recognise an ambush situation and will wait, sometimes in deep bush, absolutely stock still, for the perfect moment to launch the attack. The buffalo out there didn't lure Dimitri into a trap, but from the position we found him in, it obviously recognised the chance it would have to attack him.

'The buffalo has strength and courage beyond our imagination. It took four bullets from one of the most powerful rifles in the world to finally bring it down. The first ripped through its internal organs and lungs, but it still continued to charge. The next bullet broke its front leg, and still it carried on, ignoring the pain. The third entered its heart and still, it lived on. It was only finally put out of its misery by a shot directly into the brain!!

'It has intelligence beyond many other animals and sometimes beyond that of the humans, arrogant enough to think they can kill it without too much effort. Once Dimitri had entered that thicket to go face to face with the buffalo, he was as ***good as dead.'***

By now, Gabriel's face was flushed bright red with anger and his voice had risen to a shout. He stepped towards the client, who backed away uneasily, recognising the passion that had gripped Gabriel.

'***Not bad for a "stupid old cow", is it!?'*** he shouted, spitting the words directly into the man's face.

Gabriel felt Jackson's hand close round his arm and pull him gently back away from the client. 'Steady, steady, he's not worth it' whispered Jackson.

Although still in a temper, Gabriel forced himself to relax and he felt his self-control return. 'I'm sorry,' he said to the ashen faced Australian, turning and walking away.

Everyone understood that the priority now for Gabriel, was to return the body of Dimitri back to Maun where arrangements would be made for it to be flown home to Moscow, Russia. It would mean their trip would have to be cut short.

The camp had already been packed up by the remaining polers, and Dimitri's body was laid gently on the floor of one of the mokorros. Pavel chose to be with his friend for his last journey through the Okavango Delta.

No-one spoke on the long journey back to Ditchipi village. Where there would normally be laughter and chatter between everyone, there was only silence and gloom. Where the mood would normally be upbeat and happy, there was only sadness. At one point, Gabriel glanced across to Pavel. He could see his shoulders shaking slightly as he wept continuously for his friend.

For his part, Gabriel couldn't help a feeling of guilt. It was he who had missed all the clues about the intentions of the two Russians, the camouflage clothing and rucksacks, the way they pitched their tent and worst of all, he bitterly regretted not having quizzed them about cutting short their trip to Zambia. Each time he thought about it, he couldn't help thinking of the words, if only I'd…..

As it was, both Dimitri and the buffalo suffered the awful, and in this case, the tragically unnecessary realities of life and death on the wild African savannah.

Mishaps, Mistakes and Mayhem

The following short stories are just a small example of what can happen on safari when things don't go entirely to plan or quite simply, when the guide gets it wrong.

THE WILD DOGS

Sam was on his way from Livingstone in Zambia, back to his base in Maun, Botswana. He and six clients had been on safari to the Liuwa Plains in the north-west of Zambia. The trip officially finished in Livingstone but, as Sam had to return to Maun, clients could pay a little extra and go with him for four days of game viewing through the Moremi Game Park. On this occasion, four clients, two men and two ladies had chosen to travel with Sam.

It was a relaxed atmosphere, no early morning starts, long lunch stops and early camping in the evening. Late afternoon on the second day, they arrived at a wild-camp known as Xwai River. In order to get to the camp, Sam had to drive over a very rickety looking bridge made from tree trunks sunk vertically into the sandy riverbed and then poles laid horizontally across the top.

He stopped just short of the bridge and turned to the clients 'This bridge has been like this since I can remember, it always looks as though it's going to collapse, but it never does, although I'm sure it will one day, I just hope I'm not on it! Now, I need you all to get off and walk across, just in case.'

One or two of the clients looked down at the dark water of the river and nervously cast their eyes around, trying to spot crocodiles, and then watched from the other side as Sam expertly negotiated the bridge. The heavy Land Rover and trailer made the poles bend and jerk around as he drove over them, and they squeaked and groaned under the weight, but he kept a slow, steady pace and made the crossing without any mishap. Immediately after the bridge, Sam turned sharp left and drove into the camping area.

The camp itself comprised several large sandy areas, situated far enough apart to be private and set along both sides of a track which ran more or less down the middle. On one side of the track, the camp areas backed onto the dense undergrowth fed by the river, whilst on the other side, the camps were on the edge of a large open plain. At the end furthest away from the bridge, was a toilet and shower block. It had green painted walls and was cleverly hidden amongst the small trees and bushes alongside the river.

Sam and the others had the camp set up alongside the open plain about half way down the track, tents erected and coffee brewing over a cooking fire within just over an hour.

When everyone was settled and chatting around the dining table, Sam took the opportunity to slip away for a well earned shower. It was around 6 o'clock in the evening by this time and he'd been driving along tough sand roads, in blazing heat all day. He figured he deserved one! In reality, he needed one!

Thirty minutes later, freshly showered and shaved, Sam sauntered back towards the camp. He was in no particular hurry and took time to look into the canopies of the large trees surrounding the entire camping area, listening to the birdsong and the never ending chattering of the small, cheeky faced vervet monkeys. From experience, he knew they were just waiting for an opportunity to scamper down the branches and try and steal any food they could when he cooked the evening meal.

As Sam gazed up into the trees, his ears caught another sound. It was familiar to him, although he couldn't place it just at that time. He cocked his head to one side, trying to listen more closely. It was in the distance and very faint at first, but the longer he listened, the louder it grew and then suddenly, he knew what it was.

He whirled round to the open plain behind him, beyond the toilet and shower block where the sound was coming from and he saw 2-300 hundred metres away, a small herd of around 25 wildebeest, galloping and zig-zagging in panic. Something was obviously chasing them, hunting them. At first, Sam wasn't sure which predator was causing them to stampede, there could be several or just one. Then he caught a glimpse of a scrawny looking, black and tan coloured dog-like animal with large ears and knew this could only be a wild dog hunt.

And the hunt was heading directly to where his clients were casually drinking coffee and chatting, completely unaware of the drama that was rapidly approaching them.

As the herd got closer, he could see two or three wild dogs outside the track on the open savannah, keeping pace, ensuring that none of the prey antelope could get away before they had chosen their victim. Escaping on the other side would be impossible through the dense, riverine forest alongside the Xwai River. They were being systematically channelled into the wooded camping area. If the wildebeest managed to get to the far end of the track, thick bush awaited them and they would have to run either to the left or to the right. The river would block their way to the right and if they chose to go left out onto the plain, the wild dogs running wide would ambush them. Either way, the hunting dogs were going to catch them out, at least one of the wildebeest was doomed.

Sam immediately spun round to face the campsite, about 50 metres away and began to run towards them as fast as he could. 'Everyone!' he shouted urgently at the top of his voice, 'Get on to the Land Rover, now!! Drop everything, get on the truck!'

Although he knew that the wild dogs were most unlikely to attack humans, he was far more concerned that the stampeding wildebeest could inadvertently injure someone. Sam would take no chances and a few minutes later, his caution was proved to be well founded.

On hearing Sam's shouted warning, all the clients instantly started to scramble towards the Land Rover, only a few metres away. By now, the wildebeest and wild dogs had entered the camping area and were thundering down the track in the middle.

Sam knew he wouldn't get to the truck in time. As he ran past a large tree, he ducked away and hid behind the trunk as the herd galloped past.

The hunt would have passed through the camp area without incident, had another vehicle not driven off the bridge and turned in towards the campsite, just at the wrong moment. The wildebeest at the head of the stampede suddenly darted off the track to the left to avoid the oncoming truck, and immediately entered Sam's camping area. The rest of the panicking herd followed the leader.

In their haste to get on board the Land Rover, the clients had tipped over chairs and left various articles lying around on the floor. Most of the antelope managed to avoid the clutter left by the clients, but two or three of them tried to leap over the large aluminium dining table towards the open plain on the far side. They would all have made it out of the camp area had one of the last wildebeest not caught its leg on an overturned chair, kicking it into the path of the one directly behind it.

Unfortunately, this last animal stumbled over the chair, catching its feet and getting tangled up with the legs of the chair. For one disastrous second, it had to stop running to try and get free.

Wild dogs usually catch their prey by chasing them over long distances. They have enormous amounts of stamina and whatever it is they're chasing gets exhausted long before they do. The wild dogs then fall on the prey and literally start to eat it alive. This time however, they managed to catch their prey purely by chance.

As the doomed antelope struggled to free itself from the prison of chair legs, the lead dog took a mighty leap and fastened its jaws onto the upper part of its rear leg. It hung there for a brief second as the antelope continued to try to get away, but it was hopeless. The rest of the pack soon caught up, fell on it as one and immediately began tearing it to pieces, not more than a couple of metres from where the clients had taken refuge.

The sound of the feeding frenzy was too much for some of them and they covered their ears to drown out the sound. The stricken wildebeest was screaming in alarm and terror, the dogs were snarling and growling as they tore the flesh from its body.

It was a distressing scene for anyone to witness, and Sam, a bush-hardened safari guide was no exception.

Sam managed to sneak around behind the feeding dogs and jump up into Land Rover from the other side. He watched as Africa's most efficient and ruthless hunters gorged themselves on fresh meat.

No-one spoke for several minutes as they watched the spectacle of the wild dogs feeding. It was terrible to watch but fascinating to experience

One of the clients said quietly, 'I'm not sure which emotion is the stronger in me, wonder at nature in action or revulsion at the cruelty, but whatever, I feel strangely privileged to have seen it.'

After the initial trauma of the attack had subsided a little, Sam said, 'The wild dog pack is probably the most efficient hunting machine on the savannah. They never hunt alone, always in a group and they're organised. You may not have seen it but some dogs ran wide of the herd to ambush it if any turned to the left onto the plain. And they can run and run, virtually nothing that it likes to hunt can match the wild dog for sheer stamina; if the chase is long, the lead dog will drop back and allow another dog to take over, forcing the prey animal to keep running at full speed. They try to weaken the prey by taking chunks out of its legs and body as it's running but it's exhaustion that usually decides the issue. When the prey animal can no longer keep ahead of the pack, they bring it down and tear into it while it's still alive. There is no killing bite or strangulation as with other predators, it dies through shock and blood loss.'

'Is there much pain?' asked another client.

'The experts say not,' replied Sam, 'the shock apparently dulls the pain to a large degree. They are fascinating creatures in other ways too. They have a social system where one or two dogs remain behind when the others go hunting, to look after any pups that may be there, and there are nearly always pups around. They don't argue over it, it's just natural for them.'

'Are the puppies from several females?'

'No, only one,' replied Sam. 'The social order dictates that only the dominant dog, the leader or Alpha, will mate with the lead female dog, but it's not set in stone and other mating does take place. However, if any other females do give birth, the lead female will probably kill that dog's young in order that her pups can receive all the food they need.'

'So, if the wild dogs are here feeding, how do the pups feed?'

'The adults you see here regurgitate semi-digested food for all the young at the den. That's part of the fantastic social structure they have, and it probably accounts for the very slight build of the dogs.'

By now the pack had consumed all the meat they wanted and at the departure of the Alpha dog, they all began to trot back along the track to where their den would be, possibly several kilometres away. Even a casual glance at the pack would show that they had fed well, their entire faces and snouts were stained red with the blood of the unfortunate wildebeest.

By comparison to some prey animals, the wildebeest isn't the largest and the wild dogs made short work of eating their fill, but there was a large part of the carcass remaining, and this presented Sam with a problem.

He looked down at the partly consumed animal in his camp, and the blood-soaked earth around it. 'This is going to attract scavengers from all over,' he muttered. Turning to the clients, he said, 'We have to get rid of this carcass and the blood before the hyenas and vultures and marabou arrive, as they surely will. The smell of fresh blood will be too much to ignore. Here's what we're going to do. I'm going to tie a rope around the horns of the carcass, raise it off the ground as high as I can and then take it out onto the savannah, about half a kilometre away. Hopefully, by lifting it up, I can limit the amount of blood and guts that gets spilled out onto the ground.

'In the meantime, two of you are going to dig a pit about half a metre square next to where the carcass lay. When it's deep enough, around a metre, drag all the bloodied earth into the pit and bury it. Make sure you get it all, take more rather than less.'

Sam then took out a length of rope and both spades from under one of the seats. He tossed one spade to each of his male clients.

'There you are, let's go. The rest of you start taking all your belongings out of the tents. We're going to physically move the camp to the far end, away from this spot. I'll use some branches and bushes between two trees to block anyone else using it for now and I'll tell the park office tomorrow when we leave.'

Sam jumped down from the vehicle and quickly looped one end of the rope around the horns. The wild dogs had concentrated on the body and insides of the antelope, so the head and neck were intact. Standing on the bonnet of the Land Rover, he heaved the carcass up as high off the ground as he could and then tied the rope off on the big metal crash-bar at the front of the truck. Sam then jumped down and with a smaller length of rope, tied the two back legs of the wildebeest together and attached them to the crash-bar also. As soon as he was done, he slowly drove the sorry looking body of the wildebeest across the sandy savannah and left it out in the open, about 400 metres away from the camp.

When he returned, the two men had done what he had asked and were just digging up all the blood-soaked sand and throwing it into the pit.

'Good work, good work,' exclaimed Sam, 'just make sure you check please that there's no major blood just outside the camp where I drove the carcass away. The rest of you, start taking all your belongings to the far end and then we'll move the tents and camping stuff. I'll start to pack up the kitchen and dining table.'

Sam and his clients worked non-stop for the following hour or so and managed to move everything, the tents, luggage, camping table and chairs, the kitchen and the truck to the new area without incident.

The following morning, Sam drove past the carcass where he had left it. 'Look,' he exclaimed, 'most of it's gone.'

'Which animals would have done that?' one of the others asked.

'The hyenas would have been in first, they probably chased the vultures and marabou storks away most of the time, but after they'd eaten, the smaller scavengers such as the jackals would have come in and finished it off; if they're hungry enough, lions and leopard will also take dead meat, but only if there's nothing else.'

As they studied the near skeletal remains, Sam looked skywards, pointed into the distance and remarked, 'And it goes on, see the whitebacked vultures circling over there, they're waiting to drop onto another carcass, something else was taken during the night, and that something dies in order that others can live. The cycle of life and death here can be brutal, and it's a never ending struggle for survival for many of the species. That is how my Africa exists.'

THE FERRY

'No, no,' said Mr. Zulu the Park Ranger, 'you must cross by the pontoon.' Sam was standing in the booking office at the entrance to the Liuwa Plains National Park in Kalabo, Zambia. In order to get onto the plains, he had to somehow cross the Luanginga River with his Land Rover, trailer and six clients. In the past, he had always driven across the river, his Land Rover submerging up to the bonnet and river water swashing through the footwells. Now though, "Africa Parks" had taken over the administration of the plains and were insisting that all vehicles and people use the ferry at the bottom of a steep slope.

The ferry itself consisted of a large floating, wooden platform, a handrail along one side with a metal ring at each end. A long length of rope, attached to a stake set into the sand on each side of the river ran through the two rings and a boatman would then pull the ferry across the river by pulling on the rope.

Sam and his colleague, Diteko looked down at the river.

'See how swift the current is here, and that pontoon looks dangerous,' Diteko remarked.

'I know, but I don't think we have a choice.'

Reluctantly, Sam agreed to use the ferry, even though he knew how rickety it was. He didn't trust any ferry that wasn't steel and driven by a powerful engine but he didn't want to cause problems for Mr. Zulu.

'This is not a good idea,' he said to himself as he drove the Land Rover down the steep slope towards the pontoon. There was no track to follow, he had to weave his way around large mounds of sand. As he watched the ferry being brought over from the far side, he could see the current sweeping the platform downstream in a wide arc and the poles the rope was attached to were waving about, seemingly loose in the sand.

'Ok, I want everybody off. I'll take the Land Rover over first and then send the ferry back for you,' he said, cheerily to the clients. When the ferry nuzzled into the soft, wet sand at the river's edge, Sam could see the ferryman struggling to hold the platform steady, the swiftly flowing river was constantly trying to sweep it downstream. There had been a fair amount of rain over the previous days and the river was swollen, creating a strong current.

'Jack, take hold of the rope and give the ferryman a hand to hold it into the bank please,' said Sam to one of his clients. He knew that he had to drive onto the ferry in a straight line, that is, with both front wheels hitting the entrance ramp at the same time.

'Make sure you hold on tight when the wheels hit the platform or the ferry will push out into the current.'

'No problem,' replied Jack

When he judged the ferry was just in the right position, at right angles to the bank, he edged his way towards the platform.

Even at the slowest speed he could manage, the weight of the wheels hitting the edge of the wooden planking of the platform, forced the ferry away from the bank a few centimetres.

'Hold her, hold her,' shouted Sam urgently.

Those centimetres were critical because the current collided with the back of the ferry with greater force and the whole platform began to twist around, taking the Land Rover with it. He knew that if he continued to try and get on the ferry, the force of the vehicle's weight and forward motion would push the ferry even further away from the bank and into the current.

Instinctively he knew the situation was hopeless and he immediately stamped on the brakes and pulled the handbrake on as hard as he could to try and stop the ferry from moving. It had all happened within just a few seconds but even so, Sam had driven the Land Rover maybe a metre and a half onto the ferry. And now, instead of being in a nice straight line, he had the ferry at a crazy angle to his vehicle.

'I'm coming back,' he shouted to the others and tried to reverse off the ferry but that only made things worse. By going backwards, he "jack-knifed" the Land Rover and trailer. Now he really was stuck! He couldn't go forwards because the force of the wheels pushing onto the ferry was causing it to swing even more and he couldn't go back because the trailer had jack-knifed. 'Brilliant Sam, just brilliant!! What a mess!' he muttered to himself.

The large crowd of local people who had gathered on the river bank were enjoying the spectacle however, constantly helping with little snippets of advice for Sam, but mostly having a good laugh at his expense!! They had brought their children down to the river-side, and whole families were sitting watching the fun!

Sam looked around at the chaos he'd helped to create. It was obvious to him that the Land Rover could go neither forwards nor backwards. It was also obvious that the trailer would have to be unhitched from the vehicle, but the slope that the trailer was on, was far too steep and it weighed far too much for anyone to push it away.

'We have to empty the trailer,' Sam shouted to the clients, 'open the lid and get everything out, bags, food, tents, everything. We have to make it lighter, quickly now.'

There was an urgency to Sam's voice and all the clients jumped to obey his instruction. Sam himself didn't dare leave the vehicle, just in case!! He called his companion, Diteko over to him. 'Aupo,' he said, using his nickname, 'please go back to the town and get someone with a tractor down here, we'll have to get a tow up the slope.'

'If we're getting a tow up the slope, why are we emptying the trailer?' asked Aupo, not unreasonably.

'Because if anything happens like the rope parts or slips or anything like that and the trailer goes down into the river, we'll have clients with no clothes or food. I know it's not likely, but I'm not taking a chance.'

'Fair enough,' replied Aupo, and turning to the clients, 'ok, let's go.'

The tractor arrived just at the same time as the trailer was emptied. A towrope was attached to the back of the trailer and the tractor inched back slightly to put tension on the rope. Aupo then unhitched the trailer and the tractor was able to pull it easily up the slope to the top.

Sam assumed that he would be able to drive off the ferry once the trailer had been unhitched, but on looking down at the rear wheels, he could see that they had sunk into the soft, wet sand at the side of the river. He knew that he would have to use the Land Rover's powerful four-wheel drive to get off the ferry but he also knew that, with the rear wheels sunk deeply into the sand, driving backwards like that could possibly force the ferry away if he tried to drive off, plunging the vehicle into the river. Sam calculated the chances and figured they weren't good.

'Damn,' he cursed softly to himself, 'this is going to be embarrassing!' He glanced around the grinning crowd and then shouted to Aupo, 'tie the rope onto the towing hitch at the back of the Land Rover and take the other end to the tractor, I'll have to be towed out.'

Slowly, inch by inch, the tractor towed Sam and his Land Rover off the ferry and back up the slope. The driver could have driven the tractor much faster, but he, along with the crowd was enjoying the spectacle of the stricken Land Rover and trailer too much to end the entertainment quickly. He was playing to the audience and enjoying Sam's embarrassment. When the vehicle and trailer were both finally at the top, the crowd burst into applause, and Sam took a bow!

He paid the tractor driver handsomely for his services and then, whilst Aupo and the clients re-packed the trailer, Sam walked into the Africa Parks office and said to Mr Zulu, 'Never again, never again will I use that ferry!'

Mr Zulu simply grinned knowingly at him, he had been part of the appreciative audience.

THE HIPPOPOTAMUS

Gabriel pulled the brim of his hat down over his eyes, to shield them from the burning African sun. Even so, from where he was lying, he could still look up at the clear, blue sky over the Okavango Delta, a sky he never tired of gazing at.

He was on safari with a group of European clients and for the next three days, they would explore some of the many thousands of water filled channels that made up the Delta and experience some of the most diverse wildlife in the whole of Africa.

Earlier that morning, they had arrived by safari truck at the edge of the waterways and unloaded all their luggage, tents, chairs, cooking equipment, food, water and the thin mattresses they would lie on at night. It all lay in an untidy mess near to some hollowed-out, tree trunk canoes known as mokorros, made by local people and pushed along by villagers planting a pole on the riverbed. These would be their transport through the Okavango Delta.

The men and women who would guide them loaded their equipment into the canoes and the clients sat, rather nervously in amongst all the equipment. They were nervous because the mokorro is not a very stable craft, but in the hands of the expert "polers", there wasn't anything to worry about. Gabriel however, knew it was a waste of time trying to explain that to someone who wasn't used to the rocking motion of the mokorro going through the water.

As usual, as the safari leader, Gabriel had a craft to himself, "Privilege of Rank" he called it. He relaxed, lay down in the mokorro being poled along by Modester, a local woman, gazed up at his African sky and enjoyed the peace and quiet of his Okavango. As an African, he regarded everything about Africa as "his".

Silently, he identified the birds from their distinctive calls and birdsong, along with the distant sound of land animals such as antelope or buffalo, as they grazed contentedly on the grassy plains. Nothing could be more peaceful, he thought…. nothing!

Suddenly, Gabriel's world was in chaos!

Without warning, the massive bulk of a female hippopotamus came crashing out of the grassy reeds at the water's edge. Although he couldn't see it, Gabriel was sure that her calf would be nearby somewhere and she was taking steps to protect it.

As she came out of the reeds, her mouth was wide open, which Gabriel knew was meant as a threat to him and the mokorro; basically, it meant, "Get away from here." He could see the terrifyingly large teeth at the front of her jaws, and if she wanted to, she could almost bite him in half!

She hit the water running at a fast trot, her bulk setting up a bow-wave in front of her. Gabriel's mokorro was just far enough away to avoid her colliding fully into the side of the craft, but the wave she had created hit the mokorro side-on. Being unstable anyway, the canoe simply rolled over, tossing Gabriel, Modester, the female poler and all the equipment that was being carried in the mokorro into the Delta water.

Now they were completely in the hippo's environment and she had disappeared from view, which could mean only one thing, she had gone underwater! Gabriel and Modester were in real danger! The channel they were travelling along was around 2 metres deep, more than enough for a large hippopotamus to submerge in. Knowing that she could attack them, unseen, at any moment from under the surface and inflict very serious injuries, Gabriel immediately started to scramble to the shore, 10 metres away on the opposite side of where the hippo had appeared.

Modester however, was unable to swim. She was wearing a large chitengi, wrapped around her midriff several times, which became heavy with water and restricted her movements. She immediately started to panic and thrash around trying to stay afloat.

'Gabriel, help me, help me!' she screamed, her head sometimes dipping below the surface of the water.

Ignoring the danger of the submerged hippo, Gabriel immediately turned back and within two or three powerful strokes, reached Modester and grabbed hold of her clothing. As he did so, she tried desperately to wrap her arms around his neck.

'Relax, relax,' cried Gabriel, 'I've got you.' He managed to break Modester's iron grip on his neck and began pulling her towards the shore. They had been in the water for nearly a minute, which seemed like a lifetime they later reflected, when both of them had scrambled breathlessly up the sandy riverbank.

For a second there was no sign of the hippo, then, almost casually, two ears poked above the water, closely followed by two nostrils, then two eyes. Her calf appeared close beside her and she looked directly at Gabriel and Modester and blew a stream of water noisily through her nostrils, as if to say, "Don't mess with me and don't come back!" Once more, she sank below the surface, followed by the baby hippo.

Neither Gabriel nor Modester had seen the calf before, it must have crashed into the water immediately after its mother, but both of them knew that this was probably the reason for the attack; she was protecting her calf from danger.

They reappeared a few moments later 2-300 metres further upstream near a large pod of other hippos, all of them calling noisily in that curious, honking manner.

However, most of the equipment that was in Gabriel's mokorro now lay at the bottom of the channel, in two metres of water. There had been tents and cooking pots in big metal chests and they lay on the riverbed, as did a steel container of plates and cutlery. However, there had also been several mattresses that Gabriel was lying on and they were drifting lazily down the channel with the current, opposite to the way they had been heading.

'Ok,' said Gabriel to the team, 'the hippo has joined the rest of the pod upstream, so we should be safe enough, but I want everyone to keep watch for any of them making their way down this end. This is still their territory and they may take exception to us. I'll get back in the water and retrieve what I can. Modester, take a mokorro please and somebody else, and pick up our mattresses before they drift too far away.'

He and the rest of the clients and polers then spent the next two or three hours rescuing and drying out the water-soaked equipment, while keeping a careful eye out for the cause of all the trouble in the first place, one very grumpy hippo.

THE BOXER SHORTS

The mighty Zambezi River starts as a small spurt of water coming out of the ground in north-west Zambia, near a place called Kaleni Hills. Swollen by other rivers joining at various stages, it carves its way majestically through several countries in Southern Africa on its way to the Indian Ocean.

At some stage in the region's history, a geological event caused some of the riverbed to drop about 15 metres, forming a set of waterfalls known as Ngune Falls. They are not as splendid as Victoria Falls further down-river, but Sam always thought they were well worth a visit.

'Tomorrow, we're crossing the river and then we're hiking a few kilometres to the Ngune Falls. You need decent shoes, water, a hat and sunscreen, it's going to be hot tomorrow. We'll have some lunch at the falls and do a few other things,' said Sam at his evening briefing to his clients. He didn't explain what the "other things" were.

The next day, around 11 o'clock, they all set out in the hollowed out tree trunk canoes known as mokorros to cross from one side of the Zambezi to the other. Once everyone was ashore and ready to hike, Sam said, 'Right, let's go, follow me and keep in single file along the path.' Walking in this fashion keeps environmental damage to a minimum.

About an hour later, they arrived at Ngune Falls, the thunderous roar from which, they had heard from several hundred metres away.

'Wow,' exclaimed one of the clients. He gazed at many thousands of litres of water a minute cascading over the edge of the rocks and falling around 15 metres into deep pools, churned white with froth and throwing up a curtain of spray all around the falls.

'We'll get as close as we can over the rocks but be careful, there are lots of little potholes to trap your feet in, I don't want any broken ankles,' said Sam.

'What causes these holes?' asked Katrina.

'The rocks are ancient volcanic lava remains, known as basalt. The force of flood water and the sand and dirt taken along by the current, carves and gouges the rocks into these shapes in the same way it's shaped the channel it flows down.'

Katrina looked where Sam was pointing downstream and she could see how the river, bending left and right, had carved its passage through the dark coloured rock.

After lunch, Sam gathered everyone together and asked smilingly, 'Who wants to go swimming in the Zambezi?' Most of clients stared at him in disbelief. A couple looked back at the thundering Ngune Falls and shook their heads!

'Come on,' said Sam cheerily. This was to be his surprise for the clients. He walked a couple of hundred metres to an area where huge boulders lay in an untidy muddle. Clambering over these, he and the clients arrived at some smaller rocky ledges. Water flowed out from between these rocky outcrops, over miniature falls less than half a metre high and into small, crystal clear pools.

'This is still the Zambezi,' declared Sam. 'It diverts a little before Ngune and flows underground to here.' He pointed further down from the rocks and said, 'The water flows down there, through those small pools and joins the main river over that lip in the rocks.'

With that, he started to take his t-shirt off, followed by his shoes and socks. He emptied his pockets and slipped into the water, warmed underground by the sun-heated rocks.

'Just a warning,' said Sam, 'these pools stop at that big boulder over there. Don't climb over the rock or you could be taking the short cut back to the main river!'

Several of the clients followed his example, stripping down to their shorts, laughing all the time and getting into the water.

However, Nigel, from England decided that he didn't want to get his ordinary clothes wet, even though they would dry in a matter of minutes in the scorching heat of the day. He suffered some very ribald and frank remarks about his choice of underwear before he slipped into the water wearing a rather fetching pair of boxer shorts with pictures of Tigger and Eeyore from the Winnie the Pooh stories printed all over them!

Everyone in the water was enjoying themselves immensely when suddenly there was a shout of alarm! Sam immediately looked up to where the clients were lazing around in the pools; he was afraid one had disregarded his warning and climbed over the rock. Thankfully, he could see he still had the correct number.

'Who called out?' he demanded. As he said this, something caught the corner of his eye. He saw a pair of brightly coloured boxer shorts being swept along with the current, over the small waterfalls and down towards the big rock. He knew exactly who they belonged to as he recognised Tigger instantly.

At the same time, Sam saw Nigel splashing frantically through the shallow pools in a desperate attempt to catch up with his shorts. Everyone was in fits of laughter at the flashes of Nigel's snowy- white bum showing above the water.

'Go Nigel, go, go,' some unkind soul shouted as Nigel lunged for his boxer shorts, only to have the current whip them cruelly out of his reach. He was only centimetres away when, tragically, they disappeared through a small crack in the rocks, on their way to the main Zambezi River and eventually, Mozambique and the Indian Ocean.

Poor old Nigel! He was now about twenty or thirty metres away from everyone else, with nothing to cover his lower half.

'Someone throw me my hiking shorts please,' he shouted.

Nobody moved!

'Come on guys,' he pleaded, 'I'm naked here!'

Still nobody moved.

'What happened to your boxers then?' asked Sam.

'They just got ripped off by the current, I couldn't stop them coming off. By the time I reached down to grab them, they were round my ankles and gone.'

'Oh, bad luck,' said Sam with a smile, 'your hiking shorts are here, look, here they are!' He held them up to show Nigel not only that he had them, but also that Nigel was going to have to get out of the river naked and scramble over the rocks to get them back.

The other clients hooted and whistled as Nigel slowly got to his feet, holding his hands over his, shall we say, delicate parts at the front.

At one stage, he stumbled over a rock, 'Ouch,' he called loudly as his big toe instantly began to throb. A step later, he trod on a sharp stone and nearly lost his balance. He was swearing quietly to himself as he tried to steady himself by putting his hands out, inadvertently displaying his "delicate parts" for everyone to see.

After a few more stumbles, he gave up the fight to preserve his dignity and splashed his way noisily through the pools to where the others were standing, applauding and whooping their delight at poor Nigel's expense.

'There you go Tigger, sorry, Tiger!' said Sam, grinning as he handed Nigel his shorts.

One of the other clients said, 'Eee-yore bum is really white,' and everyone laughed even louder. 'Enough, enough,' cried Nigel, and even he was laughing as he pulled on his safari shorts, which he should never have removed in the first place.

Funnily enough, he never wore boxer shorts for the remainder of the trip.

THE LIONS ON THE TRAILER

Gabriel was on safari in Chobe National Park with seven clients, all from different parts of the world. The fact that he had so many clients meant that he had an assistant with him. Sinvula would maintain the camp whilst Gabriel and the clients were out game-spotting. He would cook the food and keep everything tidy.

It was the last evening of the trip and Gabriel was returning to camp just as the sun was setting. He couldn't return any later as the darkness comes quickly in Africa and he's not allowed to drive in the Park at night. As usual, he knew exactly where he was and how far away he was from Sinvula and dinner, maybe just a kilometre distant.

He twitched his nose to try and catch a sniff of the delicious meal that he knew Sinvula would be preparing and cooking for them. He would be barbecuing the steaks they had kept back specially for this last dinner and cooking all the remaining vegetables.

'That's funny,' Gabriel muttered to himself, 'I can't smell anything. Sinvula usually has everything boiling and cooking on the fire by now.' He kept trying to catch a whiff of cooking food as he got closer and closer to the camp, but nothing was in the air.

Darkness was arriving quickly as he approached the camp, but in the gloom, he spotted two giraffe on the plain outside his camp. They were standing absolutely still and staring at something in the distance. He was an expert in wild animal behaviour and he knew that this was a sign that the giraffe had spotted some danger, probably a predator like a lion or a leopard, hunting in the fading light. What concerned him most however, was that the giraffe were looking in the direction of his camp.

A few minutes later, Gabriel drove his Land Rover into the tented area. As he swung the vehicle around to where it was usually parked, his headlights lit up the safari trailer, which also served as the kitchen. Lying on top of the trailer, everyone saw that there were two massive male lions, probably brothers. They weren't exactly asleep, but they were definitely relaxed and perfectly content to be stretched out on Gabriel's trailer. He estimated them to be around 3 years old, healthy and well fed with magnificent, thick, dark manes of hair around their shoulders. Although they were too far away from the lions for them to be an immediate threat, once the clients sitting behind Gabriel had caught sight of them, they understandably became a little concerned.

'Ok, everyone,' whispered Gabriel, 'nobody move and keep quiet. They're not interested in us but we mustn't spook them.' He looked around the camp for Sinvula, 'Where is he?' he muttered to himself, and sounded the horn.

As if in answer, Gabriel heard a very faint voice, 'Ntate, Ntate!' He didn't know where it was coming from initially, but when he heard it again, this time a little louder, he realised it was coming from the direction of the trailer.

'Sinvula, where are you?'

'Ntate, (which is pronounced Un-ta-tay) I am in the trailer!!' Gabriel saw the lions turning their heads left and right, confused as to where this mystery noise was coming from. They didn't realise of course, it was directly beneath them.

Gabriel then looked around the camp, it was chaos; chairs were turned over, plates and cutlery were spread over the camp floor and pots that would have contained vegetables, some cooking in boiling water and some half-peeled had been knocked to the ground. Looking up into the trees, the cheeky vervet monkeys and some baboons seemed to be laughing at him as they munched on the food they had picked off the sandy ground. Gabriel figured he knew what must have happened, but his immediate concern was how to get rid of the lions and keep the clients and himself safe.

'Hold on Sinvula,' Gabriel shouted, 'we have to get rid of the lions.'

'Please hurry Ntate,' pleaded Sinvula, 'I am desperate to go to the toilet!'

Gabriel couldn't help but smile as he imagined Sinvula crossing his legs, and probably everything else he could manage to cross in the trailer.

Fortunately, it had rained earlier and Gabriel had fitted the removable side screens for the Land Rover to keep the clients dry, effectively enclosing them inside the vehicle. 'Right,' he said turning to face them in the back. 'we have to get rid of the lions, There's no telling how long they plan to stay and poor old Sinvula is trapped in the trailer. I want you all to move to the back of the truck and I'm going to drive at the trailer, revving the engine loudly. Hopefully, the lions will think we are a big animal, too big for them to take on and we'll scare them away back into the bush.' Just as a precaution, he removed his machete from its sheath and placed it by his side.

When everyone was in position, he revved the diesel engine, making as much noise as he could and drove the Land Rover directly at the trailer.

The two lions had initially watched Gabriel with total disinterest. Now, however, this huge "animal" was coming directly at them, making a noise they had never encountered before. They looked at the Land Rover with massive, frightened eyes.

When the Land Rover was only a matter of a few metres away, they both leapt down from the trailer and galloped off into the darkness and safety of the bush. When Gabriel was sure they had gone for good, he approached the trailer and banged the side. He immediately felt guilty as he heard Sinvula pleading, 'Go away, please, please!' his words strangely muffled. Gabriel opened up the trailer lid and found him hiding under a dozen or so spare blankets and tarpaulins.

'Have they gone, Ntate?' he whispered.

'Well, Sinvula,' Gabriel replied, 'if they haven't, I'm in real trouble! Come on out and tell me what happened.'

Although he wanted the toilet badly, Sinvula looked nervously around before he eventually climbed out of the trailer and ran straight into the toilet tent! When he returned, he was visibly shaking as he told Gabriel the tale.

'I was peeling the carrots for dinner and had all the steaks out on the table ready to cook. I heard a noise behind me and when I looked round, one of the lions had his front paws on the table and was stealing the meat. Then the other one jumped onto the table and they fought to get the most steaks. As they were fighting, I made a dash for the trailer, I didn't know where else to go. I heard chairs being knocked over, and the pots with the vegetables. I dived into the trailer head-first and banged the lid shut just as one of them jumped up onto the top. I could hear them growling outside and the trailer was rocking from side to side. One of them was trying to open the lid, I could feel him pulling. I prayed that they wouldn't tip it over and held onto the chain to keep the lid shut. I heard them lie down on the top and then they stopped snarling and growling. That was about two hours ago, where have you been Ntate? I was so scared!'

'Well,' said Gabriel, 'I think you've been very brave.' He turned to the clients and said 'Sorry, guys but Sinvula very selfishly let the lions eat our steaks for tonight and then he didn't stop them knocking all the vegetables into the dirt! We have nothing left for dinner except a bit of fruit.' He grinned at Sinvula, who looked at him and the clients laughing. After a second or two, he understood Gabriel's little joke and he also started to laugh. Still, he looked around nervously as he helped Gabriel and the clients pick up the chairs and pots and pans. Even though he trusted Gabriel with his life, he wanted to be absolutely sure the two lions which had scared him half to death, had indeed, disappeared back into bush, where they belonged.

THE STORM

It was late January and raining! Rain, rain, rain! It wasn't as if it didn't happen at this time each year, but Sam never looked forward to getting wet every single day. He hadn't been with Drifting Ways Safaris very long and this was his first trip with clients at this time of the year.

For most of the afternoon, the sky had been filled with dark, almost black rain clouds. Sam could see in the distance, a grey curtain of mist between the bottom of the clouds and the ground and he knew that that area was being soaked with torrential rain.

The daylight was fading fast and he was desperately looking for a place to pitch his tents for the night, a flat, sandy area. At last, he found a nice spot, but in doing so, made a very big mistake! He'd been concentrating so hard on watching the clouds and searching for a decent campsite before the rain reached him, he hadn't noticed that he was in a wide valley with higher ground on either side of him. Sam was just grateful he'd found the campsite in time and the clients could pitch their tents before night fell.

The flashes of lightning were increasing and the rolling thunder-claps were getting louder, the storm was coming their way.

'Here, take that!' He threw a shovel to one of the younger male clients, 'we need to dig some trenches around the tents to divert any excess water over there.' Sam pointed to an area away from the camp. They began to dig straight away and soon had the job done, but Sam had not anticipated the sheer violence of the storm that was about to hit them, or the volume of water that would sweep through their camp. Their efforts would be largely wasted.

About an hour after the tents had been pitched and the trenches finished, Sam was busy with preparing the evening dinner under a tarpaulin he had erected. The sky was filled with the sound of thunder and flashes of lightning were streaking across the sky. Rain had been falling steadily but getting increasingly heavy. At this stage, the drainage channels around the camp were doing their job admirably.

Suddenly, there was an almighty crash of thunder, so loud it made Sam jump and his eardrums ache. At the same instant, the sky was lit from end to end with a brilliant flash of lightning. The storm had arrived and it was directly overhead. Immediately, as if not to be outdone by the thunder and lightning, the rain began to fall in torrents, droplets the size of marbles pounding the earth. Huge puddles of water were created in minutes.

The channels gave up the struggle to cope and streams of water flooded all around the tents. The noise of the rainwater splashing onto the ground and the almost constant rumbling and crashing of thunder made it impossible to hear anyone saying anything. Sam had gathered all the clients together under the tarpaulin and they watched and listened in amazement at this display of nature's violence.

Then, as if someone had flicked a switch, the rain ceased, the thunder stopped crashing and without the lightning, the sky was pitch dark.

The storm had moved through and Sam was about to realise his mistake. In the eerie and sudden silence, his keen hearing picked up a faint rushing noise, similar to the wind blowing through bushes, but not quite the same. He listened intently, trying to figure out the noise. And as he listened, it got louder and louder.

Suddenly, he knew what was happening, 'Flash flood, flash flood,' he shouted desperately. 'Everyone, get on the truck, now, NOW!'

There was an urgency in his voice the clients hadn't heard before and instinctively, they knew there was trouble coming. Just as Sam pulled the last client onto the Land Rover, a wall of water over half a metre high came roaring through the camp.

On its journey along the river course, the flood had collected football sized boulders, loose bushes and had ripped out small trees. These now crashed into the tents that lay directly in its path. They were physically lifted off the ground by the water and then turned over onto their sides and pushed along by the debris the wave contained. There seemed to be no end to the devastation the flash-flood was causing.

As they listened to the sound of their belongings tumbling over and over inside the tents, some of the clients offered up a silent prayer, hoping beyond hope they had remembered to zip them shut, tightly!! Anyone still in their tents when the torrent struck would definitely not have survived. Sam was lucky there!

The wave collided with the vehicle side-on, physically rocking it and drenching the clients from the water that cascaded over the top.

Everyone watched helplessly as personal belongings that had been left on the ground in the race to get away from the flood, were carried off, perhaps never to be seen again. Everything in the camp, chairs, the dinner table, the barbecue grill, pots and pans, food was swept away, nothing was spared as the murky, brown flood raced through.

Eventually, the water slowed and finally stopped, its force had been spent. All that was left of the camp was chaos. The things not carried away by the flood, lay untidily in the rain-soaked, muddy soil. Where there had been tents, tables and chairs, there was now large rocks, uprooted trees and bushes.

'What on earth happened there?' asked one of the clients.

Sam was reluctant to answer, but he realised he would have to admit his mistake. 'Remember all that rain we saw falling in the distance?' he said, 'Well, I didn't realise that it was falling in an area already soaked with rain water. We've had far more really heavy and sustained rain recently than in previous years. The hills around there are rocky and the rain water just flows down the rocks and onto the ground below. So much water fell in the storm that the soil simply couldn't absorb any more and eventually, it just started to flow over the top of the ground. As it went along, more and more water joined it until it formed a river.

'This is the tricky part,' he said, 'I was so caught up looking for a suitable place to camp, I didn't realise that where I chose was actually an old, dried-up river course. Those hills on both sides of us should have given me a clue but I missed it, my mistake, I'm sorry,' he said as he held up both hands, as if in surrender. 'The water just flowed along its natural path and unfortunately, we were in the way.'

Sam looked at the clients, who all mumbled their acceptance of his explanation and apology. 'Come on,' he said, jumping down from the

Land Rover, 'let's see what we can find. Everything will be around here somewhere.'

He and the clients spent the following hour or two recovering what they could of their belongings and tents, some of which had been deposited hundreds of metres away. It was just a case really of finding what they could by torchlight and making do with what they had until daylight the following day, when they would find the rest.

After a dinner of biscuits and dried fruit, they were ready to settle down for an uncomfortable, hungry night, squashed into the tents they had found and wrapped in spare blankets.

As they sat around the campfire, Sam said, 'Listen!' There was no sound; no wind, no rain, no raindrops, no animals calling in the night, no rustling in the trees or bushes. Compared to the thunderous roar of the storm and flood just a few short hours before, the silence of the night was almost deafening.

'Look up there,' he said as he pointed to the peaceful night-sky. 'Have you ever seen so many stars?'

Glossary of Terms

Alpha	Animal regarded as the leader.
African Jacana	African wading bird.
Bale out	Rafting term to remove excess water from the raft.
Beached	Rafting term where raft becomes stranded out of the water.
Browsing	Term for eating twigs and leaves from trees and bushes.
Bush	African term for countryside.
Caprivi Strip	Narrow strip of Namibian land between Botswana and Zambia.
Carcass	Body of a dead animal.
Cartilage	Tough, natural material found in the body.
Chitengi	A large printed piece of cloth which acts like a skirt.
Chobe Nat. Park	Pronounced Chobee, National Park in Botswana.
Crash-Bar	Strong metal structure on the front of safari vehicles.
Cull	Controlled killing to reduce animal numbers.
Den	Home of wild dogs.
Eddy-out	Rafting term for stopping at the side of a river.
Elephant Grass	Tall species of grass.
Fauna and Flora	Term to include, birds, animals, trees, bushes, flowers and plants.
Ferrying	Rafting term to take the craft across the current.
Gourds	Large hollowed-out seed shell used a bowl.

Grazing	Animals feeding primarily on grass.
Herbivore	An animal that feeds only on vegetation.
Hide	A concealed shelter to observe animals or birds.
Homo Sapiens	Latin for human beings.
Johannesburg	Large city in South Africa.
Kraal	Form of stockade for animals.
Leukaemia	Form of cancer.
Loping	Long-striding run.
Lusaka	Capital of Zambia.
Machete	Large broad-bladed knife for cutting undergrowth.
Maun	Town in Botswana on the edge of the Okavango Delta.
Midden	A dung heap a specific animal will use as a toilet.
Mokorro	African canoe made from a hollowed out tree trunk.
Nkosi	African term for "Friend".
Nshima	African dish created solely from crushed maize corn and water.
Ntate	Respectful Setswana term for someone in charge.
Nyaminyami	Cultural god of the Zambezi River.
Okavango Delta	Large inland swamp area of Botswana.
Poler	Man or woman who propels a mokorro using a pole.
Predator	Animal that hunts, kills and eats other animals.
Prehensile	Part of an animal adapted for grasping.
Pride	Term used to describe a group of lions.
Regurgitation	Bringing up stomach contents to feed young.

Rifle-stock	Wooden part of a rifle that tucks into the shoulder.
Rift Valley	Valley formed when earth's crust collapses.
Setswana	Language and culture of the Tswana people .
Spoor	African term to describe trail left by an animal.
Stopper	Rafting term where current is stopped by a deep hole.
Termitaria	Collective name for termite mounds.
Thwart	Inflatable cross tube in a raft.
Tswana	Largest ethnic group in Botswana.
Wild-Camp	Fenceless tent camp where animals can roam through.
Xwai	Pronounced as "Kwy" using a soft "K" sound.

The author, Neil Robins, is a retired London police officer. During his 30 years of service however, he was fortunate enough to be able to travel to Africa on several separate occasions. As well as working on a mission station farm and helping to build schools in very rural parts of Namibia, he was given the opportunity to guide wild-camp safaris around Botswana, South Africa and later to the Liuwa Plains of Zambia.

Whilst he would always defer to the expertise and craft of those guides who were native to that part of the continent and who had worked within the safari industry for many years, he nevertheless acquired a level of knowledge of fauna and flora and the ways of Africa that would not normally be expected of someone in his unusual position. Of that, he remains justifiably proud.

These stories are based in large part on his and his colleagues' actual experiences guiding safaris in the bush, although most have been expanded and dramatised to a certain degree. The author describes them as "factional", a mix of fact and fiction.

He hopes that, as a result of reading these tales of adventure, imaginations will be fired and individuals will be inspired to see and experience for themselves, the exciting and awesome Africa.